How to Stuff a WILD Zucchini

How to Stuff a WILD Zucchini

Heather Horrocks

DESERET BOOK

Salt Lake City, Utah

Visit us at DeseretBook.com

Library of Congress Cataloging-in-Publication Data

Horrocks, Heather.
How to stuff a wild zucchini / Heather Horrocks.
p. cm.
Summary: New York playwright Lori Scott feels like a failure when her producer boyfriend calls it quits on both their relationship and her first play. On a dare, she throws a dart at a map and ends up moving to Brigham City, Utah, where she writes "The Garden Guru" column for the local paper and ends up falling in love with local firefighter John Wayne Walker.
ISBN 978-1-60641-094-3 (paperbound)
1. Dramatists—Fiction. 2. Journalists—Fiction. 3. Brigham City (Utah)—Fiction. 4. American fiction—21st century. I. Title.
PS3608.O769H69 2009
813'.6—dc22 2009001344

Printed in the United States of America
Publishers Printing, Salt Lake City, UT

10 9 8 7 6 5 4 3 2 1

To my wonderful, witty, warm-hearted, and winsome husband, Mark, who dislikes zucchini but loves and supports me in countless ways and has made it possible for me to achieve both my dreams and my own happily-ever-after

THE GARDEN GURU

Dear Dr. Dobson: I've just moved to Utah and the soil at my new home in Taylorsville is clay that clumps horribly and doesn't seem to drain. Can you give me any suggestions for preparing my garden? (Matthew)

Dear Matthew: Oh, my dear, you are absolutely right. Clay soil does not drain at all and your plants will need a better foundation. Add some organic material to improve the texture and biological activity of the soil. Peat moss is also good, as it will loosen the clumps. I wish you all the best with your new garden—you can make it work. I, also, am moving, though only temporarily. I will be taking a long-awaited three-month sabbatical to China. Never fear, my friends, I shall not leave you without gardening advice. I will provide a knowledgeable substitute while I'm gone; I will be sure to introduce that person in my last column before they try their hand . . .

Chapter One

"I am not upset." Lori Scott chucked the dart the length of her old bedroom where it thunked soundly into the center of the dartboard.

Greg whistled. "I have to tell you how impressed I am with your *non*-anger issues."

A foot taller than her own five-foot-five, Lori's older brother had maintained his track-star physique, looking lean and athletic in his official attorney's suit. As one of her favorite people, Greg could get away with saying things to her that others couldn't. Sometimes. "You're just jealous because you're not winning."

"You're absolutely right." He squinted in concentration and tossed his own dart. It landed in the outer circle. "Darn." Turning back to her with a flourish, he smiled. "So, Lori, tell me again how happy you are. Convince me."

She sighed in resignation, leaned back against her old wooden desk, and folded her arms as he crossed the room to collect the darts. She knew he wouldn't leave her alone until she told him the truth. "Let's see. Where to begin? Oh, yes, I remember now. My life stinks."

"Because your play closed?"

"If anyone could actually remember my name, I might have a chance at becoming a Jeopardy question." She swept her hand through the air dramatically like a game show host.

Greg chuckled. "I'll take 'Playwrights' for a thousand dollars, Alex."

Lori grabbed the darts from Greg's hand, turning them over in her fingers. "'The length of time it took Lori Scott's first play to flop.'" She threw a dart at the wall again. "That's what will flash onto the screen, the buzzer will sound, and then a hopeful contestant will answer, 'What is one week?'" Lori sighed. "One lousy week for one lousy play." The second dart followed the first.

Greg shrugged. "So it didn't last long. How many people can say they've even had a play on Broadway? Anyway, I still love ya."

She huffed. She had written one of the shortest-running plays ever produced on Broadway. Still aching from the humiliation, she was presently not answering calls, and had come running home to Mommy's house in Schenectady, New York, with her tail between her legs. But she couldn't stay here. Already neighbors were beginning to realize she was back, and it would be harder to dodge calls and visits from people here than from her Manhattan acquaintances.

Besides, it was said you couldn't go home again, and it was true. This place had too many memories that she'd been trying to outrun for too long. She missed the style of Manhattan—the Prada clothes and Manolo Blahnik shoes in elegant black, the nightclubs, the feeling of being where everything was fashionable. And she missed the energy and pace of a town where even the garbagemen ran to and from their trucks. But Manhattan was out of the question for now. She'd already sublet her apartment, and she didn't want to run into her ex-boyfriend, either.

No, she had to find somewhere else to go. Somewhere she could just lie low for a while. Where she could find a job and get her finances—and her life—back in order. She just didn't know where that place would be. She blinked back tears. She'd invested so much of herself into both her play and her relationship and now, just like that, they were both gone.

"I'm going to move someplace where people don't know who I am and that I'm a loser."

Greg smiled at her. "Shouldn't you put your hand to your forehead or something? For maximum effect?"

"Leave me alone, you big bully."

He pulled out the two darts and set them on the desk. Then, towering over her, he patted her head gently like she was a child. "Don't worry. Your next play will have a longer run."

"I hate when you do that." Lori pushed his arm away. "Why do you have to be so freakishly tall?"

"I think the pertinent question is why do you have to be so freakishly short?"

"Dinner will be ready soon."

Startled, they both turned toward the sound of their mother's voice. A plumper, size-fourteen version of Lori stood in the doorway, dressed in black jeans and a pink T-shirt which was partially covered by a flour-dusted apron. She smiled at her two children.

"Besides," Greg said, "can I help it if Mom wanted me around three years before she wanted you? I had a head start on the growth chart and you simply refused to catch up." He grabbed his mother and twirled her around.

"Stop that, you silly thing." Evelyn Scott laughed as she turned back to Lori. "Honey, don't you worry. Lots of people have plays that don't do so well at first. You can write another. Or maybe someone else will produce this one again." As always, her voice had just the right amount of loving encouragement.

Usually Lori would have allowed herself to be mollified, but not now, while she was steeping in self-pity. "The word you're searching for is *flop,* Mom. That's different than plays that don't do so well."

"Well, didn't you tell me Nicholas Adams, the big producer, wanted to see your next play when you finished it?"

"I don't care about plays anymore. I don't ever want to write plays again." She watched the two of them exchange a glance. Lori picked up another dart, drew back, and threw. If she imagined Nicholas Adams's face centered on the dartboard, then the dart hit him squarely on the nose. Big producer—ha! If her mother only knew.

She didn't need any more of Nick's patronizing attitude or, even worse, his attempts to convince her it wasn't natural to wait for marriage before being intimate, and his insistence that her way to success was to sleep her way to the top. With him, of course. The pig.

Lori turned and forced a smile. "Nicholas and I are no longer dating."

"Oh," said her mother. "I didn't know you *were* dating."

Greg said, "Don't worry, Lori. You know the old saying: There are lots more fish in the sea."

"How very comforting. Thank you." Lori rolled her eyes at him. "Anyway, it doesn't matter anymore. I plan on moving somewhere far from Schenectady and Manhattan, both."

"Like where?" Her mother looked worried.

Lori paused. "I'll go anywhere as long as no one there knows about my stupid play."

"Anywhere?" Greg's dark eyes lit up. "Outer Mongolia?"

"Now, Greg, she's just talking." Evelyn touched Lori's arm. "You know you're welcome to stay here as long as you want. Your room is always here for you."

It certainly was. Down to the shelf holding her stuffed animals and college textbooks and the desk she'd studied at for high school exams. The idea of moving back to her mother's home after being on her own in Manhattan made Lori feel like an even bigger loser.

She looked at her mother, and her heart softened. Lori hugged her. "Thanks for the offer."

"Lori can't move in here." Her brother shook his head. "You'd expect her to attend church, and she doesn't do church."

"Well, maybe if she did do church," her mother said gently, "her life would fall into place."

As if it were really that simple. "You mean like it did thirteen years ago?"

"Your father—"

"Mom, you know Lori doesn't like talking about Dad." Greg turned to his sister. "But Dad would like to see you."

"I bet." Lori eyed him, the old anger putting an edge on her voice. "Look, I'm glad you've maintained a relationship with him, Greg, but don't expect me to. In fact, back off."

"Okay, backing off the whole Dad subject." He saluted smartly. "Back to the play subject. Quit whining. You're only twenty-six and you've already had a play produced on Broadway. That's got to count for something."

"Not when it closes one week later."

"Ah—back to the pity party. Okay, then, are you serious about moving away? Would you just pick up and go"—he snapped his fingers—"like that?"

She did want to get away. From her humiliating Broadway flop. From the looks and whispers. From the new screenplay she hadn't been able to complete and a career that felt like it was totally the wrong choice. And especially from men like Nicholas Adams, who had proven himself to be far too much like her father.

If she really could escape her feelings of failure and discouragement with something as simple as a geographical move, she would do it in an instant. Smiling, knowing it really wasn't an option, she said, "Yeah. I think I would."

"Hang on." Greg disappeared out the door, calling out, "I'll be right back."

"Turn the thermostat down while you're out there." Sitting on her bed, Lori pulled her bare feet into a yoga pose and glanced at her mother. "I thought older women were supposed to want their houses Arctic cold."

"I guess I'm not as old as you think." Her mother paused, as if wary of upsetting Lori. "Have you had a chance to finish your screenplay? At Christmas you said you were nearly done."

Lori shook her head. "I can't seem to finish that, either. Nothing's going right for me." She hated how whiny she sounded, but she had given herself a full week to feel the pain of her world shattering—her play flopping and her boyfriend cheating on her—and she planned to make full use of the remaining four days.

Greg returned, unfolded a map of the United States, and pinned it over the dartboard before stepping back, motioning grandly. "Okay, sis. Toss and let's see where you're moving."

Evelyn frowned. "That's your silliest idea yet."

Lori laughed for perhaps the first time in the past three days. She knew Greg was teasing her, trying to cheer her up, and it had worked. The idea intrigued her.

"Oh, I don't know." Greg looked pensive. "I think sledding off the garage roof when I was ten might have been sillier."

"You didn't!" their mother protested. "You could have been maimed—or killed!"

He grinned at Lori. "What do you think? You wanna take a shot at a new place to live?"

"Sure." Her heart actually lifted at the thought, and she rose from the bed. She smiled at Greg's teasing, but it suddenly struck her that she could really do it. "I'll play along."

"You agree you'll move wherever the dart lands?" She could tell he was trying to suppress a grin. "Because otherwise, this is just a game."

More and more intrigued by the idea, Lori nodded. "I'll move anywhere the dart lands. Unless I hit water, of course."

"Promise? Because with you out of the way, all of Mom's homemade cookies are mine."

Greg might not have been serious, but suddenly Lori was. Her brother's crazy idea could solve her problem entirely. She wouldn't even have to choose where to go. She took a deep breath. She had nothing more to lose. She'd already lost her career, her boyfriend, and her pride. She'd wanted a few months away to think things through. Why not go with the toss of a dart? Wasn't the definition of insanity doing the same things and expecting different results? She was ready for different. "I promise. I'll let fate make my decision for me."

"I like the way you play." Greg handed Lori a dart. As if he realized she was taking his teasing seriously, he added, "Just to make it more interesting, though, let's say you can only move where you land if you also find a job online in one hour."

"You two quit clowning around." Frowning, her mother touched Lori's arm. "This is no way to choose where you're going to live. What if you end up someplace scary?"

"Mom, I've lived in Manhattan for two years. What could possibly scare me?" If Lori squinted, she could almost make out the East Coast and the area around New York state. Shifting her gaze to the left, she spotted what must be Hawaii.

Let fate decide? Well, maybe fate could use a hint.

Taking careful aim, she tossed the dart to the left—and immediately knew she'd gone off target. Still, the dart hit the board with a satisfying thwack. Well, living in California wouldn't be so bad. And if she'd hit water, she'd get to try again.

Greg beat her to the map, his body obscuring her view. After a pause, he started to laugh.

"What?" she demanded.

Grinning widely, he stepped aside and pointed. "See for yourself; otherwise, you'll never believe it."

She moved forward. Stopped. And stared.

No way.

"What do you suppose the odds are for something like that?" asked Greg. "They've gotta be astronomical."

The dart had landed just a few miles from the center of the seat of the church she used to attend: The Church of Jesus Christ of Latter-day Saints. LDS. Mormons. "Oh, I am so not moving to Brigham City, Utah."

Still chuckling, Greg handed her another dart. "Forget the game. You've always wanted to go to Hawaii. Why don't you just take a vacation and come back refreshed? Take your favorite brother along."

"I was *aiming* for Hawaii." She twirled her necklace, the one Grandpa Scott had given her.

"Maybe it really is fate." Her mother would think that, of course. She was the Relief Society president in her ward. And by the ethereal smile on her face, she obviously thought Lori's aim had been off because of divine intervention. "It would be good for you to go to church."

"Give Lori some space, Mom. She'll go when she's ready."

Lori spoke up. "I will not go back. I swore I never would after what Dad did, and I always keep my word." Neither of them seemed to believe her, though she thought she'd made her feelings clear numerous times.

"It's been thirteen years, honey. It's time to let go of the past. There's a reason we're supposed to forgive, and it's because our own healing can't begin until we do." Her mother sat on Lori's twin bed and smoothed the flowered quilt. "How long has it been since you called your father?"

"I don't want to talk about him." Lori realized she'd twirled her necklace into a knot, and she carefully unwound her finger.

"Well, if you don't believe in fate," her mother said, teasing, but not really, "you can stay here in your old room. I'd be glad to have you back."

But Lori already knew she couldn't stay here.

So why not Brigham City, Utah? She wanted to forget she ever had aspirations of writing plays and screenplays, and that seemed the perfect place for an ignominious forced retirement. Besides, she planned to forget all about men and relationships. Utah was full of Mormon men, and she would definitely never become romantically involved with a Mormon man. So that would work too.

Lori squared her shoulders and flashed a grin at her brother. "I said I'd go. And I will."

"Then it *is* fate." Her mother's face softened. "This could be a wonderful thing for you."

Lori laughed, seeing the wheels turn in her mother's head, expecting the Utah Mormons to be able to reconvert her daughter. Fat chance. "If it really is fate, and I'm meant to go to Brigham City, then I'll find a job online in the next hour, just like we agreed. Right?"

Greg stared at her. "You're not serious about this, are you? Because I was totally joking."

Lori shrugged. "It was a great idea."

"It was a very bad idea." He shook his head. "You need to be around family right now. Let us rally around you, and all that."

Lori shook her head. "We'll stick by our original agreement. If I can find a job in sixty minutes, I go."

Reluctantly, he said, "Okay, but if you don't, you stay."

"It's a deal," Lori said.

"I brought you a drink." Greg carried in two cold cans of pop and two glasses with ice, setting one of each on the computer desk. "Just in case you're wondering, the drink is root beer. There will be no caffeine for obstinate people going to Brigham City. You could probably get arrested just for having it on your breath."

"Very funny." Lori took a sip and enjoyed the coolness of it sliding down her throat, the chill of the glass against her hand.

He motioned toward the monitor. "Any luck?"

"There's a lady looking for an underpaid assistant at a small publishing house and a semi-well-paid newspaper columnist taking a sabbatical to China who needs a three-month replacement." She shrugged. "I doubt I'll hear back from either of them, though, especially in the next"—she checked her watch and smiled—"thirty minutes."

A tone sounded, indicating she had a new e-mail. When she opened it, she said, surprised, "The columnist wrote back. He wants my writing credentials." She stuck her small jump drive into the USB port of her laptop, pulled up her resume and samples of some articles, typed a brief note, and clicked SEND.

"Twenty-four minutes. He'll never make it." Greg pulled up a chair. "But what if he does? You wouldn't really go, would you?"

"I said I would, didn't I?" Suddenly nervous, she clicked on another job-search Web site and started a new search.

"Do you think that's wise? You don't even know anyone there."

"That's the whole point."

"Aren't you scared?" he asked in a teasing tone.

"Are you kidding? I'm scared of everything." She laughed. "Now I've gotta get back to work or you'll claim I'm cheating. And we can't have a lawyer thinking that."

He snorted. "I could sue you for that comment."

"Go for it, bro." She busied herself searching for anything else that looked like a legitimate job offer in or around Brigham City, Utah, and kept checking her watch.

Twenty minutes. Fifteen. Ten.

With only five minutes to go, she began to relax. Perhaps fate would be kinder than it had at first appeared. This time, she'd skip the dart and determine her own destiny.

She took another sip of her root beer and held the glass against her forehead. *Hawaii, here I come.*

When the theme song from *The Pink Panther* sounded from her phone, she caught Greg's eye. He raised an eyebrow as she grabbed her cell phone. "Hello?"

"Ms. Lori Scott?"

"Yes." She didn't recognize the voice.

"My name is Charles Dobson. You sent me your resume and are interested in covering my gardening column while I'm traveling."

Lori nodded at Greg. "Yes. It's good to speak with you. I am interested. Was there more information you needed from me?"

"Oh, certainly not. What you sent is more than adequate." His voice had a gravelly sound to it, and he spoke slower than she was used to in New York. "Though I have a question or two for you."

"All right."

"I can see that you can write, and that you do it well. But I need to know . . . do you garden?"

She had grown flowers in pots on the balcony of her apartment, and really, how hard could it be to transfer that knowledge to outside flower beds? Surely it was the same principle, just more sun. "Yes, I do."

"You wouldn't, by any chance, happen to be a Master Gardener?"

"No, I'm sorry."

A pause. "Oh, well, it can't be helped." He chuckled. "Congratulations, my dear. The job is yours."

That was it? Two questions? She gardened and wrote and so she got the job even though the only thing she knew about Master Gardeners was that she wasn't one? This guy was obviously desperate to leave for his Asian experience.

After the briefest of pauses, she said, "That's great," wondering if it was a lie.

"Let me tell you about the column. It's for the *Brigham City Daily.* You'll write three columns a week, five hundred words in length. They begin with a question and answer and then an article and an occasional recipe. I suppose I could write my column from China, with the World Wide Web, but I am taking a true sabbatical from all my writing."

Though he couldn't see her, she shrugged. "That sounds nice."

What was she doing? Greg was right—she didn't know anyone in Utah. She didn't have anywhere to stay, for that matter. But perhaps Charles Dobson had some ideas. "Do you have any suggestions for apartments in the area? I realize I could do the column online, but I'm also looking to get away for a while, and I'll need to find a place to stay while I'm there."

"Well, my house will be empty, but . . ." He paused for a moment. "I would prefer to rent my home to someone who is LDS. You know—Mormon. Just one of my little idiosyncrasies. Sorry. But I'll prepare a list of phone numbers for local rental properties and e-mail them to you."

"I'm LDS." Why she let those words slip out, she didn't know. Now would he expect her to attend church? And would he double her rent when he returned and learned she hadn't?

Greg grinned at her, and Lori turned away from him, her cheeks warm. So what if she hadn't been inside an LDS chapel for thirteen years? She'd been baptized, she'd attended mutual activities with her best friend Marti, and she still wore the pretty silver CTR ring her mother had given her years ago.

"That is almost too good to be true." He paused again. "Oh, the column also involves recipes, so I hope you have a few. Perhaps you know what vegetable goes best with green Jell-O?"

Where had that question come from? "Carrots. Though I've never known anyone who actually eats it that way."

"Since you live in New York, perhaps you'll find it interesting to know Joseph Smith dug up the silver plates in your part of the country."

Oh. She repressed a laugh as she got it—he thought she was pretending to be LDS just to get the house. She decided to play along. "I didn't know about the silver plates." She paused for a beat, just to put a little fun into the game, then added, "I only heard about the gold ones."

"Oh, yes," he said. "How silly of me. And I suppose you've heard about the Mormon synagogues?"

"You mean temples?" She decided to cut him some slack. "Perhaps you'd like to get a reference from my Relief Society president mother?"

As he realized she knew what he was doing, he had the good grace to chuckle. "That won't be necessary. You've got the job. And if you want the house, you've got that too. If you promise to take good care of my garden, I'll only charge you three hundred dollars in rent."

"A week?"

"A month, my dear."

Three hundred dollars a month in rent? She'd spent more than that for her last pair of Jimmy Choo sling backs. And after all, how much care could his flower garden require? A paying job, extremely low rent, and a chance to get away from the spotlight—perfect. "Mr. Dobson, you've got yourself a deal."

"And if you need a vehicle to drive, I will leave you my Ben, though I would expect you to pay the difference in insurance to have you listed as the principal driver for the next three months. And you must promise to take very good care of him. He's a classic car."

"I'm not sure I should do that. I can rent a car."

"No, really. As long as you take care of him and promise to drive him at least once a week, I'll be glad to share. Besides, if he sits in the garage for three months, he'll start to deteriorate, and right now he runs great. And you'll love Ben. Really. He's cherry-red with a 327 engine and headers. He's a real head turner, all right." He paused. "You can drive a four-speed, can't you?"

"My brother taught me."

"Good."

"Sounds like you've just made me an offer I can't refuse, Mr. Dobson. I will be very careful with your classic car."

"All right." He sounded pleased. "Your first article will be due two weeks from Monday."

Amazed, she realized she was really doing it. She was moving to, of all the unlikely places, Brigham City, Utah. "Thank you."

As she hung up the phone, her brother batted his eyelids melodramatically and pressed his hands to his heart. "Mom is right. This *is* fate."

"Jerk." Lori tossed a pillow at him.

"So now you're LDS, huh?" He caught the pillow and fell onto the bed, laughing. "I still think you're nuts."

"I probably am." Lori grinned. "Wish me luck."

"You'll need more than luck." He tossed the pillow back at her. "Better get some Prozac."

Chapter Two

This was exactly why John Wayne Walker hadn't brought a woman home to meet his oversized, bossy, and noisy family since high school—because they made such a big flipping deal about it.

It wasn't like he'd asked Dawn to marry him. He'd just brought her home for Sunday dinner. But even now, John's mother and three sisters-in-law were hustling Dawn into the kitchen to help with the dishes—as if she were already one of them.

But if Dawn fit in so well with his family, why was he having trouble breathing?

More relieved to get away than he ought to be for someone who, just two weeks earlier, had taken his relationship to a new level, John followed his father and three brothers into the den.

As he closed the door behind him, muffling the sounds of women and children, John drew in a deep breath for the first time in thirty minutes.

His father grinned widely and pointed to a fancy new Bose docking system for the latest iPod. "Check it out. My new mini sound system."

They all made appreciative sounds. John's older brother Kirk whistled. "Gotta have the latest toys, don't you, Dad?"

His father chuckled. "Gotta have rewards for all those years of hard work."

John's younger brother, Roy, picked up the credit-card-sized remote. "So how does it feel to be retired, Deputy Fire Chief Walker?"

His father, who'd retired only two months before, grinned. "Darn good."

At thirty-six, John's eldest brother, Clint, was also a firefighter/

paramedic like John and Roy, though in the nearby town of Logan rather than Brigham City. "Tell the truth, Dad. Don't you miss fighting fires?"

Their father paused for a moment. "It'll be an adjustment, that's for sure. But I'll try to plug the holes with some exciting hobbies."

Clint snorted. "Yeah, right."

Roy laughed. "That'll have to be one heck of a hobby."

"That's great," John teased, glad to have his unfamiliar anxiety fading. "Does that mean you'll go hang gliding with me and Travis next time we go?"

"Maybe a hobby not quite that exciting." Dad looked at John. "I'm glad you've brought a nice girl home, John. You know what Brigham Young said about single men over twenty-five being a menace to society—and you're seven years past that."

John rolled his eyes. "Thanks for the vote of confidence."

"Dawn seems nice." Roy raised an eyebrow and lowered his voice dramatically. "So when is the wedding?"

Irritated, John said, "You know, this is why I don't bring women around you guys."

His father pushed a button on the remote and the husky vocals of Nat King Cole filled the air. "Don't you think you ought to limit your extreme sports now that you're getting serious with a woman?"

"It's impossible for John to get too serious with a woman, Dad. He gets bored with them."

Roy had that right. Lately John always seemed to be bored, no matter which woman he was with. The more he dated, the more he realized he was tired of the whole scene. He was ready for marriage—and children. And that had led to Dawn being in the family dining room, which had led to him feeling like the walls were closing in.

Why would that be? He'd been dating her with no problem. He even liked her enough that two weeks ago he'd suggested making the relationship exclusive. At least Dawn carried her end of the conversation, was easy on the eyes, and she could make him laugh. The boredom he'd experienced on many of his dates was held at bay with her—but he still missed the spark he felt should be there, the spark his brothers seemed to have with their wives.

"Plus he has that commitment phobia thing going." Roy laughed. "In fact, I'd bet fifty bucks John hasn't even asked Dawn to our family picnic at Lagoon this Saturday."

"That'd be a fool's bet," said Clint. "Of course he hasn't."

"I don't know." Kirk raised an eyebrow. "After all, he did bring her here today and that's a first."

His father and three brothers looked at John, waiting for the answer to a question that was none of their business.

"I do not have a commitment problem. And, not that it's any of your business, but I'm ready to settle down. Just as soon as I find the right woman."

"I knew it." Roy punched the air. "He hasn't invited her."

"Since when do you guys care if I have a date or not?"

Clint put his hand to his chest. "Come on, Johnnie boy, you're killing us."

John had been thinking about inviting Dawn to Lagoon, but not here with his nosy family watching. Disgusted with the lack of privacy in his family, he said, "No, I haven't asked Dawn."

His brothers laughed, and John changed the subject. "Did you hear about the fires moving closer to Heber?"

That did the trick. His father jumped on the new topic with both feet, Roy followed suit, and Clint chimed in. In moments, they were discussing the similarities with the forest fire they'd fought the summer before in California. Even Kirk, the renegade brother who'd turned policeman rather than firefighter, could hold his own in the conversation since he'd gone up as a volunteer on several of the fires they'd fought.

John relaxed and enjoyed the guy talk.

All too soon, Roy's wife, Becky, opened the door. She'd gained some weight in the past few months, though now she just looked softer and prettier. "Ah, ha. There you are."

Dawn followed her in, smiled at John, and surprised him by taking his hand. He could feel his face flush warm as his brothers smirked.

Becky casually said, "I was just telling Dawn about our get-together this Saturday."

Dawn nodded. "It sounds like you'll all have a lot of fun. It's nice you're so close."

John felt an instant flash of resentment toward Becky. And toward Dawn. Why did he feel this resistance, he wondered. He'd been ready to ask her. Was it because she'd brought it up first? Was he really that much of a Neanderthal that he needed to make all the moves himself? He didn't know. He just knew he didn't like being pressured. He'd ask her later, away from the prying eyes of his family.

His father cleared his throat. When John looked at him, his father raised an eyebrow. His brothers were no better. They stared at him, daring him silently, except for Roy, who whispered, "Fifty bucks."

If they wanted to invite Dawn, let them. John would do it on his own timetable. He smiled at her and changed the subject again. "Did you talk with your mother? What did the doctor say?"

"There's good news." Dawn's eyes brightened. "Dad's in remission. His leukemia's gone."

"That's fantastic news!"

John's four-year-old niece, Gabi, ran into the room and between their legs. He picked her up and tickled her until she giggled and said, "Stop it, Uncle John."

"She's adorable." Dawn smiled at John. "What's her name?"

"Gabriella. She's Clint's little girl. Takes after his wife, thank goodness."

"Hey," said Clint.

"That's a beautiful name." Dawn reached out her arms, and Gabi slipped into them. Once again, John should have been glad that this woman, who he was considering asking—someday—to marry him, liked children as much as he did, but the anxious feeling returned. Maybe things were moving too quickly for his comfort.

As John's mother and two other sisters-in-law crowded into the den, his mother said, "So how far along are you now, Becky?"

Immediately phrases from the women rose, mingled, and hung in the air: "Six months along . . . October tenth . . . baby shower . . . morning sickness . . . wonderful."

Roy and Becky were going to have a baby? He'd noticed Becky looked like she'd gained a little weight, but he hadn't realized why.

It hadn't bothered John when his two older brothers, Kirk and Clint, had married their wives, but when Roy, who was two years younger than John, had married three years ago, it had been harder to handle. This news was like a fist in his gut. He ached for a wife and children of his own.

He'd been looking for "the right one" for a decade.

Maybe "the right one" was a myth.

Perhaps true love took awhile to develop—after marriage, after children, after a while.

John looked at Dawn again. As if she felt his gaze upon her, she glanced up and her face lit with a warm smile for him.

He smiled back. He did care for her. There was a warmth there for her. Was that love? He didn't know, but suddenly he hoped that the warmth he felt could be fanned into a flame. He wanted a wife who would totally light his fire, who would ignite a flame even a firefighter couldn't put out.

Perhaps he'd have to wade through those first few years of marriage to reach that point.

Maybe Dawn really was the right one.

Chapter Three

"Oh, yeah, dude. I remember that car. Old dude made arrangements for someone else to pick it up." The young man was in his twenties, his arms covered with swirling and colorful tattoos. He pushed back his long hair with one hand and held the copy of the claim ticket in the other. "Wait here and I'll get it for you."

"Thanks," said Lori. She watched Tattoo Guy thread his way back through the cars until he disappeared down a side row.

She was hot and tired. It had been a long flight from New York to Salt Lake City. As soon as she'd landed and retrieved her luggage, she'd called the number for Park 'n Jet and they'd sent a shuttle over immediately.

Right now she didn't much care what Charles Dobson's car looked like, or if it was a classic or not. She just wanted to get inside, drive to his house, and lie down. Even ibuprofen hadn't been able to knock the headache that'd started mid-flight.

A car drove up the side row and she got her hopes up, but it wasn't old and it wasn't cherry-red. Lori sighed and rubbed her forehead.

From the brochure Charles had mailed her, she knew this place had more than twelve hundred stalls, so it might take forever for Tattoo Guy to retrieve Charles's classic car. Impatient at the delay, she put her fingers to her aching temples.

Finally, an older red car headed up the middle row. This must be Charles's cherry-red vintage auto. It even looked kind of cool, in an antique kind of way. Maybe she would enjoy driving a classic.

As the young man pulled it up beside her, she blinked her eyes. It took a few seconds for the truth of what she was seeing to register. What started out as an ordinary-looking car suddenly morphed into a truck bed.

She walked around the car, shaking her head. This was a classic? Ben was the ugliest vehicle she'd ever seen. If this was Charles's classic car, what on earth did his house look like?

Dazed, she looked at Tattoo Guy. "What is it?"

"A '65 Chevrolet El Camino, dude." He grinned and hopped out of the car.

"Who designed it? The most indecisive person in the world? Is it for people who can't decide between a truck and a car?"

He handed her the keys and shrugged. "At least it's got a hot engine and the AC works. Listen, I gotta go help this other couple, dude. Thanks for using Park 'n Jet."

"Yeah. Sure. Thanks."

Still shaking her head, Lori climbed into the front seat. There was a sheet of paper folded neatly on the passenger seat.

With a sigh, she unfolded the note.

> Dear Ms. Scott,
> Please take good care of Ben; he's not as young as he used to be.
> - Charles Dobson

He wasn't kidding, either. Ben was decades older than Lori and she hoped she'd never be anywhere near as ugly. Ben was a monstrosity.

She started to laugh. *Must be the hysteria setting in,* she thought. What a hoot. And she'd promised to drive this monstrosity, at least once a week, for the next three months. If her old friends could see her now, they'd doubtless die laughing.

She was wrong. She *did* care what Charles's car looked like. And she hoped that he, right at this very moment, was riding the ugliest and most uncomfortable yak in all of China.

Lori steered the vehicle to the curb, pulled out the key, and climbed from the coolness of the car into the hot July sun. She'd stopped at a local grocery store, Kent's Market, to buy a few basics, and now she was ready to drop. At least the ibuprofen was beginning to work, because her headache, though still there, had eased a little.

At least Tattoo Guy had been right: the monstrosity on wheels had a working air conditioner. Utah wasn't nearly as humid as New York, but still hot nonetheless. Ninety-seven, if the thermometer Charles had glued to the dashboard could be trusted. It had taken more than an hour to work her way through the Wednesday traffic from the Salt Lake International Airport to Brigham City, which was at the edge of nowhere with fields everywhere. There was even a large "Welcome to Brigham City" sign overhanging Main Street. She'd just moved to Mayberry with Mormons. It was enough to make her headache worse.

Lori just wanted to go inside her new house, pull the blinds shut, turn the AC on full blast, and take a long nap.

She squinted against the blazing July sun. The fluffy clouds along the horizon did nothing to block the harsh rays. She was also going to put on some lotion, as she could already feel the moisture being sucked from her skin.

Leaving her bags in the monstrosity, she walked to the front door, still wearing the sunglasses she'd donned when her play flopped and hadn't taken off in public since then, though her pity party was now officially over.

Charles's house at 521 Hill Street was a quaint, older brick cottage with a curved door and ornate handle. It wasn't classy, definitely not New York, but cozy in a small-town kind of way. And, she noted with relief, it wasn't a monstrosity.

She caught sight of an envelope taped to the inside of the glass storm door. Her name was printed on it, so she retrieved it and pulled out the neatly printed note inside.

> Dear Ms. Scott,
> The key is safe with Agatha McCrea, next door at 525 Hill Street. Thank you.
> - Charles Dobson
> P.S. Would you mind taking care of my cat?

Lori groaned aloud.

A cat. He hadn't said anything about a cat. She didn't even like cats. She was more of a dog person.

Pushing her sunglasses up her nose and tugging on her purse strap, she sighed deeply and walked toward the next house. She hadn't wanted to meet any neighbors while she was here.

Stepping onto the porch of Agatha McCrea's house, she noticed the neatly tended flower garden.

Lori knocked and, as she waited, thought how amazing it was that these people were so trusting they would leave their house keys with neighbors. She was definitely not in New York anymore.

She raised her hand to knock again when the door was opened by an older woman whose hair was pulled back in an elaborate style of curves and curls and who sported an apron announcing "Don't Expect Miracles." The woman looked like a typical grandma, only her hair was still brown with just a few streaks of gray. The woman tilted her head and smiled. "Yes?"

"Ms. McCrea?"

"Oh, land sakes, how silly of me. You must be Lori Scott. Come on in, sweetie." She held open the screen door. "And call me Agatha. 'Ms. McCrea' makes me feel older than my years, and my years are already older than dirt."

"Oh, I doubt that."

"Let's just say I could have officially joined the Red Hat Club fifteen years ago, and leave it at that."

At the moment, Lori really didn't care how old Agatha was. Her head was starting to pound again, and she needed to get out of the heat. "I came to get the key. Charles left a note saying you had it."

"I do. Come on in and I'll get it for you. Wouldn't want to just leave it lying around, you know. It might get lost."

Lori stepped into the cool of the house. What a relief.

Agatha led her into a very feminine living room, filled with wicker furniture and soft flowered cushions, and pointed to one of the chairs. "Would you like some lemonade, sweetie? You look a little peaked."

Lori sank gratefully into the chair. "Actually, that sounds wonderful. Thank you."

"You just sit there and I'll go get us some."

Lori listened to Agatha humming in the kitchen before closing her eyes for a moment, nearly falling asleep in the chair.

When Agatha returned, she handed Lori a glass. The woman may have been in her sixties, but she moved like a much younger woman.

After draining half the glass of cool liquid, Lori leaned back with a sigh. "Thank you. That was exactly what I needed."

"Just the ticket on a hot day." Agatha placed two coasters shaped like honeybees on the table between them and sat in the wicker chair opposite. "Charlie tells me you're from New York. That is so exciting."

Lori took another sip and thought of her play flopping like a fish on land. "Not as much as you might think."

"Ah. There's a story in there somewhere, I think." Agatha leaned back in her chair and intertwined her fingers and waited.

As if Lori were going to tell this stranger her most humiliating moment. No way. She set her glass on the empty coaster and forced a smile. "I appreciate your hospitality, but I've been traveling since early this morning, and I would really like to get settled."

"Oh, yes. Of course. What was I thinking?" Agatha set down her glass, stood, and went over to the wooden mantel above her fireplace. There was a collection of little jars, about fifteen in all. Agatha picked up the first one, lifted the lid, and looked inside.

She replaced it and picked up the next one. "You know, I put things in safe places and then I can't find them later. It drives me crazy."

It was driving Lori crazy, too. She did her best not to sigh in frustration. Did everyone here in Utah move—and speak—this slowly? You could apparently fit a hundred New York minutes into one Utah minute.

"So are you a single lady? I notice there's no ring."

Lori glanced down at her ring-less fingers. Uncanny. The older woman had zeroed in on Lori's two areas of humiliation. With a wry chuckle, Lori said, "Definitely single."

"There are several men I can think of around here who will want to change that right quick. Good LDS men." Agatha lifted another lid. Lori swallowed another impatient sigh as Agatha continued to work her way from one jar to the next. Slowly. Ever so slowly. "Men who, unlike Charlie, don't plan on spending the rest of their lives as confirmed bachelors."

"I'm not looking to change my status."

"Won't matter to them, sweetie. They're men, therefore they're clueless."

"You've got that right."

Agatha lifted the lid on the last jar. "Ah-ha."

Finally.

"Here you are, Miss Scott."

"Lori, please. And thank you." Lori stood and took the keys.

"Oh, sweetie, you are like a breath of fresh air in this neighborhood. Your accent is delightful. Come back any time."

"Thanks." Heading for the door, Lori remembered the note. Reluctantly, she turned back to Agatha. "Mr. Dobson's note asked if I would take care of his cat. Do you know where I'll find it?"

Agatha laughed, a husky sound. "The cat's not at Charlie's."

Lori did sigh at that. She didn't want the bother of watching after the cat, but knew she should be worried about it.

Agatha continued, "She hangs out with my cats. They're probably out back. I'll bring her over to Charlie's house later."

Lori supposed that was all she could do about the unexpected cat problem. "Thanks."

"You are most welcome."

Before Lori could step outside, Agatha grabbed her and gave her a huge, all-encompassing hug. Lori couldn't loosen up enough to hug her back.

When Agatha released her, she smiled warmly. "Welcome to the neighborhood."

Beautiful blossoms filled the two flower beds lining the walk from the driveway to Charles's house. There must have been twenty different kinds of flowers, half of which Lori didn't recognize. It was quickly becoming obvious to Lori that she'd have to do a little research to write his flower columns. But she'd worry about that later.

For now, she just wanted to go inside, cool down, eat something, and rest.

Turning the key in the lock, she opened the curved door and stepped inside. It was about twenty degrees cooler inside, which meant it was still nearly eighty in the old house.

She paused in the small tile entryway, closed the door, and stopped. There was the doorknob and a deadbolt, but nothing else. That was it? Two locks? Where was the security system in this place? Back home she had four locks plus a chain. Even her mother's place had three locks.

In the semi-darkness, she made her way to the windows and pulled back the drapes.

Slanting open the blinds and letting in the indirect sunlight, she turned and caught her first sight of the room. And laughed. She couldn't help it.

She'd left her beautiful, elegant, black-on-white New York apartment for this? What had she been thinking? None of her family or friends would even believe this place. She'd have to take pictures.

The couch and two chairs were well kept up, not worn or torn at all, but way out of style—maybe even as old as Ben—with doilies laid neatly over the arms. A sturdy oak coffee table in the center of the room and two heavy lamps adorning matching end tables completed the furnishings. Charles must have bought them all in a different era.

The furniture wasn't the only thing that was out of style. There were old-fashioned decorations everywhere. On one end table, there were even some of the old resin grape clusters like Lori's Great-Grandma Forsythe had made in Relief Society eons ago. But at least the place was clean. And it was certainly roomier than her very expensive and very small walk-up.

Suddenly she started to laugh in earnest. Surprised, she realized her heart was a little lighter.

This was the perfect place for her to get away and hide from everyone she knew. No one would search for her here. And the more she looked around, the more she laughed. She was caught in a Mormon time warp in Brigham City, Utah, and it seemed incredibly funny.

Wiping away tears, she walked into the hallway to find the control for the central air. As she adjusted it, she hoped it wouldn't take too long to lower the temperature.

This really might be a good place to lick her wounds. To make the changes she needed to make, once she figured out what they were. She used to be happy when she was writing her plays and screenplays, but she didn't want anything to do with that now. No, for the next three months, she was going to take pleasure in simply writing three flower columns a week. Set some new goals. Think things through.

Either that—or the slower pace of life here might drive her crazy after the energy of Manhattan. Even Schenectady moved faster than Brigham City.

She lugged in her suitcase, laptop case, and the bag of groceries, leaving the heavy duffle for later. She set them in the kitchen, which held an old chrome-edged table and padded chairs. She would have been surprised to find anything else. Surely Charles hadn't intended it when he bought them thirty years ago, but the table and chairs were retro cool.

One of those old-fashioned cat clocks hung on the wall, its tail and eyes moving back and forth. There was a corkboard on the far wall with a bright orange piece of paper tacked to it amid recipe cards and the miscellany of Charles's life. Another note.

> Dear Ms. Scott,
> I thought you might like to read through my previous columns to bring yourself up to speed; you'll find them in the filing cabinet in my office, down at the end of the hall. Your new boss is Russell Neal, and his phone number is written below. Call to set up an appointment so you can become an official, paid employee and get started on the column.
> – Charles Dobson
> P.S. Don't forget to feed Fluffy; her food is under the sink. And please be sure to harvest my zucchini.

Zucchini? Lori hated zucchini. What did he expect her to do with it after she harvested it? Certainly not eat it. And there was absolutely no way she was going to can anything. Even her mother wasn't that domestic. What other requests was Charles going to spring on her?

She opened the fridge to put away her few groceries. On the bare shelves sat two hamburger patties in plastic wrap, resting on a plate alongside a whole tomato, a couple of slices of wrapped cheese, an avocado, a container of coleslaw, and condiments.

When she saw another note taped to the ketchup bottle, she smiled. Was she going to find notes all over the house?

> Dear Ms. Scott,
> If you're hungry when you arrive, feel free to use my grill out on the patio. These burgers have already been seasoned. There are buns in the bread box on the counter. Please make yourself at home.
> - Charles Dobson

The last thing she'd expected was to be amused by the older man who was renting her his house, but she was. He lived in a museum of early Relief Society craft relics, had a cat and zucchini—both of which she avoided at all costs—a flower garden, and Ben the car/truck, but he was quite thoughtful.

Maybe her mother was right. Maybe it really was fate that had brought her here. And if that was the case, then why not enjoy herself?

She wandered down the hall. There were two bedrooms and one bath. Washing her hands in the bathroom, she reached for a towel. She'd never seen a towel so thick. Something like this would have mildewed in the humidity back home. She fingered it, enjoying the plush luxury.

One bedroom had been set up as a neat and tidy office, while the other housed an old-fashioned but quite elegantly curved oak bedroom set. She laid down on top of the quilt and sighed at how comfortable the bed was. She wanted to take a quick nap, but relaxation would have to wait until after she ate; her stomach was starting to growl.

She climbed off and set her suitcase on the double-sized bed, opened it, shucked off her skirt and blouse, kicked off her high heels, and pulled on black shorts, a black T-shirt, and black Manolo sandals with black satin flowers on the toes.

As soon as she opened the French door off the dining room, the outside heat hit her again. At least the patio was covered and had an overhead fan. She turned it on and enjoyed the light breeze it created.

Charles's yard didn't seem very big, and there was no garden or zucchini anywhere that she could see, just a large hedge not too far away. A shiny gas barbecue grill took up almost one whole end of the patio.

"Lori," a woman's voice called out, and she turned. Agatha waved over the adjoining fence. "I've got Fluffy."

Lori walked over, and Agatha handed a fat white cat with the fluffiest fur Lori had ever seen over the fence. Fluffy, indeed.

"Thanks. I think." Lori took the cat, amazed at how much it weighed, and set it gently on the ground. "What does she eat?"

"Just regular cat food. A lot of it. And a bird or two." Agatha smiled. "Don't worry about keeping track of her. She'll just come back over later to visit with my cats. I always leave cat food and water out for my babies. Though Charlie denies it vehemently, she's always over here anyway, even when he's home."

As if to prove Agatha's point, Fluffy ambled over to a storage bench, leapt onto a low branch of an outstretched pine tree limb, and shot right back over the fence.

"Thanks," Lori said, grateful. She found herself liking the older woman, almost against her will. "That'll be one worry off my mind, especially since I have to take care of both his garden and his column while he's gone. I wasn't planning on the cat. Or the zucchini."

"Oh, yes, taking care of Charlie's garden is enough worry for any one mind." Agatha nodded sympathetically, then smiled brightly. "See you later, sweetie. I'm going to my Web site design class."

Web site design? Surprised, Lori watched the older woman walk gracefully back to her house.

With the cat safely in Agatha's yard, Lori figured it was time to relax and eat. She turned toward the backyard. And gasped.

The hedge had hidden the garden from view. It was *huge!* And it wasn't filled with flowers either, though they bloomed profusely around the edges of a giant square. No, the garden was filled with vegetables.

Charles's question "Do you garden?" flitted back through her mind. Lori had no idea what scale of garden he'd planted. And he expected her to take care of this? He should have held out for a Master Gardener.

As she walked toward the huge garden plot, stunned, she recognized a peach tree and an apple tree. She loved apples. But what was she supposed to do with the rest of it?

Totally overwhelmed, she suddenly wanted to move somewhere else, and forget Charles Dobson's house and his column—and especially his garden—altogether.

Unfortunately, she had given Charles her word. About his column, his house, his cat, and his monstrosity on wheels.

Even more unfortunately, she never went back on her word. But, holy cow, she wanted to turn tail and run.

She took one last long look at the humongous garden and shook her head in dismay. She'd have to learn to make it work, that's all. She could do it. She would make a success of this venture.

And to keep herself from getting depressed, she needed to eat. First burgers, then the chocolate she'd bought.

She turned back toward the house, and her stomach growled again. Time to grill a burger. She lifted the top of the spotless grill, picked up the fancy long red lighter lying across the little bars, turned a knob, and lit the grill.

Immediately, flames shot out from underneath the grill and engulfed the entire thing.

"Oh, oh, oh," she cried, stumbling back.

She was going to burn Charles's house down, and she hadn't even been here thirty minutes. If it spread to the detached garage, he'd lose Ben, too. But that would be a mercy.

Keeping her eyes on the flames, which seemed to be growing larger, she fumbled her cell phone out of her pocket and touched just three keys: 911.

THE GARDEN GURU

Dear Dr. Dobson: I remember my grandfather planting peas every spring, but they were the normal green variety. I was in a garden today that had a stunning purple-podded pea. What can you tell me about it? (Mark)

Dear Mark: You have discovered a rare beauty: the Capucijner's Purple Pod, also know as the Dutch Grey. These are an old variety, developed in the 1500s by the Capuchin monks of Europe. Almost every supermarket in Holland carries them, though they're a rare find here. When they're young, you can use the green peas inside as snow peas, or dry them for soup peas. The plant itself is very decorative and the dark purple pea pods amidst the purple and white flowers are indeed a gorgeous mix. You'll have to search for this one, but it's well worth the effort.

In other news, I am glad to announce that, after some effort on my part, I have located my capable substitute. I'll introduce her in the next column. I know she will continue the standard of excellence I have always striven for . . .

Chapter Four

"I suppose you both have dates tomorrow night, after our shift is over?" asked Roy, who sat on John's right in the fire truck. Roy was filling in for Larry, who was ill.

"From your smug tone, I suppose you think married life is so much better than being single, right?" responded John's buddy Travis, who sat on his left, behind the wheel. Travis's tone of voice left no doubt as to what he thought about marriage. John doubted there was a woman alive who could catch Travis—for longer than a month, that is. He allowed himself to be caught all the time for a few weeks, but then he'd move on, leaving the woman brokenhearted.

Sandwiched between them, John poked both his brother and his friend in the ribs. "Quiet, you two. I'm too tired to listen to you."

They'd had a busy day, and John was looking forward to relaxing at the station tonight. He wouldn't have to worry about anything except eating a good meal, watching a movie with the other guys, and getting a good night's sleep.

Maybe after he and Dawn got married . . . A chill shot up his spine. And not in a good way. What was that about? He was ready to get married, wasn't he?

Travis glanced over at him, grinned, then moved his gaze back to the road. As the engineer of their shift, Travis drove the engine on all calls, including the one they were just returning from, where they'd rescued an eighty-five-year-old man who'd managed to climb into his peach tree to help his five-year-old great-granddaughter down, but couldn't handle the climb down himself.

"And from your smug tone," Roy said, "I have no doubt you think being single is preferable to the married life."

"Well, isn't it?" Travis asked, without looking over again.

"You wish." Roy laughed. "You still didn't answer my question. Do you both have hot dates lined up for tomorrow night?"

"What does it matter?" John asked, not wanting to think about dates. He still hadn't recovered from taking Dawn over to his parents' home for dinner on Sunday.

"Oh, it matters." Travis drummed his fingers on the steering wheel in time with the music. "And the answer is *yes.* Of course I've got a hot date."

Roy chuckled. "What I've got is better."

"I dated five women last month," said Travis, his fingers quiet and still. "What could be better than that?"

"So you've got quantity. Big deal. I've got quality."

"You're just jealous, Roy-Boy." Travis grinned. "You've gotta be wishing you could date a lot of women instead of going home to your—"

"Watch it!" said Roy.

Travis laughed ruefully. "My argument just went downhill. You go home to your gorgeous, loving wife every night."

"And that's why I'm not jealous." Roy folded his arms and leaned back.

John chuckled. Travis liked to date a lot of women, but he obviously could still see the advantages of marriage, even if he didn't think the advantages outweighed his preferred life as a confirmed bachelor.

John adjusted the air conditioner vent so it blew on his chest and not in his face. With the hundred-degree July weather they'd been having, he was glad to be sitting inside.

The radio crackled. "Brush fire seven miles north of Exit 362. Three, are you close?"

John and his men were from Station Four. A member of Station Three responded immediately: "Roger that. We'll head over and take it. Three, over."

John glanced at his brother. "Still, you've gotta admit there are perks to the single life." Perks John was becoming painfully and acutely aware of every time he considered giving up his own freedom for the advantages of a wife and children.

"You're right." Roy shrugged. "You get to risk life and limb without worrying about how it affects others."

"That's just our job." Travis turned the corner, heading the engine back toward Station Four. "Yours, too, remember? You're married, but you were just as high up in that peach tree as I was helping that old guy, so what's your point?"

"I meant your extreme sports." Roy motioned with his hand. "You risk life and limb on your job . . . and then you go out and do it all over again in your spare time."

"That reminds me, Travis," John said, knowing it would bother Roy. "You wanna go hang gliding next week?"

"You bet." Travis glanced over at Roy, a smile playing on his lips. "Maybe we could line up some alligator wrestling afterward."

"Very funny," Roy said while the other two laughed. "When you've got someone depending on you, you have to give up that kind of stuff."

"Which is why you're jealous," said Travis. "You'd love to be hang gliding with us. The wind blowing past. The thrill of flying. Admit it, Roy. You'd like to still be doing that."

"Oh, I'll admit I miss the thrill of flying. But I wouldn't take it up again if it meant losing Becky meeting me at the door when I come home—and making love with someone who wants to be with me forever."

"I hate having arguments with you," Travis groused. "You fight dirty."

The dispatcher's voice filled the cab of the fire truck again. "We have a gas barbecue grill fire at . . ." Static distorted part of the message. ". . . Four, can you take it?"

John picked up the receiver. "Four here, Dispatch. Repeat the address. You cut out."

"Five-twenty-one Hill Street."

"Copy. We're just around the corner. We're on it. Four, over." John grinned at his partners. "Gear up, gentlemen. We've got another job to do."

"Aye, aye, Cap'n," said Travis as he turned left. A few streets further down, he turned right onto Hill.

Roy glanced in the mirror. "Mike's right behind us in the Rescue."

Whether it was called an ambulance when driven by an EMT or a Rescue when manned by paramedics, the vehicle Mike Patterson and Quinn Jackson drove always responded with the fire trucks.

The address tickled at John's memory. Finally he said, "That's Dobson's house." Charles was a friend of his father's, and John had been to his house for barbecues before.

The adrenaline started pumping through John's veins. A gas grill fire could go out on its own in minutes, and usually did. But sometimes, though not very often, they could explode.

Two minutes later, both vehicles screeched to a stop at the curb in front of the house. He hoped Charles was all right.

"Good response time, as always," Travis said. "Two minutes. Oh, yeah, we're good."

Three to five minutes was the department's goal, which they were able to hit most of the time.

The firefighters flung open the doors of the fire truck and clambered down, John on the passenger side behind Roy. John grabbed his gear and turned . . . and stopped dead in his tracks.

The most gorgeous woman he'd ever seen was walking down the driveway to meet them.

He stood, stunned. She was dressed in black Capri shorts and a black T-shirt, with peach-painted toenails peeking out from sandals with little black flowers and tiny straps encircling her delicate ankles. Her blonde hair was cut short and stylish and shimmered like honeyed sunshine.

Someone shoved him. "Come on, John."

Roy's voice and the shove snapped him out of whatever had caught him.

When the woman got within feet of them, he could see she had beautiful green eyes with yellow flecks. Now when had he noticed details like that? Her fantastic figure, yes. Of course. He was a guy. But eye color? He shook his head slightly, trying to clear away his foolishness.

The woman was distraught. "I swear to you, I lit the grill and instead of the fire coming up where it's supposed to, it flashed out underneath." She had a brisk New York accent and was obviously embarrassed as she related the details. "I thought the entire house was going to burn down. If I'd realized the fire would go out on its own, I wouldn't have called. I'm really sorry."

Travis put out his hand. "Travis Eckles, ma'am. At your service," he purred in his smooth California surfer-dude voice, his blond hair and tan skin matching the image he liked to project. "Show us the grill and we'll be glad to check it out for you."

John narrowed his eyes. Trust Travis to jump on any opportunity to meet a beautiful woman.

John followed the pair through the gate and into the backyard where a large hedge lined a portion of the space. He'd been to Charles Dobson's house before and knew the yard was well-tended. What he didn't know was why this woman was here. Charles was more of a confirmed bachelor than Travis was, so she wasn't a daughter. A niece, perhaps?

On the patio sat the still-smoking-but-no-longer-flaming grill. It was a brand-new model, now blackened by flames. Oh, Charles wouldn't be pleased at that.

Roy grinned. "Come on, Travis. Let's check it out."

Travis shook his head, without turning from the woman. "You take it, Roy." He spoke to the woman in a calming manner. "It's probably just a spider."

Mike and Quinn joined Roy at the grill.

"A spider started the fire?" She looked skeptical. "You're joking, right?"

Travis grinned. "No joke. There's a heat-loving spider that thrives in the gas. It nests right in the pipes and occasionally that results in a fire like yours."

She looked at John, as if for verification. He nodded stupidly and she smiled and looked back at Travis. Why couldn't he speak? Why couldn't he move?

John had heard women describe Travis's grin as irresistible. He hoped this woman didn't fall for the guy, who was a great extreme sport buddy but went through women like a forest fire burns through old-growth trees.

"Well, I guess I just learned something," she said, and her face seemed to relax. Again, John was struck by how beautiful she was.

Speak, idiot! John forced himself to get a few words out, though they certainly weren't noteworthy. "If it's a spider nest, we'll clean it out so you won't have to worry about lighting up your grill the next time."

They didn't have to do anything of the sort, but he'd do anything for this woman he'd just met. How crazy was that?

The beauty shook her head and caught his gaze in earnest. "It isn't mine. I just arrived today from New York. I'm renting the place from Charles Dobson. He's a columnist. Perhaps you've heard of him?"

"My father knows him." Looking into her eyes, John's heart raced, and it had absolutely nothing to do with the adrenaline rush of facing a potential fire.

A vivid impression hit him and wouldn't let go. A thought that was accompanied by a warmth in his chest that was a four-alarm bonfire of the Spirit.

This is your future wife.

He shook it off. What was going on? *Cupid? Is that you?* More likely his cousin, Stupid. Because that's how John felt right now. *Stupid.* What was going on with him? He knew nothing about this woman—not even her name.

The woman wore a CTR ring and was dressed in modest shorts and shirt, but that didn't necessarily mean she was LDS.

She apologized again, then said, "I'm Lori Scott. I really appreciate you guys coming out here, though I'm sorry you had to come out for nothing."

"Not for nothing." If John's chest grew any hotter, they'd have to turn the hose on him because he was going to spontaneously combust. He was surprised his uniform shirt wasn't glowing red.

"We enjoy coming to the aid of beautiful women," Travis teased. "Especially if there's no real danger."

An irrational jealousy flash-burned through John. He narrowed his eyes as Travis began flirting with Lori.

"So you're new to the area," Travis said. "Have you heard about Lagoon?"

John realized Travis was about to ask Lori to be his date du jour at John's family's annual Lagoon day, which Travis always joined, always with a new woman on his arm.

John couldn't let that happen.

Luckily, as captain, he outranked his friend. He could tell Travis to help Roy check the grill, but that wouldn't be far enough away to suit him. No, John wanted Travis out of the backyard entirely for a few minutes. "Travis, would you go get the report book from the truck?"

Travis turned to him and raised an eyebrow. "Now?"

John raised his own eyebrow. "Now."

Travis shot him a funny look, shrugged, and said, "Sure, Cap'n. Whatever you say."

That ought to keep Travis busy for more than a few minutes, as the report book was tucked securely in John's back pocket.

As Travis walked briskly across the lawn toward the gate, John stepped forward and smiled, probably looking like a doofus in the process. "Is there anything else we can do for you while we're here, Ms. Scott?"

"Lori." When she returned the smile, her face lit up, and the warmth in his chest increased. "But if you're desperate for something to do, I suppose I could start a kitchen fire."

He chuckled. "Probably not the best idea."

Again, he had the thought that she was not his usual type at all—a brash, in-your-face, black-clad New Yorker—but he was attracted to her nonetheless.

He reached out his hand. "John Walker, Brigham City Fire Department."

From behind the grill, Roy called out, "Actually, it's John *Wayne* Walker. He always forgets to tell people that."

Trust Roy to speak up when John was trying to impress Lori. "And this is my brother, Roy Rogers Walker," he said.

Lori laughed, more relaxed now. "A couple of real heroes."

And with that, John found himself saying, "My family's having a picnic at the local amusement park this Saturday. Would you like to go with me?"

A look of surprise flitted across her perfect face. "Um, I'm not sure." She ran her fingers through her honey-streaked hair and her green eyes darkened. "I've still got to get moved in and settled. Plus, there's my new job . . ."

Normally he would have backed off at this point, but Travis would be back any minute now to tell him he couldn't find the report book and John didn't have the luxury of time. "It would mean a lot to me if you'd say yes. Otherwise I'll be humiliated by going dateless. I have brothers who are even meaner than Roy."

With a surprised laugh, she looked him in the eyes for a long moment, and a wry smile curved the edges of her full lips. "I do love amusement parks. And I've never been out with a real hero before. Why not?"

Relief flooded him. "I'll call you with the information."

"All right." She rattled off her cell phone number, and he recorded it into his cell phone memory instead of the report book; he didn't want Travis to see it.

Just in time. Travis came through the gate and, with another strange look at John, said, "Couldn't find it."

"That's okay," said John.

"Got it cleaned out." Roy stood up from behind the grill and joined John.

Travis turned to Lori. "Anyway, pretty lady, where were we? Oh, yes. Have you heard of Lagoon?"

She shook her head. "I haven't."

"It's the local amusement park. The Beach Boys even sang about it." Travis smiled. "And I was wondering if you'd like to go there with me on Saturday."

Lori flashed a glance at John, and then back at Travis. "I'm very sorry, but I'm already going with someone else that day."

John smiled at her. When she smiled back, his heart thumped in his chest. It might be a miracle if he could survive being in her presence for an entire day without having a heart attack.

"Really." Travis turned to glare at John. "Well, welcome to Brigham City. Perhaps I can show you some other local sights."

"Thank you again for coming out, gentlemen. I appreciate knowing this town is safe in your capable hands."

John smiled happily, feeling lucky that she seemed to be tolerant of doofuses. "I'll pick you up Saturday at ten."

"I'm looking forward to it."

He turned and walked across the lawn, through the gate, back to the truck, and started unloading his gear, whistling all the way. He avoided Roy's and Travis's eyes.

Roy stepped next to him. "Did you just ask that woman out on a date?" He sounded incredulous.

Travis punched his arm. Hard. "Hey, dude. I was hitting on her and you totally stepped in. What is up with you?"

John smiled. "I couldn't help myself."

Roy and Travis exchanged a glance.

"This is just so totally out of character for you." Roy looked puzzled.

John shrugged. "What can I say? There were sparks."

"I thought you were a one-woman man." Travis crossed his arms. "I wonder what Dawn is going to think of those sparks."

Dawn?

The name blasted through him like ice water.

Dawn!

Chapter Five

Lori finished eating her hamburger—the one she'd managed to cook in a frying pan on the stove without setting the kitchen on fire—and cleaned up, still smiling about the firefighters vying for her time and attention and still wondering why on earth she had ever agreed to go out on a date. On the rebound was no time to be dating.

She'd felt amazingly peaceful after they'd arrived, no doubt the aftermath of the adrenaline pumping after she'd first seen the fire.

Now she wanted to relax with a good book. Grabbing the latest Grisham, she sank onto the double bed, enjoying the soft feel of the old-lady quilt beneath her arms, adjusted the pillow, and snuggled in.

She'd only read a page when her cell phone played "Girls Just Want to Have Fun."

"Hi, Marti," she answered.

"Lori, it's been ages since I talked to you. I've been so busy with girls' camp—which is finally over, thank goodness—that I haven't had time to call, but I've been thinking about you for a week."

Lori's best friend since grade school, Marti Owens, sounded like her usual perky self. Perky as in high school cheerleader for three years. Blonde. Cute. Popular. Married—in the temple, of course—to her high school sweetheart as soon as he returned from his mission and together they quickly had three adorable little kids. She was such a quintessential Mormon that it was a miracle Lori had ever stayed friends with her. Marti had also been the only person who'd been able to get Lori inside an LDS church in the past thirteen years, at least for an occasional Mutual activity.

"So how's the soon-to-be-world-famous Broadway playwright doing? Reveling in all the accolades?"

Lori groaned at the mention of her play. It was her own fault. She'd made a big deal of having a Broadway play produced, and now everyone actually expected there to be one. "I'm surprised you didn't hear the flopping sounds from Schenectady. It only lasted a week."

"Oh, Lori, I am so sorry." The caring in her friend's voice soothed Lori. "But you've still got your screenplay. Maybe you can get that optioned soon."

"Forget the screenplay." Her voice came out harsh. Deep down, Lori knew she couldn't forget it, but she feared she might never get back to it. Or, if she did, that it would bomb like her play. In fact, her deepest fear was that she'd chosen the entirely wrong career for herself. She softened her tone. "I may never finish it."

"You're kidding, right? It's a great story."

"Doesn't matter. I can't work on it because I left it behind." At her mother's place. Deliberately. She wanted nothing to do with it. This time in Brigham City was a sabbatical from serious writing for Lori as much as it was for the columnist who'd left for his China adventure.

"Are you okay? Do you want me to come over?"

Tears stung Lori's eyes. "I'd love you to, but I'm not exactly in New York right now. I'm not even in Kansas anymore, Toto."

A brief silence ensued from the woman who still lived in the same town where both Lori's mother and the man who used to be her father also lived. "Where exactly are you, Dorothy?"

"You'll never believe it." Lori started to laugh. "You will really and truly, never ever believe it."

"Stop driving me crazy with the suspense." Marti's voice took on a warning tone.

"It always drove you crazy not to know everything. I bet you're the obligatory official gossip of your ward."

Marti snorted at the insult. "Lori Elaine Scott, you'd better tell me where you are—right now."

"Or else?" Still laughing, Lori sat up on the bed. "Okay, okay. I am—believe it or not—currently residing in Brigham City."

A long pause followed, during which Lori could sense the shock on the other end of the line. "Come again?"

"Brigham City. Utah. USA."

"I'm hearing the words, but they're not computing. You, Lori Scott, proclaimed non-LDS woman forever, are living in Utah? The LDS capital of the world? Why? Were you abducted by aliens?"

That started Lori laughing again. "It does seem pretty alien here. This town is so small that the newspaper lists the missionaries, as well as a bridal registry at a nearby town's hardware store."

"Pray tell, how did you end up in Brigham City?"

So Lori told her friend about Greg's mock dare and throwing darts and her decision to move. "My mother thinks it's fate."

"I think it's absolutely hilarious." Marti's voice softened. "Though perhaps your mother's right."

"Then you'd both think John Wayne Walker asking me out is fate, too, I suppose." Now why did she have to go and mention that?

"John Wayne Walker? Wow. Is the guy as good as his name?"

"Oh, yeah."

"So let me get this straight. You move to Brigham City on a whim and you immediately have a date. I am blown away. Whatever happened to Scumbag?"

"Nicholas?" Surprised, Lori pulled at a loose thread on the quilt.

"Yeah, Nicholas Adams, Producer and Scumbag Extraordinaire. Did you finally dump him?"

"Yes." She sighed deeply and then spoke more forcefully. "Yes, I did."

"Good for you."

"Right after I found him with another woman. And I do mean *with* another woman."

"Oh, Lori, how horrible."

"It really was." Her throat tightened with emotion. "I'll never forget that awful, embarrassing, mortifying moment when I let myself into his apartment with the key he'd given me just the day before. Stupid, naïve, gullible Lori, carrying in groceries to surprise her man with a nice dinner. Well, I was the one surprised."

"Oh, sweetie. That's awful!"

"It was really for the best, though. It's made me realize my pride was hurt worse than my heart."

"Still, it had to hurt. Or make you mad. Or something."

"You're right. I was hurt. And mad. He turned out to be just like my father. Maybe I'll make Nicholas a character and have him bumped off in my next . . . play." The last word came out softly. She wasn't writing another play, not for Broadway or Hollywood, but she'd experience only more concern from Marti if she made a point of it.

"I think it's great you're moving on." Marti lowered her voice. "So tell me about this guy you have a date with. Is he handsome?"

"John has a great smile. He looks like the guy next door. You know—sandy-colored hair, blue eyes, a smattering of freckles."

"It's a sign. Your first crush was on a guy with freckles."

Lori snorted. "I was seven at the time."

"It's still a sign."

"Yeah, right." Lori related the story of the fire and the two firefighters vying for her attention. She didn't mention the peaceful feeling she'd had talking with them or how protected she'd felt that they'd come.

"Tell me more about the one who lost out."

"Well, Travis is more like a beach bum. A very good-looking, blonde model beach bum. He's been around some, I'd bet."

"But Freckles outmaneuvered him."

"Oh, yeah." Lori smiled at the memory. "Yeah, he did."

"So did you like him?"

"Yeah, I did." Lori frowned. "But you know I'm not going to get involved with anyone right now. Not on a rebound."

"So why'd you say yes?"

"I'm not sure. He caught me off guard, I guess. He was cute. And he made me laugh when he said he'd be dateless and humiliated if I didn't." There'd been something else about him she liked, though she couldn't put her finger on it. "And I do love amusement parks."

"Hold on," Marti said, and Lori could hear her talking with one of her children in the background. "I'm talking to Aunt Lori. Now go outside and play for a few minutes."

As Lori listened to the sound of children, she realized that was probably one reason why she'd gotten involved with Nicholas in the first place and stayed with him as long as she had: he was a selfish, only child and a sophisticated party guy who never wanted children.

"Okay, Lori, I'm back. Listen, I've got to go in just a minute. Please be sure to call me after your date and tell all."

"There won't be much to tell. I'll have a nice day, but I'll probably never see him again after Saturday."

"You can't fight fate," Marti teased.

Lori rolled her eyes. "I wouldn't dare try."

"So what are you doing for work?"

Lori explained about the flower column. "In fact, I need to call my new boss and set up an appointment. Give them my credentials, that sort of thing."

"Speaking of which, did you check out John's credentials?"

"Credentials?"

"I assume he's not Mormon or you would never have said yes."

"I didn't even think to ask! This is horrible!" Lori groaned. "I might have a date with an LDS guy!"

"Gotta go check on my kids, Lori. I'll call you later in the week." The phone disconnected on the sound of Marti's laughter.

John stood at the door for a long moment. The summer heat, even at eight in the evening, was uncomfortable, but he'd rather face the heat than what lay ahead.

In fact, he'd rather run into ten burning buildings than go through this door tonight. But he couldn't put this off forever.

After meeting Lori, he'd immediately called Dawn and told her he needed to talk to her when he got off shift late Thursday night. He had to let her know they weren't exclusive after all. He wasn't looking forward to hurting her, but it wouldn't be right if he didn't tell her the truth.

With a groan, he pushed the doorbell. And waited.

But only for half a minute.

Dawn opened the door, wearing the blue dress he'd told her once he liked, her auburn hair softly curling down her back.

"Hi, John," she said sweetly, fairly glowing with happiness.

Feeling guilty about what he had come to tell her, he forced a weak smile. "Hi, Dawn."

As he stepped inside, she touched his arm and leaned up for a kiss.

Caught off guard, not knowing what else to do, he kissed her—lightly—and pulled back immediately.

Her perfume was faint and flowery. She looked as pretty as he'd ever seen her.

The weight of the moment descended upon him, crushing him, constricting his breath. A drop of sweat ran down his back and another beaded on his forehead, which he wiped away with his forearm.

"My aunt's gone to a movie with friends, so we have the apartment to ourselves." She sat on the couch and patted the seat next to her.

He sat, leaving a cushion of space between them.

She laughed and closed the gap. "Come here, you handsome fireman."

He regretted sitting down at all. That was a tactical error. "Dawn, I need to talk with you."

She took his hand and smiled up at him. "Okay."

She started rubbing her thumb against his palm and he did his best to ignore it. "It's important," he said.

Her smile softened and expanded, all at the same time. "All right, John. I'm ready for this talk, too."

That took him aback. How could she know already? And why was she so happy about it? Had Travis told her? No, Travis wouldn't have done something like that. So how did she know? Or did she?

The pause expanded.

Dawn waited expectantly. When he still couldn't find his voice, she said, "John, it's okay. Maybe I can start. You know I like your family, and I think they like me. We've only been dating exclusively for a couple of weeks, but we've been together for months. I like children, and I know that's important to your family. I think we could be good together."

Call him thick, but the truth of what she was saying finally jackhammered its way through his dense skull. *Dawn expects me to propose to her. Tonight. Right here. Right now.*

When he'd said he had something important to talk about, she'd apparently assumed he was taking their relationship to the ultimate level. *But only because I'd led her to believe that.* He repressed the groan that filled his chest.

This was worse than he'd ever imagined. He had to speak before she could say anything else she'd later regret. "Dawn, it's—"

She laughed, and the light, happy sound ripped at his heart. "I haven't ever told you my feelings, but I care for you deeply. I love you."

If he didn't say the words right now, she would probably propose to him, and he didn't know if he had the strength to tell her no. Trying to let her down gently wasn't working, since he couldn't even get the words out.

Dawn tilted her head. "You love me, too, don't you, John?"

His heart heavy with guilt, he blurted out the words. "Dawn, I care for you. I do. But I've been having second thoughts. I think we're moving too fast. I think we should both start dating other people again."

She stared at him, obviously surprised. "John . . . I . . ."

"I'm sorry, Dawn. I didn't mean to hurt you." He'd rather walk on hot coals than hurt her.

"But I don't understand. I thought you were going to ask me to . . ." Her voice faded as if she already regretted her earlier words.

John closed his eyes, but when he opened them again, her hurt eyes were still there, staring at him, softly accusing him. He'd led her on and the weight of that truth ate at him. "I know. I did think about it. But I can't. Not now."

"But why not? It was only a few days ago, at your parents' house, that I thought you were considering it. What happened to change things?"

"I . . ." How could he say this? How could he just break her heart? But he couldn't lie. "I've met . . . someone else. And I just want to make sure of my feelings before we proceed. Or not."

She looked stricken and tears sparkled in her eyes. She blinked. "I don't understand. I thought . . ." Her voice faded again.

"I'm sorry." Guilt and helplessness flooded him. What was he supposed to do now? "I am so sorry."

Dawn shook her head, confused disbelief on her face. "Can we talk about it? Do I have any chance at all?"

"I don't know what will come of dating her, but I've got to find out. I'm sorry. My intentions with you were honorable."

She sniffled again. "But not honorable enough to marry me."

That wasn't entirely fair. Was he supposed to marry her because they'd dated? Because some people thought they should?

Part of him wanted to comfort her, but that would only fuel the fire of her hope, and he'd already done too much of that. An eternal decision like marriage was too important to not listen to his heart and his mind—and the Spirit—and that meant he couldn't put a ring on Dawn's finger. Not when he'd found a woman who attracted him like a moth to a flame.

Dawn took his hand again. "John, please. I love you."

As gently as he could, John patted her hand. "Dawn, I'm sorry. If I could make this easier, I would. I'm sorry for hurting you, but we have to be sure. I have to be sure."

She sighed. "I thought—"

"I know." As he stood, her hand slipped from his. "I'm sorry I led you on, but I thought . . . things were different than they were." He paused for a moment, not wanting to say anything else because any more words would only hurt her more. He had to get out of there, for both their sakes. "Good-bye, Dawn. I have to go now."

She started to cry, and he turned while he still could. He did care for her or he wouldn't have dated her, but he wasn't sure he loved her. He knew he didn't love Lori, but he thought the powerful attraction he'd felt might prove to be something special. But even if all Lori did was show him that he needed to wait for sparks and excitement, not to settle for tepid when he could have fire-hot, it would be worth it. Surely Dawn would realize that, too, after she'd had time to think things through.

"Wait. John, who is this . . . someone else?"

He stopped and turned only partway around, not looking at her eyes. "No one you know."

"Look at me, John." Her voice was soft, but strong.

He looked up and caught her fierce gaze.

She hugged her arms around her waist. "When did you meet her?"

"Yesterday."

"That's when you called and wanted to talk." Light glistened in her eyes. "You just met her and you already know you want to break up with me?" Her voice shivered with her hurt.

"Not really break up. I just think we should date other people, too. I'm sorry." The words couldn't fix things, no matter how many times he said them or how much he meant them.

As he opened the front door and let himself out, he could hear her crying. He shut the door and strode out to his truck, wishing he could know for sure that he'd just done the right thing.

And then he felt it. The Spirit was whispering to him that he had. He didn't understand any of this, but it felt right.

He certainly hoped so, because he'd just hurt a woman who truly loved him, for a slim chance at a possibility with a woman he'd just met and knew absolutely nothing about.

Chapter Six

Lori snapped her cell phone shut. It was Friday afternoon and she had already made some progress on her new job. She'd spoken with the newspaper's slow-talking secretary and set up an appointment for next Thursday morning with the big man himself, Russell Neal. Now she wanted to do some quick, comparative research so she'd sound knowledgeable.

For the next three months, she planned on becoming a fantastic flower gardening columnist. She wanted to impress both Mr. Neal and Charles Dobson, along with the readers of the *Brigham City Daily*. She was actually looking forward to doing some writing that didn't require staging or actors or producers. Just her and the blank page and some nice flower essays.

Going into Charles's overly neat and organized bedroom-turned-office, she opened the filing cabinet drawer where his note had said he kept his newspaper clippings. She was a quick researcher and should be able to pick up the information she needed by reading the column and surfing the Internet. How hard could learning about flowers be, anyway?

She found the folders quickly. Bulging with clippings, they were labeled by dates; he must have been writing this column forever. She quickly found the most recent one.

In addition to the filing cabinet, the office had a computer desk with all the related necessities, including a fancy printer/fax/copier. The desk was flanked by two tall bookshelves filled with books. She wasn't surprised to see all but one shelf filled with gardening books and biographies, all hardcovers, but what she did not expect was the shelf of paperback romance novels. Mr. Charles Dobson got more and more interesting all the time. Under the window was a sofa bed with doilies on the arms and over the back, which was a nice and cozy touch, if a bit old-fashioned.

Settling herself on the couch and enjoying the cool of the old house with its very up-to-date central air unit, Lori began to read.

Dear Dr. Dobson: My tomatoes have black spots on the bottoms. What can I do to get my plants to grow tomatoes that are red all the way through like they're supposed to be?

Tomatoes? Not flowers? There must be some mistake. Or perhaps Charles had substituted for a fellow columnist that particular day.

She set the column aside, and read the next one in the folder.

Dear Dr. Dobson: I can't figure out how to make my strawberry plants bear fruit. It's been three years and there's nary a strawberry to be found. Is there some trick to getting fruit?

Strawberries?

She scanned through the other clippings in the folder.

Squash. Green peppers. Peaches. Pumpkins. More tomatoes.

With growing dismay, she realized what her new job really entailed.

Charles Dobson didn't write a flower column; he wrote a *vegetable* gardening column, answering questions from knowledgeable gardener readers who were going to eat Lori for lunch and spit her out.

She knew absolutely *nothing* about the subject. Oh, sure, she'd eaten her share of vegetables, but she'd never planted or harvested one. Ever. Mother Earth she was not.

What had she gotten herself into? If she hadn't already agreed to write the column, she would bail out now. She was in way over her head, which was starting to ache.

She fumbled out her cell phone, flipped it open, and dialed. When her mother answered, she said, in what came out as a mournful wail, "Mom? I need help."

"Is someone in the house with you?" her mother asked, sounding concerned and obviously misinterpreting her plea for help. "Hang up and call 911. Hurry!"

"I already called 911. It just complicated matters."

"Then get out of the house while you wait for the police."

"No, I called 911 because of the fire. There's no one in the house with me."

"Fire? You had a fire?" Her mother did some wailing of her own. "I knew it wasn't a good idea for you to move there all by yourself. You need to come back home where you'll be safe."

"Mom! Stop! I'm okay. Really." Having her mother so upset actually helped calm Lori. "The fire was in the barbecue grill and some very nice and good-looking firefighters came over, but it had already gone out. It was caused by a spider nest in the tubing."

That silenced her mother for a moment. "A spider nest?"

"That's what I said." Lori laughed at both of their overreactions. "Now I know where I get my freaking-out gene from."

Her mother sounded calmer when she spoke again. "So if there's no one in the house, and your grill's not on fire, why were you so upset when you called?"

Oh, yeah, the vegetables. For one brief moment, Lori had forgotten her dilemma. "The columnist I'm replacing doesn't write nice little essays about flower gardening. He writes about vegetables. His readers ask questions and I'm supposed to answer them, and I'm going to flop again, miserably."

"I'm sure you'll do fine, honey. What can I do to help?"

"Just help me figure out what I'm going to do."

"Well, you can find the answer to almost every question on the Internet nowadays. And it might be too soon for you to know any of your neighbors yet," her mother said, "but maybe some of them garden. You could ask them some questions."

Lori hadn't known how uptight she had been until she felt herself relax. "Mom, you're a genius! I'll talk to Agatha next door. I bet she knows about vegetables."

"Glad I could help," her mother said. "So, have you unpacked all your suitcases and boxes yet?"

"Just my suitcases so far."

"I'd open the red box soon if I were you. It has something important in it. It's in the duffle bag you took with you."

Her mother must have gotten her a going-away gift and Lori hadn't even brought it in from the monstrosity-on-wheels yet. The car/truck. Cruck? Trar? "I guess I'd better go open it then. Thanks, Mom."

"Love you, Lori. And, honey, lock all your locks."

Yeah, all two of them.

Intending to retrieve the box from the car hidden in the detached garage, Lori pulled open the front door—and found a man standing there, his arm outstretched toward her. She jumped, her heart racing, before realizing it was the other firefighter, the blond model guy—Travis—reaching for the doorbell. "You startled me," she said.

"Sorry. Great timing, huh?" When he grinned, a dimple appeared on his left cheek, but not his right. With his lanky good looks, he could definitely make a bundle modeling clothes for trendy magazines and department stores. "Are you just leaving?"

She opened the screen door and the heat of the day blasted her. "No. Just going out to the car to bring something in, but I can do that later."

"Can we visit for a while?"

Pushing back her impatience, she said, "Sure."

She glanced at the two wrought-iron chairs sitting next to a matching wrought-iron round table that held a cluster of flowerpots, sheltered in the shade of the covered porch, then nodded her head toward the inside of the house. "Come on in. It's too hot to sit out here. It's gotta be over ninety today."

"Ninety-five." He stepped inside, casually handing her a single red rose as he entered.

"Thanks." Surprised, she raised it to her nose, enjoying its delicate scent. "Mmmm. Smells good."

"'A rose by any other name would smell as sweet.'"

"Shakespeare," she blurted out, surprised even more. So the model could quote the Bard. But then that was a pretty popular line. It didn't mean he'd actually ever read the plays.

"Romeo and Juliet." He grinned again. "Business major with a journalism minor, neither of which I use in my current profession."

Who knew? Good looks, roses, and a literary background, too. "Let's go see if Charles has a vase."

Travis followed her into the kitchen where she rummaged through cabinets until she found a clear glass vase. Rinsing out the dust, she filled the vase with water, trimmed the rose stem, and quickly stood the flower inside.

Travis paced the room, stopping in front of the bulletin board. "This Dobson dude must really like to cook."

"I guess so," she said as she centered the vase on the table. "The rose really is beautiful. Thanks again."

He turned away from the board. "A beautiful rose for a beautiful lady."

"Thanks," she said, repressing a smile. Oh, yeah. Travis was definitely a player. Which made her extra wary. "Would you like a glass of water or a soda or something?"

"Water would be great. Thanks."

He had a lot of nervous energy—enough that it was agitating her, too. She grabbed a bottle from the fridge and handed it to him.

He twisted off the top and took a swig. "I was wondering if you'd like to see the Kennecott copper mine while you're here. It's a little drive, but it's worth it. It's one of only two man-made objects that can be seen in space—I think the other one is the Great Wall of China—and it's really quite impressive. Actually, I guess there are three if you count that huge man-made island in Dubai." He grinned. "I told you I'd find another sight to show you."

"That's very kind of you, Travis." She motioned toward the kitchen table. The reference to China made her wonder what Charles was doing right now, and if he was having as difficult a time adjusting to the foreign culture as she was.

"Kind, obedient, thrifty, yada, yada, yada." Travis took a seat. "I was a Boy Scout, too."

"So you're one of those guys who help little old ladies across the street?"

"My specialty." He smiled and the dimple appeared again. The lopsided effect was very cute—a fact she suspected he knew and used to his advantage. "Along with helping young ladies enjoy their visit to our fair state. Well, my adopted state—I'm originally from sunny California. So is next weekend okay?"

"To be totally honest, Travis, it sounds great, but you know I'm going with John on Saturday. Plus I've got to get some work done right away, and I'm a little nervous about what it will entail. Maybe after I see what my writing workload is going to be on this new job. Can I take a rain check?"

She wondered about a man who seemed willing to move in on his friend's date. She was pretty sure she wouldn't be available for any rain checks.

He shrugged, seeming to take her semi-rejection in stride as he took another swig of water. "That's fine, as long as you don't mind me checking back with you later."

As long as you don't mind me putting you off when you do, she thought. He was cute, but there was something about him that she didn't quite trust. Maybe he reminded her too much of Nicholas; flattering words came too easily to them both. "Sounds like we have a deal."

"You said you have some stuff in the car? The Boy Scout in me wonders if I can carry it in for you."

"That would be great." She found the car keys, led Travis outside to the detached garage, and pushed the garage door opener.

As Ben was revealed, Travis chuckled. "Your vehicle?"

She grimaced. "I would never have paid money for a '65 Monstrosity."

"Yes, an El Camino is definitely that." He chuckled again.

"I have to drive it once a week."

"I recommend after dark."

She laughed, and pointed to the black duffle bag in the truck portion. He hefted it and she held open the front door for him, directing him to the kitchen table.

"Thanks. I wasn't looking forward to wrestling it in by myself." She pulled up the duffle bag flap. "My mother said she sent me a gift."

She rifled down through the clothes until her hands hit something solid, and she pulled out a rectangular red box, about the size of a shirt box, only deeper, and tied with curled, sparkly red ribbon. "This must be the one."

"Your birthday?" He leaned back against the kitchen counter and crossed his arms, looking fabulous while he did so.

"No. Just my mother being nice, I guess. But you probably don't want to stand around watching me open gifts from my mother."

"I don't mind spending time with you."

"Okay, but it might be pretty silly. She gives gifts like no one else. Last Christmas, she gave me and my brother toy pirate swords, complete with clanking and swishing sound effects."

"Sounds fun."

"Actually, it was. We had sword fights for days."

Untying the ribbon, she pushed it out of the way. Next she lifted the bright red lid . . . and froze.

"What is it?" Travis asked, stepping closer in curiosity.

"My screenplay." Her mother had sent it—despite the fact that Lori had told her she didn't want to work on it, despite the fact that she'd wanted a break from her writing, despite the fact that she'd stuck it in an old ugly box and hidden it under her bed in her mother's house. Despite all that, her mother had found it and wrapped it gaily and sent it anyway.

"I'm impressed. I didn't know you wrote screenplays."

"I don't. Not anymore."

Travis smiled. "Maybe you'll go back to it."

"Maybe." But not for the next three months, during which she'd keep the box under her new bed and only write Charles's *vegetable* gardening column.

That meant she couldn't let anything else get in the way of talking with Agatha. She really hoped the older woman had some wisdom to offer her because Lori was fresh out.

She looked at Travis and smiled. "Sorry. Listen, I've got some stuff to do. Can we talk later?"

"Absolutely." He grinned again as he headed for the door. "I look forward to cashing in that rain check."

"Actually," said Agatha, "Brigham City isn't the edge of the earth—but you can see it from here."

"That's reassuring."

"So are you all settled in?" Agatha set a plate of delicious-smelling, still-warm homemade cookies on the kitchen table in front of Lori, along with two glasses of milk, and sat down beside her.

The combined kitchen and eating area was filled with chrome from the fifties, completely unlike the Laura Ashley flowered cushions and wicker furniture in the living room. But, like Charles's kitchen, it was delightful and fit the older woman and her apron perfectly.

Lori's mouth watered at the delectable scent of chocolate chip cookies and she picked one up. "Almost. I'm still unpacking."

"And entertaining firemen." Agatha smiled. "Did they fix your barbeque?"

"So . . . you saw them." The adrenaline rush caused by the flames was a vivid memory even two days later. "The fire was caused by a spider in the pipes, of all things."

"In the venturi tubes. I've read about that." Agatha nodded as she picked up a cookie and took a sip of her milk.

Lori tilted her head in amazement. "That's right. How did you know the name of the tubes?"

"Oh, sweetie, I am a font of useless information." She waved her half-eaten cookie for emphasis. "Just call me the Trivia Queen. Go on, ask me something."

Lori supposed it was too soon to throw out the gardening questions that had brought her over, so she searched her mind for a piece of obscure information. "What was the first thing Thomas Edison recorded on his new invention, the phonograph?"

"Mary Had a Little Lamb." Agatha nodded. "Not that I attended the actual event, you understand."

"Oh, I know."

Agatha laughed. "That was a joke, sweetie."

The older woman might speak more slowly than New Yorkers did, as everyone did here in Utah, but her mind certainly hadn't slowed down. Lori gave up fighting the temptation, and took a bite of her cookie. "These are delicious."

They spent a quiet moment savoring the rich flavors of a warm-from-the-oven chocolate chip cookie.

"So, have you met any nice men yet?"

Lori couldn't help but smile. "Well, two of the firefighters asked me out."

"I knew you'd be swamped with men in no time at all. Which one are you going out with?"

Lori smiled again as she remembered. "John Wayne Walker."

"Fine name. Fine family, too. I know his father. I read in the paper that Deputy Fire Chief Walker retired a month or so ago."

Amazed again, Lori said, "Do you know everything that goes on in Brigham City?"

"Oh, dear, no. Brigham City has gotten far too large for that."

Large? Ha! Compared to Manhattan, Brigham City was practically a village. No, that was too big. A *hamlet.* Even compared to Schenectady, it was still small. Hicksville perhaps was too strong a word, but Brigham City reeked of small-town quaintness.

"I have a hard enough time keeping track of my immediate neighbors. Take Charlie, for instance." Agatha rolled her eyes. "Though perhaps he's a bad example. I mean, can't you just tell from looking around his house that he's a reprobate?"

"A dinosaur, maybe." Lori chuckled. "It's obvious he chose his furnishings a long time ago."

Agatha laughed and tapped Lori's arm. "You aren't just whistling Dixie on that one, sweetie. Charlie is a cutie, though, that's for sure. I've always thought he was a looker."

"I didn't see any pictures of him. Well, other than at the top of his columns." Lori thought he was okay-looking, but nothing special.

"Oh, that one's ten years old, at least. To my knowledge he hasn't added a single personal touch to the house since his mother died two decades ago. All the decorations are Relief Society craft projects his mother—or his grandmother—made."

"My favorites are the grapes."

"Ha. I say give me just one hour in that house and I could fix it right up." Agatha's eyes sparkled with humor and mischief.

Lori fought a smile. Agatha's home wasn't much more modern, but she could at least add a feminine touch.

"Not that he'd ever let anyone in to change things, though. For a fancy-dancy newspaper columnist, he's a regular stick-in-the-mud."

Lori couldn't have asked for a better segue into her gardening questions. She hoped. "So what would you change in his garden?"

"Oh, his garden is in excellent shape. That's one place Charlie's hard to surpass. Even for me."

"He asked me to harvest his zucchini."

"I'm not surprised." Agatha narrowed her eyes. "I'm not surprised Charlie has let you stay in his home, either. Or let you drive his beloved eyesore of a vehicle. Gives a horrible meaning to the word hybrid, doesn't it?" Agatha laughed. "He must trust you a great deal."

"I don't know about that. But he's asked me to write his gardening column while he's gone, and I needed a place to stay while I'm here."

"Why, I am impressed. Another fancy-dancy newspaper columnist next door, only you are definitely no stick-in-the-mud. Tell me all about what else you've written."

This lady didn't miss a beat, but Lori didn't want to talk about her play. "Oh, nothing special."

"Young lady," Agatha said, wagging a finger in her direction, "Charlie would never have hired you unless you were both a top-notch gardener and a first-class writer. So I know you've written something impressive, and I'm hoping you'll share with me what that is." She waited expectantly.

Well, what would it hurt to tell her? Lori sighed. "I recently wrote a play that made it to Broadway."

"Really?" Her eyes widened. "How exciting."

"It flopped one week later."

Agatha winced. "Oh, that must have hurt."

"It did." Lori worked to keep the self-pity from her voice; she almost succeeded.

"So you needed a break and that's why you came to Utah?"

Could this woman read her mind? But somehow it didn't bother

Lori. Despite her initial reluctance to meet Dobson's neighbors, Lori liked Agatha. "Yes, I did need a break. Both from writing and from men."

"But you accepted a date with John Walker."

"I know. Don't ask me why, because I'm not sure. But it's certainly not going to become a relationship."

"Ah, I suspect we'll need more time than we've got today to hear that part of the story."

"That part of the story is over."

"Even more intriguing." Agatha smiled and took a sip of milk. "We'll save it for our next visit."

Lori had no doubt Agatha could weasel the story from her. If only Lori could weasel some gardening answers out of Agatha first. "I'm wondering when you usually harvest your vegetables. Just to compare notes."

"Oh, the usual time, sweetie."

Well, that was helpful. "It's just that I don't know if the Utah harvest comes in at a different time from New York's."

"In about two weeks, we'll have more zucchini than we can shake a stick at. When do you harvest back east?"

"About the same." Lori tried for a casual tone of voice.

Agatha squinted her eyes in concentration. "The frost usually hits here a few weeks earlier than in the Salt Lake area. Except this year has been warmer than normal, so I'm hoping for a longer harvest time."

"What do you do with all the zucchini after you harvest them? Other than the usual, I mean."

"The usual being baking them into every type of recipe imaginable, including cookies and cakes, as well as freezing them?" Agatha shrugged and grabbed another cookie. "Mostly I give them to neighbors and let them worry about it."

This wasn't working. Maybe Lori could look through the questions from Charles's readers and then just periodically ask Agatha the questions outright. Except that this woman probably read each column and Lori would only get away with it once. She'd better make it more official. "I wonder if I could do an interview with you about your garden for Charles's column."

Agatha chuckled. "An interview, huh? I'd be glad to, but I'm not sure Charlie would like that."

"Why not?"

"Oh, he just thinks I don't know much, that's all. But he's wrong."

This was the moment of truth. "Well, would you be willing to answer a few questions for some of his readers?"

Lori waited to see how Agatha took the question.

"I think you'd be much more qualified to do that than I am, my dear."

"I'm not so sure," she let slip out, then glanced at Agatha to see if her dejected tone of voice had given too much away. "I mean, I do know gardening. I'm looking forward to doing the column."

"I have a strange feeling about that."

Lori tried to think of something to say, but before she could, the corners of Agatha's mouth quirked up and then the older woman was laughing, a good old-fashioned belly laugh. "You mean to tell me Charlie left his beloved column to somebody who doesn't know a darn thing about gardening? Oh, that is too precious for words."

Lori's cheeks flamed and she stuttered out some sort of silly defense. "I'm a good journalist. Really."

Agatha raised her hand and struggled to stop laughing. "I'm sure you are, sweetie."

As her laughter slowed to a more hiccupy sound, Agatha said, "Don't mind me. It's just that, well, you can't possibly know how much I'm enjoying this. You're like a breath of fresh air and, heaven only knows, Charlie's house needs a good airing out. So does Charlie, for that matter."

Afraid Agatha would reveal Lori's ignorance to everyone, she said, "You won't tell him, will you? Or the paper?"

"Heavens, no. This is just too wonderful for words. I would never breathe a word of it to him. Or anyone else, either." She grabbed a tissue and wiped the moisture from her eyes. "My dear, you have lightened my day. Now don't you worry about a thing. Your secret is safe with me. And if you need help—any help at all—you be sure to ask me."

Embarrassed at being exposed as the gardening ignoramus she really was, Lori could only hope Agatha would keep her word.

Still chuckling, Agatha took a deep breath to compose herself. "I would love to tell you how to harvest Charlie's vegetables. And to answer some of your other questions."

"Thank you. I appreciate it so much."

"On one condition."

Lori waited, willing to trade her beloved Jimmy Choo sling backs for some help at this point. Well, maybe not those.

"I'm a member of the Spade and Hope Garden Club. You've missed the annual garden tour, but the annual potluck is coming up, and we're allowed to bring a friend. You must come with me. Because anything I've forgotten about vegetable gardening, those ladies will probably remember. You can ask them all sorts of questions."

Relieved, Lori said, "I'd love to go."

Chapter Seven

Though Lori had only met John a few days before and this was their first date, she clung to him more and more frantically the higher they were hoisted. Then, with a heart-cringing lurch, they stopped. She had no idea how high they were, but it sure looked to her that they were higher than any of the other rides.

"Should I pull the cord?" asked John, grinning at her like he was having the time of his life. He was on her right; he'd paid extra so that it was just the two of them in the giant swing rather than the three it could accommodate.

They'd been pulled high into the sky, in a harness that, when John pulled the cord, would swing down low and back up in a huge arc, and then back down in a death-defying, stomach-dropping, scream-inducing swing. What had she been thinking?

"I've changed my mind!" She looked out over the amusement park with a moment of sincere regret. The Ferris wheel had looked so tall from the ground, but she couldn't even see it now for the trees. Why hadn't she agreed to ride the Ferris wheel instead?

He said, quite casually, "Does it bother you to think that the people who clipped us into this equipment are making minimum wage?"

Lori groaned. "Stop."

He reached for the cord.

"Wait! I'm not ready!"

He teased, "Are you sure you don't want to just get it over with?"

She drew in a deep breath and clutched the jacket. "Okay, go for it."

"Yee-haw!" John yelled as he pulled the cord that sent them hurtling in free fall toward the ground.

They dropped down, down, down.

As they flew toward the people on the ground, adrenaline flashed through Lori and she screamed.

Beside her, John laughed.

The giant swing smoothly arced up, rocketing them forward.

Between screams, Lori began to laugh—until their momentum carried them up the other side and they began to slow. "Oh, no! We're going to drop again."

And they did. And, sure enough, Lori screamed again.

It took long moments and several passes over the watching, laughing, pointing crowd below for the swing to lose enough momentum so that the minimum-wage Lagoon employees could pull them back down to the stand where they had climbed into the swing to begin with.

Legs shaking, Lori began to shed the equipment. "I can't believe I let you talk me into that."

As John stepped out of his safety vest, he grinned. "Wanna go again?"

"Absolutely not! It was horrible!" But she was laughing as she said it.

Grinning, he took her hand, and she let him lead her down into the crowd. With her heart still pounding faster than a rock band's drummer, she was glad for the reassuring warmth of his hand. Normally, she'd have pulled her hand back almost immediately, if she'd even taken his to begin with, but being scared out of her gourd had a way of lessening her inhibitions.

Had he planned it this way? She didn't think so. There was something sweet and disarming about John, not planned or contrived. Nope, he was just a nice guy, and she was a gal with a racing heart who was overthinking things again.

He checked his watch. "It's nearly four. We'd better head over to the pavilion or we'll miss out on the food. And you do not want to miss my mother's brownies. Or the Colonel's chicken and coleslaw."

As they walked in silence, Lori thought about how her

expectations for the day had been exceeded. So far the date had been pleasantly—even surprisingly—enjoyable. John had picked her up at Charles's home at ten, and they'd driven nearly an hour down to some small town, where he'd taken her to a Chinese restaurant for an early lunch before driving to Lagoon. Since they'd entered the park, he'd purchased cotton candy, popcorn, and a cherry snow cone for her.

Now she was growing more curious about the family she'd be meeting in mere minutes. And a little nervous. How weird was it to be meeting a guy's family on your first date? After all, she'd dated Nicholas for more than a year without ever meeting his parents. Things were definitely different here in Utah.

It might be awkward for a few moments, but she'd never see these people again in her life, so how bad could it be?

She'd enjoyed John's company so far, and she hoped his parents would be as easygoing as he was. "How much of your family will be here today?"

"My three brothers, their wives and kids, and my parents. Oh, and my best friend Travis, whom you've already met. And my other best friend Quinn and his wife and their two kids. That's it."

"That's it?" She shook her head in overwhelmed disbelief. "When my family gathers, we need only three chairs—one for me, my brother, Greg, and my mom."

"You make your dad sit on the ground?"

"He divorced my mom about thirteen years ago." She wasn't about to reveal the soap opera and betrayal that hid behind those relatively simple words.

"I'm sorry to hear that."

"It was probably for the best."

John looked at her and frowned slightly. "Still, it's always sad when any marriage breaks up, especially when there are kids."

"It was hard," she admitted and then, determined to change the subject, said, "My gosh, it's hot. Do you think it's over a hundred today?"

"We could go rushing through the air again. You didn't seem to notice the triple-digit heat while we were on the swing."

"You're right." Lori laughed again and slipped her hand from

John's, becoming a little too aware of the contact between herself and the man who was still practically a stranger. She didn't want to meet his family and friends holding his hand. "I was far too worried about dying on that free fall to worry about the heat."

"I was beside you." He shrugged. "I'd have kept you safe."

She stopped and turned until she faced him. She studied him for a long moment. Tall, broad, and well-muscled. The strong-but-not-so-silent type with freckles. The guy with a job practically requiring a cape and a big "S" on his chest. He saved people all day long.

"Yeah, I bet you would have," she said softly.

Was that a blush on his freckled cheeks? Before she succumbed to the "aw, cute" feeling hovering close by, Lori said, at top New York speed, "Come on, take me to the pavilion. Quickly. After four hours of riding rides, I am starving to death right before your eyes." She lifted the back of her hand to her forehead for effect, just as her smart-aleck brother Greg had shown her.

"Nah, you look just fine to me." John took her hand from her forehead and intertwined his fingers with hers. Again.

Wait a minute. How had that happened? He was persistent, she had to give him that. But she wasn't sure she was okay with holding hands with John Wayne Walker.

Oh, sure, he was cute. Attractive. Attentive. Available. And his obvious interest was flattering. Being around him made her happy and uncomfortable all at the same time.

Other Utahans may move and talk slowly, but this guy was moving way too fast.

Such confusing emotions. He wasn't anything like Nicholas, but he was still a man and, therefore, a potential emotional land mine.

So what was she? A New Yorker or a mouse?

She wasn't going to get involved with him, especially since he did have the fatal flaw of being Mormon—she could see the line of his garments through his shirt. What difference did it make if she indulged in a little innocent hand-holding? So what if her bruised ego needed an emotional bandage and holding John's hand seemed to provide that? So what if she'd just met him? Holding hands certainly didn't mean they had any kind of a relationship; surely John realized that as much as she did.

If he wanted to hold hands as friends—she did consider him a new friend, didn't she?—then who was she to object? As long as he didn't try anything more, which she would put a stop to immediately, she would just go along with the hand-holding, especially since it felt so warm and comforting.

Having decided that, Lori smiled and held his hand as he led her toward the pavilion and his humongous family.

"There's Mom," John said. "Come on, I'll introduce you."

"This is your family?" Even though he'd warned her, Lori's eyes still widened at the sight of all the people.

"Yup. With a few friends mixed in." John laughed. "And just to warn you, I've brought other lady friends to events, and the family always makes a big deal out of it. You think they'd be used to the idea by now."

Lori was used to a family being a manageable size. This was an unruly crowd: four couples and lots of children of all ages, some seated at the pavilion tables, others lounging on blankets or pulling cans of soda from coolers, all talking and eating and visiting at once. A noisy, overwhelming family.

John took his hand from Lori's and placed it on the small of her back. With his other hand, he pointed to an attractive and petite middle-aged woman rearranging buckets of chicken and coleslaw on a central table. "Lori, this is my mother, Irene Walker. Mom, meet my new friend, Lori Scott."

"Pleased to meet you, Lori." With a warm smile, Irene put out a small hand and shook Lori's. "I'm glad you could join us."

"Let me introduce Lori to everyone before they eat, Mom."

He turned to Lori. "This is always the interesting part. Our father made sure of that. First I have to explain that my father, William Walker, was nicknamed 'Wild Bill' on the job as a firefighter, so here is my father, 'Wild Bill' Walker. You can call him Bill for short. Dad, Lori Scott."

John's father was a husky man with a moustache that matched

his name. He had a hint of freckles scattered across his face and arms, and his hair had faded from what must have been the same sandy color as John's to a light gray with glints of red in the sun. He enveloped Lori's hand with both of his and smiled broadly. "It's good to meet you. Welcome."

"Thanks for having me."

Three men who had to be John's brothers stood. They all looked to be the same height—well over six feet, give or take an inch. All with sandy hair and freckles, all younger clones of their father, minus the moustache.

John laughed. "Okay, here goes. These are my brothers, all named by my father."

"The deal was I got to name all the girls." John's mother smiled. "Only we didn't have any girls."

"And you're about to find out what kind of movies my father watches. My oldest brother, Clint Eastwood Walker, and his wife Julie. My brother, Kirk Douglas Walker, and his wife Opal. And my youngest brother, Roy Rogers Walker, and his wife Becky. I won't even try to introduce all their children to you."

She laughed. "All famous cowboys. How wonderful."

One of the brothers—she didn't have them straight yet—said, "Well, at least the actors who played them."

Despite herself, Lori was charmed by the men and by their wives.

John's mother patted her arm. "Just don't let John get out of line. When he was little, if there was a commotion, it was either John and Clint, or John and Kirk, or John and Roy."

"Mom, I think she got the point."

Lori smiled at him. She could feel these people watching and assessing, and that made her nervous. Surely John had brought many dates home before. After all, he had to be in his late twenties or early thirties. So why were they watching her so intently? John realized they weren't dating, didn't he? Of course he did. He'd called it a date, but this wasn't a date. This was a family circus.

She waved to Travis as he joined the group. When he saw her, he grinned and walked up to her, taking her hand and kissing it like a medieval knight. Beside her, John said, "Hey! Watch it!"

Travis let go of Lori's hand and turned to John. "Are we on for more hang gliding?"

"Sure."

"Just wondering if you were concerned about your safety yet." He grinned at John and turned back to Lori. "John and I hang out and do dangerous things together."

"Like alligator wrestling," said Roy.

"Really?" Lori looked to John for confirmation.

John rolled his eyes. "No. Don't listen to either my crazy brother or my even crazier *former* friend here."

Travis leaned in closer to her. "In my hometown of Ventura, California, we do wrestle alligators occasionally."

John put his hand on Lori's arm. "Let's get out of here before we need hip-high boots."

The next half hour passed in a pleasant whirl of conversation, laughter, and fried chicken, John always at her side as he laughed and joked with those around him.

She liked him. And his family. They were a warm, caring sort of crowd.

Becky asked her, "How does it feel to date a firefighter?"

Her husband, Roy, said, "As if you don't know."

John leaned toward Lori, teasing, "You light my fire."

Lori joked back, "Well, you put mine out."

The others laughed.

"You want some ice for that burn, John?" said Roy.

Travis saluted. "You'd think a firefighter would know how to handle a burn."

John scowled at his friend. "Get lost, surfer boy."

Lori was amazed at the way men talked with their best friends. Men and women were definitely different regardless of whether they lived in New York or Brigham City.

When Lori had finished eating, John took her paper plate and tossed it in the trash. "Would you like a pop?"

Pop? Oh, he meant soda. "Sure. Thanks. A . . ." The only person drinking a caffeinated soda was Travis, who held a Pepsi in his hand. Wasn't that a no-no? The Utah equivalent of beer, or something? Shouldn't he be drinking it from a brown paper bag? "A root beer, please."

John handed her an A&W. Without opening it, she held the chilled can against her warm forehead. "Ah."

Suddenly a young boy of about five rushed up and flung himself at John. "Uncle John!"

"Lori, this is my good buddy, Evan." While still sitting, John lifted the boy and tossed him in the air in a single smooth move. "Okay, Evan, what's today's password?"

"Oh, no, Uncle John. Not the password!"

"Oh, yes." John wrapped his arms around the boy, who was struggling—though wearing a big grin—to get free. "Tell me the password and you can go free."

"Ah, heck," said the little boy.

"Nope. That was yesterday's password."

"Okay." The little boy sighed deeply in exaggerated resignation. "Tickle me, please."

"I'd love to." John tickled a laughing, squirming Evan.

The sight touched Lori. A big, strong man like John playing with a small child. The way her father used to play with her before . . .

Lori shook her head. Oh, she was so not going there.

A couple joined them, the woman holding a baby. They were apparently Evan's parents as they both looked lovingly down on the little boy.

"Lori, these are Evan's parents and my good friends, Quinn and Tricia Jackson, and their new baby girl, Emma. This is my friend, Lori Scott."

Though the couple smiled warmly, Lori didn't miss the quick look that flashed between them.

Tricia hugged her and said, "I am very glad to meet you."

Evan said, "Let me go, Uncle John. I said the password."

John set him down and reached out his arms for the baby. "And how is my girl today?"

"How old is she?" Lori asked.

Tricia smiled at her baby and said proudly, "Three weeks."

Lori blinked. The woman must have a personal trainer to have a flat stomach again only three weeks after her second child. She couldn't be larger than a size two—four tops.

"Go get some food," John said. "I'll take care of Emma."

Lori watched John, amazed at how gentle and tender he was with the infant. He cradled her tiny body in his strong arms, and the sight touched something deep inside of Lori. He'd make some lucky woman a wonderful husband and father for her children. And, for an instant, Lori felt a pang of regret.

John held out his thumb in front of Emma and she grasped it with her tiny fingers. He murmured baby words to her. Finally, with a smile, he turned to Lori, and said, "Sorry, I'm being selfish, holding the baby when I know you women like to do that."

Before Lori could shift so as not to take the baby without being obvious, John placed Emma gently in her arms. Lori fought rising panic. What was he doing?

He looked down on her with a happy smile and said, his voice soft, "Now that's a pretty picture."

She forced a smile for John, her body tense as she held the child. Luckily, John's mother called out to him and he turned his gaze away so he didn't seem to notice.

Emma cooed and reached her tiny hand up toward Lori's face. The baby was soft in Lori's stiff arms, but she couldn't relax to enjoy the moment. She couldn't even try to relax because she had to steel herself against the emotion holding a baby brought—and it wasn't enjoyment.

Tears burned Lori's eyes and she blinked. Hard.

She would not cry here.

Not now.

Not in front of these virtual strangers.

She steeled her heart and turned her gaze back to the child, but she couldn't do it without pain.

It had been years since she'd held a baby, and the last time she'd sworn that she never would again. She'd realized long ago that it wasn't worth the momentary pleasure of holding someone else's child to put herself through the torture of wanting something she herself could never have.

Lori looked up at John, who had turned around and was looking at her with a dangerously soft expression in his eye.

Someone like John Wayne Walker, however, would definitely want children of his own. So it was a good thing she'd only be here a few months. She'd be leaving the state long before either of them had a chance to get involved.

In fact, just to make sure, she wouldn't accept any more dates with John while she was here. She would enjoy the rest of their time at Lagoon, but that was it. From now on, she'd concentrate on her job writing about vegetables. She certainly had enough to learn about zucchini to keep her busy.

"Lovely child," Lori managed to say as she handed Emma back to her mother.

THE GARDEN GURU

Dear Dr. Dobson: I recently watched Disney's Cinderella *with my granddaughter and I must admit I fell in love with Prince Charming all over again. While I was watching the fairy godmother do her Bibbidi-Bobbidi-Boo magic, I started wondering if the pumpkin she turned into a coach was based on a real vegetable. Do you know? (Cheryl)*

Dear Cheryl: Yours is indeed an unusual request. The answer is yes. In 1883, the Burpee Seed Company introduced its Rouge Vif D'Etampes pumpkin, which had been popular in France since the early 1800s. Cinderella's fairy godmother could not have chosen a better vegetable to turn into a coach as it is one of the more ornamental pumpkins. Plant one and you will harvest great fall decorations.

And now, dear readers, though my temporary substitute will have already been busy writing, you won't see her columns published until next week. So let me introduce an accomplished gardener and writer, Ms. Lori Scott, who will answer your questions while I am in China. I shall return an older and wiser man . . .

Chapter Eight

"So, what do you do for downtime from your dangerous job?"

"Usually Travis and I find other dangerous things to do."

"Yeah. He seems like a dangerous-things kinda guy."

An unfamiliar shock of jealousy jolted John. Did she like dangerous-things kinda guys?

"But you, now." She shook her head and pondered seriously. "You don't seem like a diehard adrenaline junkie. No, you seem more like your brothers."

"Is that an insult?" he teased. "Because I don't have to go out with a pretty lady to get insulted. I can get that at work, at home, and at family get-togethers."

"It's not an insult. You just seem more like the settling-down kinda guy. Someone who knows what he wants and goes for it."

She blushed and took a few small steps forward in line. His eyes settled on her legs.

Finally, it was their turn to climb on the ride. John made sure both he and Lori were strapped in securely; then the ride started and the laughter and screaming followed. He was glad it was her doing the screaming and him doing the laughing or he'd have been really embarrassed.

As the ride ended, she turned to him, her eyes sparkling. "That was great. Let's go on another one."

Amused, he said, "I take it you like rides."

"I can't get enough of them. I used to go on all the monster rides with my brother, Greg."

Becky and Roy were waiting for them under a tree. Becky fanned herself with an empty paper French fry container, looking uncomfortably warm.

The four of them walked back from the edges of the park, until Becky saw a snow cone stand. "I want one of those, please."

"Another one?" Roy complained. "You've had three already."

"So I'm craving cherry snow cones. Go buy me one. Now." Her words would have had more weight if she hadn't been teasing, but Roy ordered another one, nonetheless.

"Would you like another one, too?" John asked Lori.

"No, thanks." She shook her head, lightly touching Becky's sleeve. "I'm only eating for one."

Becky laughed. "Cravings are an incredible force in the universe."

"You can say that again." Roy handed over the snow cone.

"Thanks, honey," Becky said and leaned up to kiss Roy's cheek. Roy had to bend way down so Becky wouldn't spill her new treat.

"Hey, let's go on *that!*" Lori pointed.

John repressed a groan. Captivated by Lori, he'd forgotten to keep track of where they were—smack dab in the center of the park alongside the white beast.

She was pointing at the one ride in Lagoon that John hadn't gone on since he was a kid. The one thing in the entire park—maybe in the entire world—he had an unreasonable fear of.

The old, white, wooden roller coaster.

Becky caught his eye, but John pulled his gaze away and tried to distract Lori. "How about the parachute ride instead? It's just over there. Or the Hammer. Or the Tilt-a-Whirl. They're more fun than this rickety old thing. Hey, let's ride Wicked again."

Lori laughed. "I've never been on a wooden coaster and I'd really like to go."

John wasn't a coward, not by any means. He could do dangerous things, with or without Travis, but in this moment when he was going to have to admit to the woman he wanted to impress that he didn't dare go on this ride, those moments flashed through his brain in mere seconds. It was like seeing his life flashing before his eyes, but only the most adventurous moments: hang gliding on the breeze; skydiving, free falling until finally pulling the parachute's ripcord; swimming with dolphins in the Caribbean; diving in a shark cage off the tip of South Africa.

He could run into a burning building—over and over, if need be—to save the people inside. He could, and had, spent harrowing hours on countless rescue teams. He'd even helped his Aunt Violet clean out her garage—once.

Lori raised an eyebrow and the corners of her mouth edged up as she waited for his answer, clearly amused by his hesitation.

With effort, John drew his gaze away from Lori to stare at the rickety old ride. It loomed like something from one of his nightmares. He didn't know what it was about that thing, but he'd always been afraid of Lagoon's white roller coaster. The fear was irrational. He couldn't explain it, and he didn't want to try. He'd ridden it once as a young boy and been terrified out of his mind. He didn't want to ride it again—ever. He didn't dare attempt this coaster, not even to impress Lori, in case he freaked out and unimpressed her even more.

John forced a smile and prepared to tell Lori the humiliating news that he was indeed too chicken to ride.

Before he could, Becky placed a hand on Lori's arm. "Lori, would you mind terribly if John sits this one out with me while Roy goes on the coaster with you? This is Roy's favorite ride and I don't want him to miss it. Plus I'd like to talk to John . . . about the couples shower he doesn't want to attend." She grinned.

Lori glanced at John, who nodded in a way he hoped looked encouraging, as if he was indeed just being nice to Becky and not as if he was incredibly relieved to be let off the hook. He didn't care if Becky wanted to talk about a couples shower, something he normally would have run from in a second; he'd even be willing to attend this one, just in gratitude.

Lori smiled. "Sure."

John grinned. "Okay. See you in a few minutes."

Roy punched his arm in passing, took Lori's arm companionably, and they walked casually to the end of the long line, him in his clodhopper sneakers and her in her sexy black high-heel sandals.

Incredibly relieved and grateful, John found a shady bench for his pregnant and very sweet sister-in-law. They sat quietly for a moment. Without looking at her, he said, "Okay, talk me into coming to your stupid couples shower."

She laughed. "I'm thinking thanks are in order first."

"You're right." He patted her arm. "Thanks."

"You owe me big time, you big scaredy-cat."

So his rat fink brother had spilled his guts. Thank goodness. "Thanks for saving me from total humiliation. I'll pay whatever price you ask. I'll even go to the shower."

"Good answer."

Becky brought what was left of her snow cone up to her mouth and ate while John watched the line snake up and around slowly. Roy and Lori wove through the barricades. As they reached the first turn, a familiar figure cut through the crowd and hopped over the chain to join them.

Travis.

His buddy was wasting no time moving in on Lori.

"Wow," Becky said in mock awe, "I don't think I've ever seen you clench your jaw so tightly before."

He gestured toward the line and opened his very tense jaw to mutter, "Do you see them?"

"I see my husband, your girl, and your buddy."

"Doesn't it bother you?"

"Am I missing something here?"

"I don't want Lori to get caught up with Travis. Did you know he calls each of his many women 'honey' so he won't mix up their names?"

"Really? I've heard of guys who do that but I didn't think I'd ever meet one."

"I mean, Travis is a great guy and all. He'll risk his life to save yours, but I didn't think he was the type to go behind your back and steal your girl."

"*Your* girl, huh?" Becky put her hand on John's arm and he turned to look at her. "I think you and Lori make a great couple. You look like you belong together."

John hadn't planned on admitting his feelings to any family members yet, but found it easy to confide in his favorite sister-in-law. "I like her a lot."

"The family has noticed how different you act when you're with her," Becky said. "You actually *talk* to her. A lot."

He glanced back at Lori in time to see Travis lean close and say something that made her laugh.

Pausing for a moment, Becky asked softly, "What about Dawn?"

John didn't want to remember the haunting look of hurt in Dawn's eyes. "After I met Lori, I realized I wasn't ready to settle down with Dawn. To settle for. I told her we needed to date other people. I told her I had met someone else."

She nodded.

"It's far too early to tell, but . . ." He looked into Becky's eyes again and said the words he had wondered if he'd ever be able to say. "I want to see if Lori might be the one. The one I *could* settle down with, commit to, create a family with." He leaned back and tasted the foreign words on his tongue. Delicious.

"I just have one more question for you." Becky shook her head, amazed. "Who are you and what have you done with my bachelor brother-in-law?"

In a quiet corner of Lagoon stood Pioneer Village, which offered a taste of pioneer life through a walking tour of historic buildings and museums as well as quaint shops and a bakery filled with delicious treats. Lori loved the place and felt like she'd been transported back to the wild days of the Old West.

Leaving the pioneer cabins behind, Lori and John crossed the street toward Pioneer Village's business district. John placed his hand briefly at the small of her back and the spot sizzled. Well. She was certainly physically attracted to the man, which just made her more determined to keep her distance, and she took a step away.

"So," he said, "what are your dreams?"

"Oh, no, you don't. You tell me yours first."

"My dream? That's easy. I always wanted to be an astronaut. Or a cowboy." He grinned. "Or a fireman."

"Are you telling me you're already living your dream life?"

"Pretty much." John shrugged. "Okay, your turn."

Why not? After today, she'd never see this handsome guy again. She'd tell him her old dream, the one she'd given up on. "I always wanted to write. But big things—plays, screenplays, bestselling novels." She glanced at him. This was the point where most people's eyes usually started to glaze over.

His remained bright and interested. "Those are great goals."

"This place would make a great place for a writing field trip."

"Really? What kinds of places do you go for those?"

"Depends on the characters. A racetrack for a NASCAR driver hero, a bed-and-breakfast for the floor plan for a cozy murder mystery—"

He grinned. "The fire department for a fireman hero?"

"I don't know." She smiled and teased, "Do heroes hang out in places like that?"

"Who else you gonna call? Not Ghostbusters." He grew serious. "So tell me more about your writing dreams."

"I wanted to get the Oscar for best screenplay. I wanted to produce movies." Here's where most people thought she was, as Grandma Scott used to say, "too big for her britches."

He tilted his head. "That's awesome."

More relieved than she should have been at his positive response, she shrugged. "Yeah, well, it would be if my first play hadn't flopped after one week."

"One week? Ah, man." His voice was full of sympathy.

"Yeah. My name was up in lights on Broadway for seven full days. Pretty pathetic, right?"

He stopped and put his hands on her shoulders. "Are you kidding? That's fantastic! And your next one will be there longer until you have a play that everyone in the country is talking about. Your name will be in lights in huge letters." He released her to motion broadly with one hand. "A *Lori Scott* play."

She liked the image he'd created, but then she sighed. "I don't know if I could go through that disappointment again."

He leaned toward her and lowered his voice conspiratorially, "I betcha another snow cone you could."

She laughed. "You'll have to do much better than that."

"How about dinner at the nicest restaurant in town?"

He was saying all the right things, that was for sure, and she was warming to him, but she was determined to resist that feeling. That feeling could only get a woman into trouble. And she'd had enough of man trouble.

She'd learned the hard way that men couldn't be trusted. She just needed to remind herself of that whenever her pulse started racing at this fireman's touch.

"So how about it? Dinner?"

She looked up at him and paused. She should tell him no. She should just get on with what she came here to do, but she found herself saying, "If you still want to ask me next week, I'll consider it."

He grinned. "Count on a call next week."

As they strolled along the crowded, rustic wooden sidewalk, a gunfight broke out. A staged one, but the explosion still made her jump. They stopped to enjoy the show and after the shooting and shouting died down, they moseyed on down the boardwalk.

"Hey, look," said John. "Let's get our picture taken."

The window of the old-fashioned store showed a poster with photos of people in Old West apparel. She smiled at the thought. "Why not?"

They stepped inside and into another era. Not much larger than the miniscule cabins, the room was crammed with Old West artifacts: fake guns, polished sheriff badges, elaborate hats with feathers, and vintage clothing.

A man dressed for the time period, complete with watch and chain draped across his vest and sporting a handlebar moustache—was that a job requirement?—welcomed them and introduced himself as Mr. Bailey.

They waited behind another couple, who took *forever* to decide which costume to wear.

Somewhat surprised she'd allowed herself to be talked into this, Lori picked out a saloon girl's purple dress. John chose a sheriff's vest with badge. Of course.

Finally, with the other couple done and gone, the photographer positioned John and Lori in front of a rich maroon brocaded material draped and tied with a heavy golden tassel. John sat on a wooden stool, and Lori stood behind him, her hand demurely on his shoulder, acutely aware of the contact.

John turned his head toward her and his face was very close to hers. Too close. He smiled and . . . was he leaning toward her? Again? He was. Was he really going to try to kiss her, right here in public? Was she going to let herself be kissed?

No. She couldn't. She placed her finger on his chin to stop him.

He cocked an eyebrow.

She teased, with a slightly shaky voice, "I never knew John Wayne was quite so quick with the ladies."

Quite seriously, he said, "John Wayne always won the woman."

The photographer said in a raspy voice, "Amen to that."

Lori laughed. "In the movies, maybe."

"Okay, counting down from five to the perfect Old West photo: five, four—"

"Wait. This isn't quite right," murmured John.

"What isn't?" the photographer asked.

"Keep counting, Mr. Bailey," said John and he grinned up at Lori. "Come here, saloon girl."

"Three—"

Reaching up and around, he pulled Lori onto his lap and leaned in for a kiss.

"Two—"

Startled, Lori's eyes opened wide. Surely he wouldn't kiss her. He wouldn't dare. But she was too surprised to move or make a sound other than a sputter.

"One."

When John kissed her, she didn't pull away, not even when the flash went off.

And that was how Lori Scott was caught enjoying a kiss with a Mormon guy—on film.

Chapter Nine

"I'll have to call you back, Mom," Lori spoke softly into her cell phone. "I'm about to have a meeting with my new boss."

"All right. Good luck, honey. I want to tell you all about your brother's new girlfriend."

Alone in the small waiting room except for the secretary at the desk, Lori couldn't resist asking, "Are you sure you mean my brother? Because Greg doesn't date."

"He happens to be dating a very nice girl. Her name is Kelly."

"Are you kidding? I'm having trouble taking this in."

A beep sounded from the desk and the secretary motioned. "Mr. Neal can see you now, Ms. Scott."

"Gotta go, Mom." Lori put her cell phone on silent and nodded to the secretary. Brushing a piece of lint off her black business suit, she straightened her maroon silk blouse and grabbed her portfolio. She'd read enough of Charles's previous articles to fake her way through this appointment without getting fired outright, which was good, because she couldn't take losing a job faster than she'd lost her play.

She'd also read enough columns to sound quasi knowledgeable on the subjects of growing, harvesting, and even cooking vegetables, as long as Mr. Neal didn't ask her too many in-depth questions.

"Thank you," she said to the secretary as she walked past the desk and through the indicated door into a surprisingly small office. She'd expected more lavish accommodations, something more . . . well, more Manhattanish, she supposed. This office was done in oak; in New York, it would have been black, glass, and chrome.

And the man behind the desk was not what she'd expected,

either. In New York, he would have been dressed to impress and intimidate. Instead, the tall, beefy guy who stood and came around the desk when she entered was dressed in boots, jeans, and a green golf shirt. He looked like he might have played football twenty years before. His brown hair was buzzed short on top, military style. Slightly freckled, his face had a look of permanent mild sunburn.

Placed prominently on his desk so all visitors could see it was a photo of him with his wife and five children, sitting in front of trees with vivid orange, red, and rust-colored leaves.

He smiled and put out his hand. "It's good to finally meet you, Ms. Scott."

His hand dwarfed hers. "Likewise."

He motioned to one of two chairs in front of the desk. When she sat, he settled into the other one.

"Please, show me what you've got."

She raised an eyebrow. Oh, no. Not this. She couldn't—she *wouldn't*—work for another Nicholas.

His sunburn turned the darker red of embarrassment. "My wife is right. The only time I open my mouth is to change feet." He chuckled at himself and shook his head. "I'll tell you what. Let's try this again. Please show me what you've got in your portfolio."

Realizing she was hypersensitive, she relaxed and opened her portfolio notebook.

It didn't take long to go over her background: degree in literature from New York State, jobs in theater, magazine credits, play written and produced. She'd debated leaving off the flop, but finally decided it still looked good on a resumé.

Throughout the review, he was attentive, making sounds of encouragement and appreciation of her accomplishments. He was, it seemed, a nice guy, warm, open, and personable. And his attention was focused on her work and not on her. How refreshing. She decided in those few minutes that she liked him.

"Very nice credentials." He leaned back and nodded, putting one foot across his other knee. "I won't take up your time with a lot of other questions, Ms. Scott. If Charles thought you'd do a good job, I'm sure you will."

She remembered the few questions—hadn't there been just

two?—Charles had asked in his desperate haste to leave the country. She almost felt guilty, like she should confess her ignorance. But she kept quiet.

"Let me give you some basic info about the column."

Lori pulled out a pad and pen to take notes.

"We've got you set up as a guest columnist until Charles returns in three months. I'll have my secretary give you our standard employment forms; just fill them out and fax them back to us. Once that's done, e-mail me your articles each week by Wednesday noon. The e-mail address is on my business card. Your paychecks will arrive twice a month, mailed to Charles's address. I hope that's correct. He said you'd be staying there."

"Yes. It was very generous of him."

"Not if you have to take care of his cat, it wasn't." Mr. Neal chuckled. "Or his garden."

"They are quite intimidating," Lori confided.

"And I hope you don't have to drive his El Camino."

"Yes." She smiled. "Yes, I do."

"My condolences. Just don't dent it."

She smiled ruefully. "I already set his barbeque grill on fire."

"His brand-new grill?" He laughed deeply at that. "Probably best we don't mention that to Charles." He dropped his foot back to the ground and leaned forward, resting his elbows on his knees. "Good luck with your plays. I see you had one produced on Broadway. I'm impressed. That must feel great."

"It felt fabulous." For a couple of days.

"I don't know if you're aware of it, but there is a huge film industry in Utah. And, if you'd like, I have a contact for Sundance Film Festival tickets, which is in January. It's a must-see."

"I probably won't be here by then."

"It'd be worth a special trip back."

"I'll keep that in mind, Mr. Neal."

"Rusty, please."

She smiled and nodded. "Thanks, Rusty."

"I almost forgot. You can write about any vegetable in July, but August is traditionally zucchini month."

"Zucchini? For all four weeks?"

"Yes. Sad to say but our readers love zucchini. My wife alone must have over a hundred recipes for the awful stuff. Don't tell Charles I said that, though, because I'll deny it. The official position of the *Brigham City Daily* is that zucchini is great."

"August. Zucchini. Right." She wrote a note on her pad that may have appeared to Rusty to be about zucchini and articles but was, in truth, a series of question marks interspersed with the letter Z. After all, what did Lori know about zucchini? Zip, zilch, zippo—that's what. But that didn't matter because she was faking her way through this whole thing anyway. She smiled widely. "I'll get right on it."

"Good." Rusty nodded with her, though she was pretty sure he wasn't thinking what she was thinking, which was that she hoped those gardening books in Charles's house and his old clippings of August articles would give her a clue as to what she could possibly say about zucchini that hadn't already been said. What did one say about zucchini, anyway? "Green" and "yucky" covered it for her. She wondered what Charles's readers would say to that. She might be in real trouble here.

"We have a competitor writing a gardening column for the Logan paper. Logan's not too far from here. It's about twice the size of Brigham City. Anyway, Mark Williamson owns Anderson's Seed and Garden and he's very popular."

Oh, great. She not only had to live up to Charles Dobson's standards, but also had a popular columnist as competition.

"I'm sure you'll have no problem matching him."

Lori forced a smile. Sure. No problem at all.

"It's been a pleasure to make your acquaintance, Ms. Scott." Rusty stood and held out his hand. "I'm looking forward to reading your stuff."

"Lori. Please." After standing, shaking his hand, and gathering up her portfolio, she walked back through the newspaper offices, feeling like the rookie *Daily Planet* reporter—what was his name? Jimmy somebody—who'd been assigned to track down the Man of Steel for an interview. Or like she'd just received a Mission Impossible message.

As she pushed open the door and was hit with the blast of July heat from the street, she thought back to the fateful dart toss that had started all this.

She was going to call Greg and ask him about his new alleged girlfriend. And, while she was at it, she was going to chew him out for getting her into this whole mess.

Walking from the newspaper agency toward the cherry-red monstrosity, Lori speed-dialed Greg's number. She'd placed her portfolio on the passenger seat and climbed into the driver's seat before he answered.

"Hi, sis. How are you doing in the big, bad city?"

She could hear the smirk in his voice, which added to her irritation. "I have you to blame for being here."

She started the El Camino to get the air conditioner running and sat in the parking lot as she talked, slipping on her dark glasses so no one would recognize her in this vehicle.

"It's not my fault. I was joking. You took it and ran with it." He chuckled. "All the way to Brigham City, Utah."

"Zucchini Capital, U.S.A." She sighed. "Why didn't you stop me? You know how irrational I can be."

"That's part of your charm." He sounded amused.

"Speaking of charm, what's this dating news Mom told me?"

"Ah. Sweet Kelly." He sighed romantically, but she couldn't tell if he was teasing or serious. "Sister Sorensen's niece. She is a beautiful sight. I'm thinking I may even propose to her."

"Ha. Liar. I don't believe you."

"Well, I may. Some day. Not this month. Perhaps not even this year."

"Are you dating exclusively?"

"Kelly is the only woman I'm dating."

"What are you thinking?"

"You make it sound so horrid. I happen to like her."

"What happened to never getting married and not risking doing to a family what Dad did to ours?"

"Lori, you gotta get past that. I can't live in that place anymore.

It's time to move on. I don't say it as much as Mom does, but you've got to quit hanging on to your anger and hurt. You gotta let it go."

"Just like that?"

"Thirteen years later is not 'just like that.' We were kids. Dad is sorry for the pain he caused us. He'd tell you himself if you'd just talk to him."

"Okay, time to move on to another topic."

"Hey, you brought up Dad, not me."

"Whoops, there's a lot of static on the line. Gotta go."

"Ah, Lori, come on—"

"'Bye, Greg. Talk with you later." She slammed the cell phone into the pocket of her purse and drew a deep breath, waiting until she'd calmed down before driving home.

When Lori pulled into the subdivision twenty minutes later, she was almost looking forward to the daunting task of weeding at least a little of Charles's garden—it should burn off the rest of her anger—before fixing an easy lunch and relaxing all afternoon.

But as she pulled into the driveway, she was amazed to find a man watering her front lawn.

John Wayne Walker.

Her heart fluttered a little, almost as if she was glad he was there. But she wasn't. She refused to be.

It had been five days since she'd seen him, and he looked good. He wore jeans and a light blue, short-sleeved, button-up shirt that brought out the color of his blue, blue eyes. His hair was just a bit mussed up. He looked delicious, but she couldn't afford to have him around, not after their kiss. How was she going to get rid of him without seeming rude? Or did that matter? She was from New York, after all. She could handle this guy.

She climbed out of the car, drew in a breath of mid-day heat, and frowned in irritation. "Do firefighters ever actually go to work?"

"I work forty-eight hours on and get ninety-six off." He moved the end of the hose toward her, as if to splash her with the cascading water, but stopped short of actually getting her wet. He shrugged and grinned mischievously. "I came to offer my services as a tour guide. Would you like to catch some local sights this afternoon?"

She ignored the question. "Why are you watering my lawn?"

"Because it needs it." He swept the water back to the lawn. "For a gardening expert, you don't have much of a green thumb."

"You're only getting away with saying that because you have a hose in your hand."

He adjusted the sprayer to a mist and pointed it toward the flowers along the walk. "So . . . what about that guided tour?"

"Fuhgetaboutit," she said in a thicker-than-usual New York accent. She sighed deeply. She didn't want to be rude, but how else was she going to get rid of him? And suddenly the answer came to her. She'd just mention the awful task ahead of her and surely he'd find some excuse to leave. "I've got to weed Charles's garden. For hours."

"Doesn't sound like nearly as much fun." He laughed. "But I'll help you anyway."

"Are you kidding? Have you seen Charles's garden?"

"I have, one morning when a beautiful lady lit a barbeque grill on fire."

Surprised, she studied him. She didn't think he'd even seen anything but her the day of the fire because he hadn't seemed able to take his eyes off her. She'd been flattered then and she was flattered again remembering it, but she fought that feeling. John was apparently more observant than she'd realized.

"Plus Charles is a family friend. I've been here before." He set the hose down to let it water the big pine tree in front. "Should we head back to the garden now?"

"Wait."

He looked at her expectantly. Raised an eyebrow. Waited.

Finally, she relaxed. Why was she fighting? She could use his help. Who knew, maybe he'd even prevent her from pulling up any vegetables by mistake. She sighed. "You're crazy. You know that, don't you?"

"Probably." He grinned.

"I've got to change. I'll meet you in back." Shaking her head, she headed toward the front door. Maybe she couldn't get rid of him, but she was definitely not going to kiss him again. She'd enjoyed that far too much for comfort.

Chasing a woman was new to John—and he very much liked it.

Grinning, he tossed another weed on his pile. It'd been Lori's idea to have two separate piles, and his had grown to nearly double the size of hers, not that it mattered. All that mattered was that he got to spend time with her, another chance to get to know her better.

He glanced over at Lori, who seemed to look gorgeous no matter what she wore. She'd slipped into her regulation black shorts, this time with funky hot pink sandals and a matching T-shirt that wasn't overly tight, but still revealed her slender curves.

Her uncharacteristic frown only made him more determined than ever to cheer her up.

A light breeze fluttered the leaves of the three quaking aspens set at the back of Charles's yard. The sun still had plenty of time in the sky, and the air still shimmered with heat, but not nearly as much as earlier.

"I think I'm ahead now," Lori said.

John glanced pointedly at the two piles of weeds. "Um, no."

She smiled sweetly. "Are you sure you haven't been stealing some of my weeds?"

He chuckled. "I'm just a better weeder. Admit it."

"Well, there's a news flash for you. Yes, I admit it. You are a better weeder. You're probably a better gardener, too."

"I doubt that. You're the garden columnist. An expert in the field—as it were." With a grin, he stood up and stretched out his back muscles, then took a sip of the delicious lemonade she'd served. She followed suit, leaning back, her hands on the small of her back. He moved his gaze away to someplace safer. "So I have to wonder why you're really here. You're obviously not a garden columnist by trade. What really brought you to Brigham City? Are you a spy or something equally exotic?"

"A spy? Hardly. I'm a writer, I live in a fashionable penthouse, and I never, ever garden. Except for flowers in pots." She sighed deeply. "You want to know the truth?"

He looked into her eyes. "Yes, I do."

She held his gaze for only a moment before looking away, wrapping her arms around herself. "Okay. My Broadway play flopped. My lousy rotten boyfriend found another woman. And I needed some space to think things over."

He frowned. "Boyfriend?"

"Not anymore. He never should have been—ever. I should have spotted the weasel signs much earlier."

He relaxed a little. "It's an easy enough mistake to make."

She looked at him earnestly. "Do your parents have a good relationship?"

Uncertain where this was leading, he answered, "Yes. Sure."

"You say it like it's a given."

He shrugged. "They were married in the temple."

"So were mine." Her tone was bitter. "And my dad still left my mom and my brother and me thirteen years ago, even though he was sealed to all of us."

Encouraged by her sharing and wanting to be careful of her obviously hurt feelings, he said quietly, "I'm really sorry, Lori. That must have been tough. It's gotta affect everything."

"Yeah. Like the Church."

"The Church?"

"I was raised and baptized Mormon."

He smiled gently. "I suspected as much. You do wear a CTR ring, after all."

"But since my dad left, I feel Mormonism is too phony."

"Hey," he said, trying to keep things light, "I'm Mormon."

"I know." She didn't sound antagonistic, but she wasn't smiling either.

He leaned back against the fence. "Do you think I'm a fake?"

She stared at him, her arms still crossed. "I keep looking for signs of it, but I haven't found any yet."

He didn't know whether to be insulted or not. "You're looking for phoniness in me?"

"Don't take it personally. I do it with everyone. Especially guys." She shrugged. "Especially Mormon guys."

Grateful for his own happy childhood, he decided not to take her comment personally. "I'm really sorry your family had such a rough time of it."

"Don't be. I'm okay." And with that, she went back to pulling weeds. "I think you ought to know that I usually avoid Mormon guys."

"And how do you do that?"

Tugging at a small weed, she tipped her face up at him and smiled brightly. "I don't go to church."

A twinge of disappointment flickered through him. "Ever?"

"Ever." She returned her focus to the weeds.

Wow. John turned so she couldn't read his expression while he figured this one out. He reached for another weed.

He was phenomenally attracted to a woman who wasn't even active in the Church? How could she possibly be the woman for him? And if not, why had he gotten such a strong impression that she was?

For some reason, Lori had been brought into his life. Maybe he'd misread the impression. Did she need to be reactivated? Was he supposed to help her? Maybe, but John thought there was something more going on. The impression he'd gotten had been pretty specific.

Though discouraged, he wasn't about to back off now; Travis or someone else might move in. Travis, who wasn't Mormon and so wouldn't scare her like John did.

He might not be able to talk her into changing her mind, but he could certainly issue a personal invitation to attend church with him this Sunday at eleven. That would give him plenty of time to convince her and plenty of time for her to get ready.

John wanted to see where this relationship could go, but he was going to have to be very careful. He planned on a temple marriage.

He waited until the next time she stood, and then spoke casually. "Hey, what if you come to church with me next Sunday? That way you can see that most of the people in my ward aren't phony. In fact, most of them are very sincere."

Stretching her back, she rolled her eyes. “Yeah, right.”

She was being sarcastic, true. But he smiled anyway. He was going to take her words at face value and she’d said yes! “All right. I’ll be here at ten-thirty.”

He caught another eye roll before she leaned forward.

He’d obviously have to do some more convincing on Sunday, but he’d cross that bridge when he came to it. For today, he’d lighten up and have fun with her, so she’d actually want to spend more time with him.

Chapter Ten

As if.

Lori rolled her eyes a third time, pulled another weed, and wiped her arm across her forehead. She hoped her little revelation had given John second thoughts. She was not the woman for him, and now she had let him know it. She refused to be pushed into going to church.

His voice floated over to her, low and rich. "I have to admit, I thought you'd know more about plants than you seem to."

John's change of subject surprised her. She figured he was going to push, and then she could get ticked off and ask him to leave, and then she could be left alone. Like she'd wanted all along, right? But his light tone invited a response in kind. "I thought I'd be writing flower articles. Flowers I've actually grown. Vegetables I've seen on my dinner plate, but never in their natural habitat."

"How on earth did you get Charles to let you write his beloved column? He's like the most finicky guy ever."

"I think he was kind of desperate," she admitted.

"I doubt that."

"And I misunderstood what exactly he needed." She sighed and pointed to one of the plants. "Okay, let me prove I'm not a gardening expert. I don't even know what this plant is. Do you?"

"That, my fair lady, is zucchini." He laughed heartily. "Now that I know you can't identify plants, I can hardly wait to read your column."

"That's zucchini in the wild, huh? There sure seem to be a lot of them on the plant."

"The zucchini on this plant is nearly ripe, which means the

others will soon be ready. I count eight plants, so you're gonna have to harvest more zucchini than a family of ten can use."

Overwhelmed, she stared at the section he was pointing at, shaking her head. "There's no way I can harvest all those, no matter what I told Charles."

John lowered his voice conspiratorially. "Maybe you could just stop watering them and let the survival of the fittest weed them out." He grinned. "As it were."

Shocked, she said, "I can't deliberately kill a plant."

"I'll tell you what. I'll come over and help you harvest the zucchini. Then we can doorbell ditch some to the neighbors." He laughed. "Yup, your articles are gonna be doozies."

She pulled a weed and tossed it, whapping him in the chest. "Oh, I'm *so* sorry. I'm *such* a bad shot."

He raised an eyebrow menacingly and took a step toward her.

"Now, none of that. Get back to weeding." Even though she was trying for tough, she couldn't manage it with her laughter.

He advanced on her. "I think I need to teach you something about plants, Miss Column Lady."

He grabbed her arm, and she widened her eyes. Wait. She wasn't supposed to be flirting with this man. Again. At this rate, he'd be kissing her again and she couldn't have that. Could she? Even having that thought meant she was in trouble. She held up her hands. "Uncle. Really. I give."

He held her arm for a moment longer, as if trying to decide her fate. Finally, he smiled slowly. "What's the password?"

"Oh, no, not the password."

He nodded. "Come on."

She closed her eyes and sighed. "Tickle me, please."

And he did. And she laughed. Finally, he released her, and they both were laughing.

He said, "Okay, I'll let you go. For now."

Awareness of him tingled up her spine. John had a quick wit and a sharp mind. He was gung ho, helpful, confident, and intelligent. And he did interesting things to her heart rate. That was a dangerous combination.

"Nah." He shook his head and took another step forward. "I think I'll get you now, after all."

At the teasing threat in his eyes, she took off running. She'd outraced Greg often enough, but before she'd reached the patio, John caught her around the waist and swung her around. They tumbled lightly to the ground and laid on the grass in the shade from the hedge, his arm holding her firmly against his side.

"Uncle!" She laughed. "Let me go!"

"Not good enough." Still holding her, he leaned over, plucked a small rose from the bush by the edge of the patio, and held it above her head. "Now . . . tell me something about yourself I don't already know. Or I'll have to feed you this delicious weed."

"That's not a weed. Even I know that."

"I was wondering. Now, quit stalling, pretty lady."

"Um, okay . . . I need a good zucchini recipe?"

He chuckled and, with her side pressed so close to his, she could feel the rumble of it. "Nice try. My mother has a great recipe you can have. But I want something better than that."

She pulled back so she could breathe normally, but he still held her. "Okay. Okay." Her heart thumped in her chest. "I've been thinking of giving up writing altogether."

He raised his eyebrow. "Really?"

"Really. I've never told anyone that before. Except my mom."

"Wow." Slowly, he released her. "Why?"

"Because I'm afraid I've lost my touch. Or maybe I never had it." Self-conscious after her revelation, she touched his forearm. "Now it's your turn. Tell me something about yourself. Something you're afraid of."

He paused for a long moment. "Fair enough." He paused again and then shook his head. "I'm afraid to ride the white roller coaster at Lagoon."

"Really?" Surprised, she studied him. "But you fight fires and do all sorts of other scary stuff."

"I know. I can't explain my fear. I went on the beast as a child, I was terrified, and I haven't been able to go on it since."

"But you hang glide and wrestle alligators with Travis, right?"

"We made up the alligator part. But I have gone swimming with sharks."

Looking up at his face, she shook her head in amazement. "Does anything else scare you?"

He smiled warmly and she could feel herself blush.

"You know, I did have some scary moments in Sweden—"

"You were in Sweden?" she asked. "When?"

"On my mission. Thirteen years ago. Now are you going to be quiet and let me finish my story?"

She did the locking-the-mouth-shut motion. Normally, she didn't like to talk about missions and temples and other Mormon stuff, but, for some reason, she didn't mind as much with John. As long as he didn't seriously expect to get her back to church.

"Now where was I?"

"Sweden."

"Right. When I was in Sweden, we had an apartment with a bathroom you could just hose down when you wanted to clean it."

"No way. You're making that one up."

"Cross my heart." He made the motion. "And my first day out, when I was the greenest of all greenies, my senior companion knocked on a door answered by a woman. Guess what she was wearing?"

Lori shrugged. "A snow suit?"

"A birthday suit. My companion immediately averted his eyes and said if she'd like to put on some clothes, we had a message for her. I, on the other hand, just stood there in shock with my mouth hanging down to my knees."

Lori laughed at his expression. "Did she? Get dressed, I mean?"

"She did. And it turned out the woman, Helga, was later baptized. It was the best experience of my life. Well, second best. The best—" John's voice cracked with emotion and the air around him seemed to crackle with some kind of power that touched Lori's heart. "The best was blessing a very sick little four-year-old girl who got better."

Lori couldn't move. She could hardly breathe. She hadn't felt the Spirit this strongly in years. She'd deliberately avoided it, and yet here it had caught her by surprise in the garden.

"Teaching Helga—and all the others—was when I truly gained my testimony of the Church. God's Church. Jesus' Church. Our church."

Caught up in the overwhelming emotion, Lori didn't dare speak. She blinked back tears. She was not going to cry.

"It wasn't until I was on my mission that I took Moroni's challenge seriously. I read the Book of Mormon three times before I prayed to see if it was true. So I always challenge everyone to read the Book of Mormon, and then pray about it."

He paused, and the only sound was a bee buzzing past. A dog barked down the street. A bird called out in the trees next door. Still Lori couldn't find words. She wouldn't have dared use them even if she could for fear her own voice would crack with unshed tears.

He breathed in deeply. "Okay, I'll be quiet now. I guess I got carried away."

He'd gotten carried away, all right. Like her father, who used to tell her to read the Book of Mormon, and look what he'd done. He'd had no qualms about lying—and much worse.

To give John credit, he did seem sincere, which was the only reason she wasn't ordering him off the property.

But this clinched it. She was definitely not getting involved with him. Oh, sure, if he wanted to help her weed, she'd accept the help. But no more dates. No more kisses. And definitely no reading of the Book of Mormon either. For her, that book was closed forever.

"So," he said, "are you going to say anything?"

She blinked past the Spirit, smiled, stood, pulled another weed, tossed it on her pile, and said, "You're falling behind, mission man."

"You always beat your brother at darts? That's great." John opened her back door and let her step in ahead of him—the same action would have sent many a Manhattan feminist into fits, but she found it charming in John. "Did you bring your board?"

Lori shook her head. "I haven't been too lucky at darts lately. That's what landed me here in Utah."

"That sounds intriguing. Tell me more."

As he followed her, she told him the details. By the time they entered Charles's kitchen, he was laughing.

The cool air inside felt fantastic. They washed and dried their hands. Lori filled two glasses with ice, poured more lemonade, and they each took a long swig, and sighed happily.

"Thanks." He took another sip. "This tastes really good."

"Old family recipe," she teased.

He eyed the Crystal Light container still sitting on the counter and raised an eyebrow. "Hmm."

"How do you know my mother's maiden name wasn't Crystal?"

"Go toward the Light, huh?" He chuckled, and it seemed so natural to Lori to have him in her kitchen, joking with her.

Lori took a deep drink of lemonade, enjoying the iced liquid sliding down her throat and the cool air in the kitchen. "Thanks for helping with the weeds."

"You're welcome."

She sat down and motioned to the chair opposite her. "Have a seat."

"Actually, I'd prefer to stand and relax my back. Bending over for two hours is not my natural position."

"You're telling me. My back and shoulders are killing me."

He set down his glass on the table and came behind her chair. "Let me rub them for you."

"Oh, no, that's okay," she began as he grasped the tops of her shoulders and began to knead the muscles. It felt really good, and she sighed deeply. "That's wonderful. Where'd you learn to do that?"

"Just relax. Your muscles are very tight." His fingers moved up to her neck and she tipped her head forward. "My sister-in-law Opal, Kirk's wife, trained as a massage therapist and she forced all us guys to learn a couple of easy techniques."

"Bless her heart."

His fingers felt marvelous, but the warmth from his hands—and from his body, so close behind her—was making her whole body tingle with awareness. He was standing far too close and making her want things she shouldn't want. After another few moments, the feeling overwhelmed her. She shifted out from under his hands. "Thanks, that felt great."

As she stood, he picked up his glass to take another sip.

She grabbed her near-empty glass and changed the subject. "Would you like more?"

"Thanks." He looked amused, and she was aware of him watching her as she refilled the glasses from the pitcher in the fridge. Her face flamed hot.

He took the offered glass from her, and the warmth of his fingers as they brushed hers zinged through her.

"Tell me more about yourself," she said, and immediately regretted her words as too forward, too foolish, too intimate.

"Do you want to know something else I've never told anyone?"

"Sure."

John leaned a hip against the counter, crossed his arms, and smiled slowly. "Okay. I've never told anyone that I've always wanted six."

"Six?" she said dumbly. As opposed to sex, she supposed, which was what her last boyfriend had wanted, and which he'd found with a theater bimbo. A thought flashed through her mind of Nicholas, the man she'd left behind in New York—correction: the man who'd left her behind—and she realized there was no hurt there. Her ego was bruised, but her heart was not.

John was already a much better friend than Nicholas ever had been. And she planned to keep it that way. When she became romantically involved with men, things never went the way she wanted them to.

"Six." His smile deepened and his eyes warmed. "Children."

Stunned, she forced a smile. "Wow. I'm impressed."

Under her words, sadness coiled its way through her, a feeling so strong she was amazed by its power. She thought she'd worked her way past this, but obviously there was more yet to go through. The pain could still catch her by surprise.

"How about you?" he asked. "How many children would you like?"

She blinked once, swallowed, and forced out the words, glad her voice could still sound normal. "I've always wanted children. I've just never really thought about how many."

That was a lie. Her gaze slid away. It didn't matter how many children she wanted. She braced herself against the coil of sadness still working through her like a tendril of smoke, gray and wispy and hurtful.

John's revelation just reinforced what she'd known all along. She and John were not meant to be any kind of a couple. In fact, it was almost pathetic to consider. He wanted kids—*six of them!*—while she . . . Well, she couldn't have even one.

And that fact hadn't bothered her for a long time. Not until she'd begun spending time around John Wayne Walker.

It was good she'd be leaving soon.

"Okay. Your turn," he said.

"I had a ruptured appendix when I was fourteen."

"Ouch."

"It led to an ugly infection and I was in the hospital for several days while I healed." She wasn't about to reveal any more of the story to him than that. Some things were better left unspoken. Forever.

THE GARDEN GURU

Dear Ms. Scott: Let me be one of the first to welcome you to The Garden Guru. I'm somewhat of an expert myself and for several years I have been compiling a book on the subject of controversial vegetables. My personal favorite is the Brussels sprout. How do you weigh in on the subject? And what is your favorite way to cook them? (Stanley)

Dear Stanley: Being a writer, I believe books can change the world, so good luck with yours. On the upside, Brussels sprouts provide vitamins A and C, folic acid, and fiber. But despite that, in a 2002 survey, Britain awarded them the "most hated" status (as have most children, regardless of their heritage). If you can avoid overcooking them (which releases sulphur compounds), it is claimed the vegetable has a delicate, nutty flavor. You might be interested to know that the official "speed eating" record is forty-four sprouts in one minute. And that is an extremely frightening thought.

As for me, my favorite method of preparing Brussels sprouts for cooking is to cut off the base, discard the entire thing, and order out a gourmet vegetarian pizza. . . .

Chapter Eleven

Saturday night Lori attached her first completed column to an e-mail for Mr. Neal. It was past midnight and her muscles were well aware she'd been weeding too much over the past few days.

She still had several days before her deadline, but she wanted to send the first column now so she wouldn't risk forgetting later. Plus she wanted to send it in early because she knew she was going to have to work harder than the average gardening columnist. She planned to do lots more recipe research and testing over the next month—starting with John's mother's recipe. She was going to leave nothing to chance. She intended to write an excellent column that would make everyone think she was an expert on the topic of zucchinis. And, in another month, perhaps she would be an expert.

If she lasted that long.

After clicking SEND, she yawned, stood and stretched, then made her way to bed.

She pulled on her sparkly, red-and-black Betty Boop shorts-and-shirt jammies and settled herself into bed, touching the lamp on the nightstand with her fingers to turn it off.

In the darkness, she yawned again. Tomorrow was Sunday and she was looking forward to sleeping in late. And, after she'd had enough sleep and awakened without her alarm clock, she planned to get up, do her Tae Bo workout, and eat a late and leisurely breakfast. Maybe she'd even stay in her power jammies all day long. An entire day to herself sounded perfect.

She relaxed into the sheets, preparing to fall asleep immediately. But she couldn't. She kept thinking about her mother and brother, wondering what they were doing. In fact, she was fighting off quite a wave of unexpected homesickness.

After lying in bed for a while, her mind racing, Lori rolled to her side to try to get more comfy. Her muscles were sore, but that shouldn't keep her awake. After all, she was really tired; she needed her rest.

With her eyes closed, she thought of the other day when John had weeded beside her for two hours, and smiled. She did enjoy his company.

John's words in the garden that day about praying about the Book of Mormon flickered through her mind and heart. And in that instant, her soul ached to talk with her Heavenly Father. She couldn't help but slip out of bed and kneel.

It had been a long time since she'd prayed. Years. Ever since her father had left and never returned.

"Heavenly Father," she began, then paused. "I know I haven't been good about praying, but I'd like to start again."

She paused again. Then, hesitantly, she prayed to her Father in Heaven. A peaceful feeling warmed her heart, and her thoughts turned again to John and what he'd said about reading the Book of Mormon.

She groaned, ended her prayer, and climbed back into bed. She glanced at the clock and sighed. She'd been tossing in bed and praying for forty minutes and seemed further from sleep now than when she'd climbed under the covers. Her eyes burned with fatigue, but her brain was buzzing and wouldn't quiet down.

Fifteen minutes later, she groaned again. This was insane. She flipped back the covers and swung her legs out until she was sitting on the edge of the bed.

She couldn't get John's words out of her mind. Why did he have to bring up religion? And why on earth should she care about the Book of Mormon? She was not going to read it. No way. That book was for losers and hypocrites. Her father had read from it every single morning and look what he'd done.

But it didn't seem to matter that she didn't care. The feeling kept coming to her that she needed to read it. So, okay, in the interest of sleep, she'd read one verse. One stupid verse. That was all. That certainly ought to be enough to bore her to sleep.

She padded into the office, turned on the lights, and searched the shelves until she found a well-worn, brown leather-bound copy. Inside the front cover was the name "Delores Dawson." Since Agatha had mentioned Charles was a confirmed bachelor, Lori guessed it had been his mother's.

She climbed back into bed, pulling up the covers and keeping only the nightstand lamp lit. Once settled, she opened the book and flipped through to the first page. She smiled. She'd be asleep in no time. She began to read.

I, Nephi, having been born of goodly parents, . . .

For some reason, the words hit her hard. Lucky Nephi. His father hadn't been out chasing other women while still married to his mother, hadn't left his wife to care for Nephi and his siblings on their own, hadn't cast his family aside for another woman.

Perhaps going to sleep while reading would work better if she didn't bring her own emotion-charged baggage into the book. Lori had been born of a goodly mother, at least, and she'd try to concentrate on that.

With a sigh, she forced herself to read on.

. . . therefore I was taught somewhat in all the learning of my father; and having seen many afflictions in the course of my days, . . .

Lori stopped again. She could certainly identify with the affliction part lately—her play flopping, Nicholas dumping her, ending up halfway across the country from her home and family.

She sighed again. Deeply. At this rate, she'd be up all night just getting through the first verse. She started again.

. . . nevertheless, having been highly favored of the Lord in all my days; yea, having had a great knowledge of the goodness and the mysteries of God, therefore I make a record of my proceedings in my days.

Lori was surprised that she read the next verse. And the third. And by how quickly she relaxed as she read. Must be all the weeding and fatigue finally taking effect.

It wasn't long before her eyes closed and she settled into a peaceful sleep.

Dressed in her power jammies the next morning, Lori finished her Tae Bo workout in the living room, pushed the coffee table back into place, and slipped into the kitchen for another glass of the lemonade she'd mixed last night.

So far the day had gone exactly according to plan. She'd slept in until nine. Worked out. Now it was time for breakfast, then relaxing for the rest of the day. No church. No interruptions. No stress.

She wiped her face with her workout towel, draped the towel over a kitchen chair, pulled out a bowl, and dumped in some home-baked granola. She hadn't baked it, of course—that'd been done by the folks at her mother's favorite health food store and deli back in New York.

She flipped open the *Brigham City Daily*. There was a reminder of Peach Days the first week in September. More missionaries listed. Stories of decidedly local interest. Quaint. More Mayberry with Mormons stuff.

Lori poured milk over her granola and lifted her spoon.

The doorbell rang.

Oh, she was so not answering the door today. It was just past ten on a Sunday morning in Brigham City—shouldn't all her Mormon neighbors be in church already? Was a Jehovah's Witness making the rounds while the competition was distracted?

She tried to ignore the bell, not even getting up to peek through the window to see who it was. She was just going to sit here and eat her breakfast and wait for them to leave.

She took a couple more bites; the doorbell rang again.

With a roll of her eyes, she continued eating.

The doorbell again. Two rings, this time. Whoever was there was really persistent. But so was Lori.

When the obnoxious intruder started to knock—loudly—she began to get mad. Someone was ruining her day of rest.

She rose, ticked off and ready to tell this person—no matter which religion they happened to belong to—to get off her porch and stay off. Lori swung open the front door—and stopped, mouth open, too surprised to speak.

Dressed in a charcoal-gray suit, white shirt, and tie, John Wayne Walker stood on her porch, smiling and looking incredibly and wholesomely handsome. He glanced down at her jammies and back up to her face; his grin widened.

Her anger faded and was quickly replaced by embarrassment. "Umm—" That was as far as she got. She tried to re-summon her anger but the fickle emotion wouldn't return.

He tipped the brim of an imaginary Stetson. "Hi."

"Um." She tried not to look down at her jammies and, to his credit and her relief, he didn't look down again either. "Hi."

"Can I come in?" He looked and sounded amused.

"I'm not exactly dressed for receiving guests." She started to recover her voice—and, finally, her attitude. "What will the neighbors think if you come in while I'm still in my jammies?"

"They'll think you're absolutely scandalous, of course." Now he sounded extremely amused. "As do I."

She rolled her eyes. "I can handle being labeled scandalous, but can you afford the blot on your spotless reputation?"

He laughed, the sound rumbly and comforting. "I can survive a smudge or two. Are you going to make me stand out here all morning? It's hot."

She opened the door and stepped back. "Excuse me a moment."

Quickly, she grabbed her red silky robe from the bedroom, regretting its faded look and frayed hem. Better than the jammies, at least. Tying the sash, she came back out to find John relaxing in the doily-armed, pillowed chair. "Why aren't you in church, mission man? Surely you're not the kind of guy to play hooky."

"Nope." He eyed her robe. "It is lovely, but somehow I thought you'd dress up more for the occasion."

"Hey, you caught me totally unaware, without even a courtesy call first."

"I did invite you to come to church with me, remember?"

Ah, yes. She didn't like being pushed and light tension filled her muscles. She forced a smile. "Tell you what. You can watch me eat breakfast and I'll wave as you leave for church. I told you I don't do church, remember?"

He grinned. "Technically, I remember you saying—and I quote—'Yeah, right.' Therefore I, of course, assumed you meant you were going. You do keep your promises, don't you?"

Was he consciously playing one of her convictions against another? Or was it just coincidence that he was pushing her to keep a promise to go somewhere she'd promised never to go again? "I did not promise, though if I had, of course I would."

He widened his smile without saying a thing.

She frowned. "You are absolutely infuriating."

"I've been told that. Never believed it, though."

"Believe it. I am so not going to church with you. Besides, I'm expecting some Jehovah's Witnesses any minute."

"Let me see if I can tempt you." He leaned back in the chair and his voice grew quiet. "I attend a singles ward, along with a lot of other very nice people. And I thought you could use a few friends while you're here."

She sighed. Deeply, darkly, dramatically.

He chuckled, apparently even more amused than before.

"Don't push the church thing. You're lucky I like you at all, in spite of the fact you're a Mormon."

"Thanks. I like you, too. So are you coming to church with me or not? I don't have all day to wait for your decision." He glanced at his watch. "We have to leave in forty minutes. Can you possibly make yourself presentable by then?" He pulled a face as if it was distasteful just to look at her.

If he hadn't obviously been teasing, his voice warm as honey sliding over her senses, she'd have been offended at his words. As it was, he caught her by surprise—again—and she laughed. The laughter released whatever tension there had been between them.

"Why on earth would I go with you? I repeat—I have not been to church in thirteen years."

"Then I say it's about flipping time." He eyed her from head to foot and back. "That outfit has got to go. Hurry back."

She stood, uncertain. She couldn't believe she was even considering it.

He motioned to her. "Shoo. Go on. You don't have much time. And I don't like being late."

She crossed her arms. "I don't like being pushed."

"I'm not pushing. I'm encouraging."

She shook her head, frustrated. "I can't."

He slipped from the chair and knelt on the carpet, putting his hands together imploringly.

Surprised, she took a step back.

"Please, Ms. Scott. Please come with me to church. You will liven things up considerably."

"What on earth are you doing?"

"I'm begging—not pushing. Groveling, even, to get you to go."

She started to laugh at the sight of this big, brawny man down on his knees, clowning around just to convince her to spend time with him. "Oh, fine, you big bully. I'll go with you to church—but only to see how you look when you're struck by lightning for sitting next to me."

He chuckled again. "I'll take my chances."

With a roll of her eyes, she turned and stomped away. Behind her, John began whistling a merry tune. A Primary song, if distant memory served her right: "I Am a Child of God." The man was sneaky. Oh, yes, he was.

As she carried her clothes into the bathroom and hung her dress from the hook on the back of the door, Lori couldn't believe she'd let John talk her into going. What was she doing? She hadn't been inside an LDS chapel for thirteen years. She couldn't just go back, could she? Just to meet some new friends?

But she was in Brigham City, Utah, where you couldn't swing a cat without hitting either an LDS person or an LDS church. If she wanted friends while she was here, chances were high she might actually have to associate with some Mormons. Besides, Marti was Mormon and she was a great friend.

Lori was used to hanging out with singles in New York, but she had to admit she didn't have any really close friends in Manhattan. Her best friend had always been Marti. Lori hadn't made friends easily, not after her dad left. She'd climbed within herself and pulled up the walls and hadn't let many people in.

John had shown himself to be a good guy, and he was right—it would be nice to have more friends. At least more acquaintances. The thought of being alone didn't seem as appealing now as it had even a week ago. The loneliness was beginning to overwhelm her.

She supposed, as long as John was willing to just be her friend and not push for more, she could be willing to open up a little to friendship. He hadn't tried to kiss her again since Lagoon, so perhaps he'd also realized it would be wise not to cross that line again.

And if she could meet other people while she was in town and help ease her unexpected loneliness, she was open to that, too.

She almost laughed as she turned on the water in the shower.

Bring on the Mormons and pull out the lightning rods—Lori Scott was going to church.

Chapter Twelve

Though Lori would never admit it, especially to her family, she actually enjoyed the first two hours of church. After the sacrament (which she hadn't taken because she'd have felt like a hypocrite if she did), she'd enjoyed the talk by a missionary recently returned from Brazil, and even the next one by John's bishop. She enjoyed them more than she would have guessed, but that hadn't taken much—after all, she'd steeled herself to endure all three hours, for potential friendship's sake.

The Sunday School lesson had been rambling, and John leaned over at one point to whisper, "Too bad the usual teacher is sick; he's always well prepared." But sitting next to John had still been a pleasant experience, and she'd been reminded about Christ's healing Atonement.

Now, unfortunately, John had deserted her at the Relief Society door for the third hour, and she was currently sitting next to the pretty, slightly chunky woman in her thirties who had welcomed her at the door, introduced herself as Jeanette Harmon, led her to a seat behind the piano, and now couldn't seem to stop talking. Lori heard precious little of what the teacher had prepared, but a lot of gossip.

She hoped to make it through this class and have John take her home. She'd been there two-and-a-half hours and had given up on finding any friends today.

Lori was relieved when, partway through the class, they sang a rest song. Afterward, the piano player took the empty chair by Lori.

The woman was Hispanic, with glossy, thick, black hair falling past her shoulders and soft feathered bangs framing her heart-shaped face. Her skin was a warm, creamy brown. She leaned toward Lori and whispered, "Hi, I'm Serena Martinez," with the slightest hint of a Spanish accent in her rich husky voice.

"Lori Scott." She hoped she wasn't going to have both women chatting to her throughout the last twenty minutes of the lesson.

Jeanette said, her voice a little too loud. "I was just telling Lori about the ward and about John's dating habits."

With a nod, Serena whispered, "Oh, that's wonderful. I'm sure she's interested in talking about the man she came with."

Startled, Lori looked at Serena to see if she was being sarcastic or not. The sparkle in her eyes and the slight smile told Lori she was, and Lori liked her immediately.

Jeanette frowned. "She needs to know his reputation. We women have to stick together, you know."

"Oh, yes," whispered Serena. She patted Lori's arm. "You watch out for John Walker, *amiga.* He loves them and leaves them."

With a suspicious glance at Serena, Jeanette turned her attention back to Lori. "Your black dress is quite lovely."

"Thank you," said Lori, forcing a tight-lipped smile.

"And those shoes. They must be very expensive."

Lori glanced down at her black Jimmy Choo sling backs and replied with a hint of ice in her voice, "Yes, actually, they were."

Serena smiled and whispered. "I would die for a pair of Jimmy Choos. You are so lucky."

Jeanette frowned. "You shouldn't be so caught up in material things, you know."

"Oh, I know," Serena whispered. "That's why you have to choose just a few of the best ones."

Jeanette made a disapproving sound—a sort of *humph*—and turned to listen to the lesson. Quiet. Finally.

Amused by Serena's comment, Lori twirled her necklace, wishing she could leave and find John, but having no idea where he'd be right now. The next time she came with him, she'd tell him she wanted to leave after Sunday School. Maybe even right after sacrament meeting.

Wait a minute. What was she thinking? There wouldn't be a next time. This had been a disastrous friend-finding excursion.

The quiet pause proved to be too good to be true. Jeanette leaned toward Lori again and whispered, "I just think you should know that John likes to play the field. He's dated all of the women in the singles ward at one time or another. He's broken more hearts than Don Juan."

Lori was actually relieved at this news, because it proved John really did want to be just friends.

The teacher glanced in their direction and then away.

Jeanette didn't even lower her voice. "I just don't want you to get hurt."

"That is so thoughtful of you." Lori crossed her arms and leaned away, trying to put as much physical distance between her and the other woman as she could while still sitting next to her.

Jeanette was everything Lori didn't like about Mormons—the fake smile and too-sweet church voice. Lori certainly knew plenty of non-LDS people in New York who weren't very nice, but she was perhaps oversensitive to women in the Church playing false. Ever since Sister Fiona Bennett had made Lori feel like she was something special, when all Fiona really wanted was to get to know Lori's still-married father better.

With a shake of her head, Lori pushed away the ugly thought.

Serena touched Lori's arm lightly. "I'm going to the restroom. Would you like to come with me?"

"Yes," Lori whispered back, grabbing her purse. She followed Serena out of the room and down the hall, grateful for the escape—and even more grateful when Jeanette didn't follow them.

As they entered the restroom, Serena grinned. "I thought maybe you could use some rescuing."

Lori smiled back. "Thank you for being so perceptive."

"Jeanette can be a bit . . . overwhelming." Serena leaned back against the long counter with a warm smile. "Just so you know, I am not going to mention John or his dating habits."

"Thanks."

Serena turned to wash her hands. "Unless, of course, you beg me to."

"John and I are just friends."

"Good. He could use a good friend. All the women here are trying to get him to the altar."

Lori didn't get the feeling Serena was asking, but she answered anyway. "Not me."

"Me, either. I prefer my men more salsa and less meat-and-potatoes." Serena dried her hands. "Where did you move from?"

"New York. Manhattan."

"Really? Sweet." Serena tossed the paper towel in the trash can. "Would you like to find someplace to sit and get acquainted, or do you want to go back in with the dragon lady?"

Lori thought of Jeanette, picturing her more like a spider spinning webs of gossip, and shuddered. She'd narrowly escaped that web. "I'd much rather sit and talk."

They found an unoccupied couch in the foyer. While they chatted, Lori learned that Serena loved snow and skiing and being in America and that her family—mother, father, and two brothers—had moved from Mexico to Utah when Serena was six.

"I was very homesick when we first moved, because I left all my friends behind. How about you? Are you homesick?"

Lori nodded and found herself confiding, "Yes."

"Would you like to go to lunch sometime?"

"I'd love it." And she really would. She had found a friend after all. They exchanged phone numbers and e-mail addresses.

When John walked around the corner, Lori's heart lightened. But when a curvaceous redhead came into view clinging to his arm, she was surprised by the flicker of emotion. Jealousy? Surely not. Just surprise.

John hadn't seen Lori yet but seemed to be scanning the hallway in both directions as he walked past. Lori almost stood and waved, but found herself staying put while the pair continued down the hall and out of sight.

She turned to Serena. "I think I'd like to ask that question now."

"*¿Sí?*" Serena nodded. "What do you want to know?"

"Has John ever dated anyone seriously?"

"Tough question. Easy answer." Serena leaned closer. "Up until recently, everyone thought Dawn—the redhead walking with him just now—might be the woman who finally got a ring from him."

"Really?" Another flash of jealousy hit Lori; this time, there was no mistaking it. Jealousy she shouldn't be feeling for a friend she barely knew.

"But since he brought *you* to church," Serena continued, "I'm thinking they must have broken up."

"But she was with him. Like a couple."

"I haven't seen them together for a while."

Except for walking the halls together at church. "Who do you think broke up with whom?"

Serena motioned with her hands. "Dawn is not the only woman who has hoped for more with John, but he has always held himself back. If they broke up, he did the breaking. But maybe her heart hasn't gotten the message yet."

Yeah, that's what Lori was thinking, too. She wondered how she could get John to tell her more.

Friend to friend, of course.

As they crossed the church parking lot toward his Dodge Ram pickup, John watched Lori walk in those ridiculously sexy black high heels, her slim hips swaying in that elegant, simple black dress.

She glanced at him, her silky blonde hair framing her pretty face, her rosy soft lips parting in a smile.

"So," he asked, "did you meet any new friends?"

"Oh, yes." She looked up at him with a mischievous twinkle in her eye. "And I heard all kinds of interesting rumors."

"Really."

"Oh, yes. About all the guys and their dating patterns."

"Really." Uneasy about what she might have heard from Jeanette, who had latched onto Lori as soon as he'd left for priesthood meeting, John asked, "And what exactly did you learn?"

"Well, I heard an awful lot about you, in particular. You seem to be very popular with the ladies."

She didn't say anything more, which drove John insane, but she just walked beside him, swinging her little black purse and humming lightly.

He endured the silence until they reached his pickup, when he opened her door and held it for her while she climbed into the cab. "So what exactly did you hear about me?"

Her smile widened as she slid gracefully up, swiveling her long legs and high heels inside. "Oh, this and that."

Frustrated, he shut the door and walked around to the driver's side. As soon as he was seated, he turned to her. "You're deliberately teasing me."

"Yes. Yes, I am." She laughed, a delightfully light, tinkling sound. "You deserve it for dragging me to church. Do you know how many years I've sworn I would never do that? And don't you dare mention this to my brother. Greg would never let me forget it."

"Did you at least enjoy it?"

She shrugged, but her mouth fought a smile. "It was okay."

"Admit it. You enjoyed it."

"Okay, I know you well enough to know you won't stop until I say something. So yes, I, Lori Scott, who swore never to go back to church, returned and actually enjoyed it. There, are you happy now? Can we go home?"

Her words were tough, but her voice held an undertone of laughter.

John was pleased. Not only had he gotten her to church—but she'd liked it. He smiled and started the truck. "So now will you tell me what everyone said about me?"

"Oh, it was great. I learned you are quite the operator and that you have dated all the women in the singles ward—"

"Hardly all." He was glad Lori hadn't seen him with Dawn on his arm; it had taken all his persuasive powers to get free so he could find Lori. But Jeanette could have told her anything. "Who told you this stuff?"

"My sources prefer to remain anonymous," she demurred. "But I was told you've dated many, many women."

"I have." He even sounded defensive to himself, and that wasn't right. "I haven't wanted to get serious with anyone or lead anyone on."

"Ah. But I also heard that some people thought you *were* getting serious with a certain redhead."

Oh, boy. Busted. What did he say now? He wouldn't lie about it, though he wished he could. "Okay. Yes. I was considering it."

"So, friend to friend, what changed your mind?"

He paused, carefully—and frantically—trying to come up with a true answer that didn't state the obvious: *I met you.* Finally he settled for, "I realized she might not be the one for me, after all."

"Well, at least hearing all these stories made me realize you were telling the truth about just being friends. It seems like there's quite the competition to see who can get you to the altar. Bets are being laid and a club is being formed."

"You planning to join?"

"Not me, mission man. I'm leaving in less than three months, remember? Charles will be back on October fifteenth. I've gotta get back to my Manhattan penthouse and my glamorous nightlife."

Ouch. That reminded him that he didn't have much time to get to know her—and that he was not nearly sophisticated enough. He'd have to walk a fine line, getting close enough, but not so close he'd scare her away.

And he had less than three months to do it.

He'd have to bump up his schedule a little. "Mom told me to be sure to invite you over for Sunday dinner tonight."

He'd have to call his mother before then and make sure she realized it was her idea.

Lori opened her cell phone, but hesitated with her hand above the buttons. John was coming to pick her up in an hour for dinner at his parents' home. What was she doing? Had she lost her mind? Totally confused by her attraction to John and her seeming willingness to go along with whatever he suggested, Lori needed to talk to someone, but who?

Not her mother, who would only get her hopes up. And no way she'd call Greg. No, she needed to talk with a girlfriend, but she didn't know Serena well enough yet. With a nod, she pushed speed-dial seven.

Marti picked up on the fourth ring. "How was the date?"

"It wasn't a date. He just took me to . . ." She faded off before the word *church.* Marti didn't know about that non-date.

"To some amusement park. I know. How was it?"

"I have to admit it was really fun."

"I'm so glad. And now, where else did he take you that you're so obviously trying to keep secret from me?"

Lori laughed. "I never could keep anything from you."

"Especially when you nearly say it. Tell me."

Lori groaned. "First, you have to promise never to divulge what I am about to say to anyone. Not your husband. Not my family. Not your family. And especially not Greg."

"Wow. Sounds great. I promise. Now tell me everything."

"John took me to church today."

Marti whistled. "So let me get this straight," she said, sounding amused. "You're living in Brigham City and you're dating a Mormon guy who convinced you to go back to church."

"Yes. Kind of. Not exactly."

Marti chuckled. "Any lightning strikes?"

"Don't make me regret having told you."

"I'm just trying to wrap my brain around this one. I have to ask you this, Lori, though it's painful." She paused dramatically. "Are you, like, being assimilated into the Borg?"

Amused by the thought, Lori said, "Of course not."

"Well, then what else could possibly account for this sudden change of heart? Oh, wait, I know." Her voice grew excited. "Did you call your father?"

Lori snorted. "As if. I didn't call to talk about him."

"Okay. Remind me exactly what you did call to talk about? Because this bogus Mormon-guy-taking-you-to-church story doesn't fly." Marti's voice dripped with disbelief. "Did aliens abduct you? Do you have amnesia? Head trauma? Heat stroke from spending too much time weeding?"

Lori sighed. "I don't know why I called you, anyway."

"Because you love me and I love you. Okay, I promise I'll be serious, because this certainly sounds serious."

"He's taking me to his parents' house for dinner."

"You're meeting this guy's parents today?"

"No. I met them last week at Lagoon."

"You've already met his parents? Wow! He's a fast worker, isn't he?"

"You have no idea." What she loved most about Marti was that it didn't matter how long they went between phone calls or visits, it was like they'd never been apart. She could tell her anything, and Marti would give just enough sympathy, but not so much that Lori would indulge in tears. "The guy actually wants six kids."

"Oh." Lori could hear Marti's sigh across the states. "That could be a problem."

"Only if I were dating him. He's just a friend, remember?"

"Just a friend. Gotcha. Well, in the case of *friends*"—she stressed the word—"who want six kids, perhaps he'd consider adoption."

"Adoption?" Pain flickered through Lori. "He wants his own children, not someone else's."

"Lori, have you told him?"

"Of course not. Why would I? We're just friends."

"Maybe you need to bring up the subject."

Pain coiled around her heart and squeezed her lungs. "Maybe *I* don't want someone else's children."

"But you are so good with my kids. You'd be a wonderful mom. And adoption might be a way for you to be a mother. Forget the *just-friends* guy. Some day you'll meet Mr. Right. And when you do, adoption could be a great idea."

"I'd rather not talk about my inability to have children."

"Hey," Marti said with a slight edge to her voice, "you brought it up."

"I know. I'm sorry. Maybe I shouldn't have called."

"Are you kidding?" Marti's voice softened. "Now tell me what's really wrong."

Lori hesitated to say her real feelings aloud. But this was Marti, who knew her better than she knew herself. Finally, she admitted, "I actually like the guy. And I don't want to like him. I just want a friend while I'm here."

"So just be his friend. And when that drives you crazy, call me and I'll talk you out of getting too serious."

Lori laughed. "Can it really be that simple?"

"Yes, Miss Analyze-Everything-to-Death. You can be friends, even if you're attracted to the guy. Just don't let him kiss you."

Lori couldn't suppress a chuckle. "He already did."

"What? You're kidding! When?"

"At the amusement park."

"You're in bigger trouble than I thought." Marti's voice lowered conspiratorially. "Did you kiss him back?"

"Hey, I know what—let's talk about you instead."

"You *did* kiss him back."

"How are the kids?"

"You're trying to change a very interesting subject."

"Yes, I am indeed changing the subject."

"O-kay then. The kids are great. Kimmi just brought home a paper flower she made for me in Primary . . ."

Chapter Thirteen

"My grocer was Korean, my doorman was Russian, my building super was Israeli, my deli guy was Chinese, my laundry guy was Italian, my newsstand guy was Egyptian, and my favorite falafel guy was Pakistani." Lori drew in a deep breath and smiled. She was rambling because she was nervous, because she wanted John's family to like her. "That's one way Manhattan is different from Utah."

Seated on Lori's left, John's sister-in-law Becky touched her forearm lightly. "It must be a blast living there."

"Yeah," said Clint from further down the table, "but I bet you've never had funeral potatoes at your fancy New York dinners."

Surprised, Lori blinked. "Funeral potatoes?"

Roy chuckled and motioned toward her plate at the grated potatoes mixed with cheese and what Lori guessed was sour cream or a cream soup or something similar. "They're called funeral potatoes because they're served at luncheons following funeral services. But they're Clint's favorite, and so my mother, playing favorites, also serves them when we have Clint's favorite pork chops."

"Oh. Well, they're great." Lori laughed lightly. "I'll have to call my mother tonight and tell her I have now experienced funeral potatoes."

Lori looked around the long oak table at the ten other adults seated there, many of whom she'd already met at Lagoon: John's parents, his brothers and their wives—Clint and Julie, Kirk and Opal, Roy and Becky—his friend Quinn, and Quinn's wife, Tricia.

John and his brothers all resembled their father with matching sandy-colored hair, freckles, and boy-next-door looks. Only the eye colors—and obvious taste in women—varied.

An argument erupted at one of the three tables set up for

children, and Clint turned around. "Kevin, knock it off. Leave your sister alone."

Even with the main table and three others, the huge dining/kitchen area was still roomy. The entire house was large. The rambling ranch house had an old-fashioned feel, but she found to her surprise that she liked the cozy, rustic look.

"What else do I need to know about Utah?" she asked.

"There's no gambling in Utah," said John's father, Wild Bill. "So people drive to Idaho to buy a gallon of milk and play the lottery."

"You're kidding. There's no lottery here?"

"Nope," said John. "The Church frowns upon gambling."

Clint laughed. "Except for the U versus Y game. That rivalry brings out the betting spirit, even among Mormons."

"I'm betting on the Bees this year," said Roy. "That Callister kid is gonna be a good running back. He's fast."

Wild Bill nodded seriously. "I bet they have a good chance at taking State this year."

Lori asked, "Which college team has the Bees?"

"The Bees are the Box Elder high school team." John nodded. "We know all the players."

"On a high school team?" Yup, Mayberry with Mormons. Only this time it made Lori smile. "That's different from New York."

"And always remember, once you're married, if you're called a ten-cow wife," said John's mother, Irene, with a laugh, "take it as a compliment."

Lori was skeptical. "Now you're pulling my leg."

Roy lifted Becky's hand and pointed to her ring. "Now *this* is a ten-cow ring."

"Oh, no way," Clint said. "Julie's ring is a ten-cow job."

Kirk said, "Opal's cost eleven cows, easy."

Lori laughed. "I still don't get the cow thing."

Becky put down her fork. "It's from a movie—*Johnny Lingo.* The bigger the ring, the more cows you would be worth in the Pacific Islands."

"No matter how you define it," said Roy, "John is going to have to spend a small fortune to outdo his brothers."

Oh, dear. Time for a change of subject. Lori's cheeks warmed. Seated to her right, John caught her gaze and chuckled.

The conversation swirled noisily around her, almost overwhelming, but she liked it. It was a fast and furious energy that reminded her of the high-octane rush of living in New York. As Lori watched John's family members tease and laugh together, she could feel the undercurrent of love—and it seemed to include and enfold her with warmth.

John bounced his four-year-old niece, Gabi, on his knee, feeding her little bites of funeral potatoes in between his own. "Is that yummy, honey?"

When Gabi nodded her cute little blonde ponytailed head, John looked over at Lori and winked as he continued to baby talk. "Are you really cute?"

"Uh-huh." Another bounce of Gabi's ponytail. "I cute."

John looked back at the little girl on his knee while Lori found herself suddenly struggling to catch her breath. Was this really how family dinners were supposed to be? Happy and rambunctious? With a mother and father at either end of the table?

Was this what her own family could have been like—*should* have been like—if her father hadn't deserted them?

Anger flooded her as she realized this was exactly what her father had right now with Fiona and the Hideous H's. He'd replaced Lori and Greg with a totally new family and never looked back. Lori would never forgive either her father or Fiona.

John leaned close, his brows furrowed and his low voice concerned. "Are you okay, Lori?"

As she looked into his blue eyes, she breathed deeply and let the anger drain away. She wasn't going to ruin this beautiful moment by dwelling on her own broken family. "Just thinking."

"About?"

"What a great family you have."

"I like 'em." He glanced at his brother, Roy. "Well, except for Roy on certain days."

"Hey," said Roy. "What'd I ever do to you?"

"Besides team up with Clint and Kirk to tie me up and feed me to the wolves?"

"Bandit was hardly a wolf." Roy snorted. "Worst he could have done was lick you to death."

Across from Lori, Quinn asked, "So tell me—which John Wayne movie will we all be watching after dinner today?"

John explained, "It's our tradition to watch a western, but I can take you home before, if you'd like."

"I bet Lori would like *The Quiet Man,*" Clint said.

"Nah." Roy shook his head. "A New York socialite won't like a movie where John Wayne spanks Maureen O'Hara in the end. Literally."

"Where else can you spank someone?" asked Clint with a grin.

"He does?" asked Lori, appalled.

"What a chauvinist," said John with mock indignation.

The others laughed.

"She deserved it, though," Roy said. "She'd led him on a merry chase."

"Oh, Lori, if you could see your face right now," said Becky. "Don't let them get to you. They're just teasing you. They're all talk. They're really just kitty cats."

"Please. We prefer you use the correct term." Now Roy acted indignant. "Lions."

"Or tigers," said Clint.

"Or bears, oh my," said Becky. "You guys are so full of it."

Quinn alternated between tickling his son, Evan, who'd finished eating and now sat on his father's lap, and leaning over to warble at his infant daughter, Emma, cradled in Tricia's arms. Again, Lori was struck by how Quinn seemed to adore his two children. And she just knew that was the kind of doting father John would be.

In a smooth movement, John swung Gabi up into his arms as he stood. "We'll be right back, folks." He returned a moment later carrying a newspaper. "Hey, everybody, I want to show you Lori's first Garden Guru column." He passed the paper to his father and it began to make its way around the table.

The family was generous in their praise, and Lori's heart warmed at the family fire.

On her left, Becky whispered, "I'm glad you came today."

Lori looked at her and smiled. "Thanks. Me, too."

Becky leaned in so close that her words went no further than Lori's ears. "I just thought you'd like to know that John is a totally different man around you. You bring out the best in him."

Lori whispered back, "We're just friends."

Becky smiled. "If you ever want to take it up a notch, you could. John really likes you."

Lori glanced at John to see if he'd heard, but he was still busy playing with Gabi.

"Trust me on this," whispered Becky.

Lori couldn't suppress a smile.

Wild Bill's voice carried loudly. "Lori, did you know John's grandfather was a firefighter, too?"

"I didn't. That's great."

Becky whispered, "His parents like you, too."

"Everyone except Kirk is a fireman. He's the black sheep of the family." Clint shook his head sadly. "Went and became a cop."

"Oh, that is a shame," Lori said with a laugh.

Kirk held up his hand. "Change of subject, please."

"Or what?" John laughed. "You'll arrest us?"

"I've been wanting to haul your behind in for quite some time, John," Kirk said, obviously teasing. "But, fortunately for you, ugly isn't against the law."

"You know what they say . . . if a citizen needs help, they call the police, and if the police need help—"

In unison, all the men—even Kirk, though in a sarcastic voice—said, "They call a fireman."

"Yeah, yeah," Kirk said. "You firemen are all talk."

Roy said, "Lori, do you know the difference between firemen and policemen?"

She shook her head while Kirk rolled his eyes and said, "Don't you have any new ones, at least?"

Roy laughed. "Firemen never wanted to become policemen."

While the men tossed that conversational ball around, Lori asked the women, "I need some good material for my column. Can you ladies tell me what you do with zucchini?"

"Yuck." Becky pulled a face. "I hate zucchini."

The other women noted Lori's e-mail address and promised to send recipes.

"Oh," gasped Becky, moving her hand on her large belly.

Concerned, Lori asked, "Are you all right?"

"Sure. It's just the baby moving. Catches me by surprise."

"That must be an incredible feeling."

Becky grinned, grabbed Lori's hand, and placed it on her distended belly. "Feel for yourself."

Shocked at the contact, Lori wanted to jerk her hand away, but didn't want to offend Becky. Then Becky's stomach rolled beneath her hand and a bulge poked out on the side.

"That's a foot or elbow or something," said Becky with a half smile, half grimace. "Ouch. And a fist in the ribs."

Awe filled Lori as she felt the tiny life inside Becky move, followed by a wave of sadness. Still with her hand on Becky's belly, unable to move because of the wonder of it all, she whispered, "It must be fantastic to be pregnant."

"It is," Becky whispered back. "You'll love it."

Lori looked up to see John watching her. And suddenly it didn't matter if his parents liked her or not, because when he smiled softly, feelings she didn't expect or want skittered through her. She pulled her hand back.

John wanted children to dote on and she could never give him any. The two of them were totally incompatible.

And that knowledge had never hurt her so much as it did while she looked into his blue eyes that seemed to caress her very soul, reminding her of what she could never have.

John glanced at Lori again. She sat next to him in his Dodge Ram pickup, looking out the side window, away from him, very quiet. The only sound was the air conditioner cooling the hot night air.

She'd stayed to watch *Silverado* with his family, and she seemed to enjoy the time with them, laughing and joking. It was only after she'd gotten into the pickup with him and they were alone that she'd seemed to withdraw into herself.

He drove on, resisting the urge to reach out and take her hand. She was far too skittish. He wondered who had hurt her in the past. Or was he imagining things? Overwhelmed with protectiveness, he wanted to shield her from harm, keep her safe, take care of her.

Pursuing her was a challenge because she obviously resisted his every attempt at involvement. But he had to admit he was enjoying being the one chasing for a change.

He glanced at her again, her face beautiful in silhouette and her hand within reach of his on the seat.

He parked his Ram in Charles's driveway and went around to open the passenger door and give Lori a hand down. She was incredibly graceful, especially for a woman in heels.

They walked to the house in silence, not companionable, but awkward. At the door, she fumbled with the keys, and he hoped her nerves were a good sign. If he made her nervous, then maybe she liked him, too. He would prefer it, though, if she were relaxed and comfortable around him, as she'd seemed to be on other occasions.

When she finally opened the door, she looked up at him and said, "I had a very nice time with your family, John. Thanks."

Before he could blink, she stepped inside. If he didn't speak up quickly, she was going to close the door on him, and he didn't want to go. Not yet. "Invite me in for a minute?"

She paused with her hand on the edge of the door. "I don't think that's a good idea tonight, John."

"Then can I take you out Friday? There's a theater down in Perry, not too far from here. We can go to Maddox Ranch House first and then to the Heritage Theater. I think you'd love it."

"Thanks, but no, really." She shook her head. "I don't want anything to do with the theater right now."

A pang of some strong emotion he couldn't identify—hurt? jealousy? determination?—struck him hard. Did she not want anything to do with theater? Or with him?

He was amazed at how much he wanted this woman. Not just physically, though there was certainly that element. He wanted to spend time with her—every waking moment, it seemed—to laugh with her and talk with her and . . . kiss her.

Mixed emotions didn't begin to cover what he was feeling. He was hurt at the thought of walking away without knowing if he'd see her again. Jealous of her time away from him. Overwhelmed by the strength of his longing for her.

And he realized he already cared enough for her that he couldn't just walk away. He was going to keep asking, even if she kept saying no. And maybe he'd luck out and she'd say yes. He was no longer afraid of commitment.

Lori looked at John, wishing she could invite him in, but afraid of the feelings he and his family had roused in her tonight. "Good night."

"You can't turn me down forever. I'll keep asking until you say yes. I'll wear you down with my sheer persistence." He quirked an eyebrow. "I'll ask you out every single day, sometimes twice, and occasionally on bended knee."

Lori couldn't help but laugh at the image, his words breaking her resolve to keep her distance. "You would, too."

"Of course I would. I always go after what I want."

A tingle worked its languorous way up her spine. "And what exactly do you want?"

"To get to know you better."

The tingle spread.

"On dates, not just pulling weeds in Charles's ridiculously huge zucchini patch. I enjoy your company, Lori Scott. And I think you enjoy mine. And that's a rare thing."

"Rare?" She snorted in a most unladylike fashion. "You've dated half the singles ward."

"Only the female half." His mouth curled up in a smile. "But you'll notice I want to spend my time with you."

"You just like a challenge," she said, afraid it was true. "I don't fawn over you, and so you think you need to fix that."

"There could be some truth to that. I'd like to find out."

Disarmed by his honesty, Lori was tempted. Why not enjoy a few dates while she was here? She'd be in Brigham City ten more weeks. It wasn't like she was going to marry him or anything. And she did enjoy his company.

"What do you say? Will you date me, Lori? Be my girlfriend?"

At the word, the tingle swirled to her fingertips and toes. "Are you just expanding your playing field?"

"Exclusive dating while you're here. Just you and me." His blue eyes grew intense. "What do you say? Will you go out with me?"

Flattered, she wondered why she shouldn't take their friendship up a notch to short-term romance. It would just be a holiday romance—something more than friendship, but less than commitment—ending naturally when she returned to New York. Why not allow herself the boost to her wounded ego?

She wouldn't be leading him on, after all. She'd already told him she wasn't active LDS and didn't want to be involved with the Church, so he wouldn't be expecting that from her.

No, she concluded, he really did just like the challenge she presented. Even if he got bored after a few dates, she'd be no worse off than she was now. And it'd be nice to have a few months of romance before hitting the brick wall of reality. "I'll be leaving for New York in ten weeks," she reminded him.

"I know." He grinned. "Want to have fun while you're here?"

Why not? Yes, she would date him and have fun.

The fact she couldn't have kids wouldn't matter, as she'd be gone long before the relationship turned serious. She'd dated Nicholas for more than a year; three months was nothing.

They could have fun, no one would get hurt, and he was a handsome fireman. How perfect could a holiday romance be?

She drooped her shoulders and made her voice tired. "Just the mere thought of your legendary persistence wears me out."

His grin widened. "So you'll go out with me?"

"Okay, okay. You win. But no theater events."

He took a step closer, until he was only inches from her. "Great. I'd like to seal our new arrangement." He leaned down and she widened her eyes.

Yikes. He was going to kiss her. Again.

Quickly, she put her hand to his mouth. "Not so fast, mission man."

He kissed her fingers and shot her a cocky grin. "Good night,

Lori. I'll pick you up Friday at six for a non-theater event. And I'll call you from the fire station tomorrow."

She watched him stride to his pickup, climb in, wave, and pull away like a knight on his dark metallic-blue charger.

Still smiling, she closed the door.

She, Lori Scott, was officially dating a Mormon.

And glad of it.

Chapter Fourteen

With a scowl, John clipped his phone back on his belt as Travis wheeled the engine into the station house, shut down the big vehicle, and pocketed the key.

"Still no answer at the Scott residence?" asked Larry, seated between John and Travis.

"No," John grunted as he opened the large door. It was killing him that he couldn't leave the station and see Lori. But he didn't want to talk about it with Travis. Or Larry. Or anyone else, for that matter.

"Maybe she just turned off her phone," said Travis, obviously bored.

"Maybe."

"So leave a message." Travis grabbed his gear.

"I already did." Two of them. And he didn't want to make himself more of a pest. He and Lori had been dating now for two weeks, but he still didn't feel secure in their relationship, though he found himself thinking about her more and more.

"Let's clean up and eat. I'm starving," Travis called out from the gear room.

John wished he could take Lori to dinner again. They'd gone to restaurants several times in the past two weeks: halibut at the Idle Isle, steak at Maddox Ranch House, the Fiesta Sampler Platter at Café Sabor in Logan. They'd gone to see three movies—one of them even an action-adventure rather than the chick flicks Lori preferred.

On the previous Saturday, he'd driven her down to American Fork, nearly two hours away, for the long hike up the trail to Timpanogos Cave. She'd held his hand in the darkness of the cave and, when the lights were turned back on, oohed and ahhed over the beauty of both the climb and the cave.

He'd even helped her pull more of those horrible weeds that insisted on proliferating in Charles's garden.

Silent, John dropped his boots in his large gear bin and stuffed his gloves on top.

It had been nearly two days since his shift began and he'd last seen Lori, and he seemed to be having withdrawals. He'd been at the station house for thirty-six hours. With the day work over, but twelve more hours on his shift, he had nothing but television or reading to entertain him for the evening—unless, heaven forbid, there was a fire. He knew, from last night, that all he'd think about would be Lori and her silky blonde hair framing her perfect face, her black clothes framing her perfect body, her smile lightening his heart.

"You're mooning around like the Bees just lost their home game to Bear River." Larry tossed him a hose. "Here. Go wash down the truck to take your mind off . . . who is she again?"

"The blonde with the spider in her venturi tubes." Travis turned back to John. "You know, you never acted this way with Dawn . . . or with Jill or Trina or—"

"It's none of your business. That's who it is." John's voice was harsher than he'd intended.

As Larry came out of the gear room, he raised an eyebrow. "A mite touchy, aren't you?"

John barely heard the banter. If only he didn't have to sleep at the fire station tonight. If only he was off shift. If only Lori would answer her flipping cell phone.

Larry said, "I bet five bucks on the blonde."

John turned and the hose hit Larry square in the legs.

Larry jumped back. "Hey! Watch it!"

"Oh, sorry, man," John said with a grin. "How clumsy of me."

"Yeah. Whatever. Two can be as clumsy as one." With a matching grin, Larry grabbed Travis's hose, and soon all three of them were in the fray, dripping wet and laughing.

Afterward, Larry said, "Hope no one calls a fire code now."

John chuckled as he coiled the hose. His earlier tension was gone. Buddies were great.

"Not to change the subject or anything, 'cause you guys know I love talking about women," said Travis, "but I hear conditions are right for another big burn down in California."

The California fire four years ago had been a bad one. They'd all volunteered, along with countless firefighters from other states, but it had still taken two weeks to get the flames under control and to save the houses in the fire's path.

John's phone burbled. Finally! Lori was returning his call. His heart lifted as he flipped open his cell. "Hi."

"Hi, John." A woman's silky voice caressed his ear, but disoriented him—the caller was definitely a woman, but not Lori. *Dawn.* "I hope you don't mind me calling."

Not sure what to say—he hadn't exactly broken up with her definitely, just discouraged her, and then he hadn't called her for weeks after he started dating Lori exclusively—he mumbled something along the lines of, "That's fine."

At his strained tone of voice, Travis glanced his way, tilted his head, and mouthed, "Who is it?"

John waved him off and turned away as Dawn continued. "I need a favor. We have a problem with our faucet and I'm not sure what to do. It's leaking a lot of water. I was really hoping you could help us out." Dawn lived with her aunt and taught school in Logan.

He'd felt protective toward Dawn for months. Not to the extent or with the strength he felt toward Lori, but he found now that he couldn't just turn off that emotion. But he also couldn't give in to guilt or misplaced responsibility now, not when he was pursuing a romance with Lori. An exclusive relationship. He gave the first excuse that popped into his mind. "I can't leave work, Dawn. Why don't you call your home teacher?"

"We already did, and he didn't know what to do." John could almost see the slight pout of Dawn's pretty lips as she spoke softly, wistfully. "John, I really need your help."

At her words, guilt flooded him. Before he could stop himself, he said, "Okay. I'll stop by tomorrow after work and fix it for you."

"Oh, thank you. You're so wonderful. I'll see you tomorrow, then. I can hardly wait. Okay, it's a date, then."

Before John could explain that it wasn't a date, she'd disconnected. With a groan, John put his phone away.

Unfortunately, when he turned around, Travis was right behind him, standing with arms crossed. "That was a woman-related groan, wasn't it?"

John slapped his palm to his forehead. Twice.

"The blonde or the redhead?"

"Dawn."

"I'll help you out, ol' buddy, ol' pal." Travis turned on another hose and wet the station house floor under the engines. "I'll date one of them while you work on the other."

John shook his head, picking up another hose.

"Dawn is way too obsessed with getting married, though. How would I avoid getting engaged to her?" Travis mused.

"Like you do with all the women you've dated," called out Larry from the gear room. "Love 'em and leave 'em."

"Oh, that's cold, dude," said Travis. "I just don't want to let women get too attached to me. Otherwise, I'd break their hearts and how cruel would that be?"

John narrowed his eyes. Perhaps Travis could help him out of this. "Hey, Travis, ol' buddy, ol' pal, you might be right. I'd be happy to give you an opportunity to date Dawn."

"Your kind offer is a little suspect at this moment, dude. What have you gotten yourself into now?"

John tried another tack. "You owe me."

"Nobody could possibly owe you as much as what I'm afraid you're about to ask. Come on. What's up?"

Reluctantly, John told him about Dawn's request.

"All right." Travis grinned. "Slight revision to the plan. You go help poor helpless Dawn and I'll keep Lori busy while you're gone. There. Problem solved."

Jealousy struck John hard and fast as he realized Travis was probably exactly the kind of worldly guy Lori was used to dating. "Keep your hands off, dude. Lori might be my future wife."

Now why did he have to go and tell Travis that? He was glad the other guys had already gone into the station house to change into dry clothes.

"Whoa, dude." Travis blinked. "You serious?"

"Yes. No. I don't know." John was sounding like an idiot, and an indecisive one, at that. "It doesn't matter if I am or not. You just stay away from her."

"Okay, dude, I get the message. Loud and clear." Travis lifted his hands. "Lori is all yours."

Travis took a few squishy steps in his wet socks before turning back toward John. "But just so we're clear, so is Dawn and her leaky faucet."

John groaned again.

THE GARDEN GURU

Dear Ms. Scott: Do you have any gardening club affiliations? And, if so, what are they? I'm trying to decide if I should join a club. I'm not an expert like you and Dr. Dobson, but just a beginning gardener. I'd appreciate any help you can give me. (Tammy)

Dear Tammy: The Spade and Hope Garden Club in Brigham City is helpful to beginners and advanced gardeners alike. They provide an annual summer garden tour, annual spring plant sale, and informative conversation. You can learn a lot from these knowledgeable gardeners. I highly recommend you attend the next meeting; you and your garden will be glad you did. The annual dues are minimal. For more information, call . . .

Chapter Fifteen

As a decadent morsel of cheesecake drizzled with strawberry sauce tickled Lori's taste buds, she looked around the grassy area. Apparently, one of the Spade and Hope Garden Club members owned the Alpine Nursery in Perry and had offered up a large expanse of lawn with a large pond next to it, nestled in the trees, for their annual each-member-may-bring-one-friend potluck dinner.

She counted five tables in all, five people seated at each. Two long tables had been pushed together, end to end, to hold the food.

She'd caught a ride with Agatha, and they were seated at a center table with Agatha's gardening cohorts: Victoria, Lisa Anne, and Norma. All past sixty, all gardening experts, and all—except for an amused Agatha—impressed with Lori's supposed expertise as the Garden Guru substitute.

Her expectations of a slow-paced evening had been realized, but she was so grateful for the help she didn't mind. And the dinner itself was delicious, consisting of each woman's specialty dish: salads of all kinds, two soups, many casseroles, punch, and dessert.

Now Lori took the last bite of her cheesecake, savored the flavors, and sighed. "Fabulous."

Lisa Anne, a wrinkled, tight-curled, blue-haired woman in her eighties, smiled. "I do love a girl with a hearty appetite."

In her seventies, Norma tossed her stylishly cut and dyed—Lori assumed—dark brown hair. "I prefer the peach pie myself."

Victoria, the youngest at sixty-four, radiated sadness. Her eyes showed pain and she couldn't seem to work up a smile. "I used to have a good appetite."

Agatha motioned dramatically. "I told Lori you ladies would be generous with your best zucchini recipes."

Norma patted her dark hair. "She ought to get the recipe from—"

Agatha shook her head as she interrupted. "No use. We need to share some of ours."

Lori nearly chuckled. She hadn't figured out Agatha yet, other than that she was an eccentric lady.

Victoria said, with a hint of Eeyore's mope in her voice, "I'd be glad to share my zucchini-strawberry cake recipe. Maybe you could all come to my house and I'll fix it for you."

Agatha shot Lori a glance and said, "We'd love to. Just let us know which day."

"I'll look at my calendar and call you," Victoria said, with the first hint of excitement she'd shown since Lori arrived forty-five minutes ago.

"No one has even noticed," Norma said impatiently, patting her hair. "Do you like what my hairdresser did this time?"

Agatha snorted. "I preferred the red."

"Not me," said Lisa Anne. "I like the brown. It flatters your face, Norma."

"No, no, no." Agatha shook her head. "It ages you, hon. The red took ten years off your face."

"Really?" Norma tilted her head, as if studying that thought. "Well, then I'd better go red again."

Better red than blue, Lori thought, looking around.

Agatha turned to Victoria. "How have you been doing?"

Victoria sighed. "I've been very lonely."

Agatha explained to Lori, "Victoria's husband passed away three months ago."

"I'm sorry to hear that," said Lori.

Victoria sighed. "I know it sounds horrible, but I'm angry at Ted for leaving me alone. I'm so angry at him, and I miss him so very much."

Lori was struck, out of the blue, with the woman's loss.

Agatha patted Victoria's hand. "It'll get better with time."

"The counselor says I'm still stuck in the anger phase of grief." Victoria sighed and forced a faint smile. "I don't want to be stuck, but it's hard to get out."

A horrible thought slammed Lori. Could *she* be stuck in a stage of grief? The *first stage* of anger? *Thirteen years* after her father left? She blinked. No, surely not.

A woman stood and, over the clatter and chatter, invited everyone over to look at a huge sure-to-be-prize-winning tomato.

As the women at their table rose to their feet, Agatha asked Lori, "Would you like to join our little club?"

Lori nodded. "Yes. Though I'm certainly not in the same league as these ladies."

"They're quite competitive about their gardening skills, aren't they?" As the other women wandered off, Agatha lowered her voice. "Most of 'em are all talk. Don't you worry about a thing, sweetie. I'll help you keep your secret."

Tossing her purse on the bed, Lori pushed the speed-dial number for Marti.

"About time you called. I am going absolutely crazy here with my family."

Lori laughed. "You love your family. In fact, you married far too young so you could start said family, remember?"

"Well, tonight I've had just about enough of them, thank you very much."

"What's up?"

"Where do I begin? Bryce got his Wood Badge for his work as a Scout leader and so the kids and I went to his award ceremony. We were assigned the punch, and I'd already discovered a big dried punch stain on the front of my dress earlier in the day. I washed it out—only when we drove to the church, more punch leaked out of the container onto my dress. In the same exact spot."

"Oh, Marti, I'm so sorry." Lori made a sympathetic sound, which, unfortunately, sounded a lot like a chuckle.

"Oh, wait. That's not the worst of it. We got the big jug all set up on the table and I was helping a few kids push the button and hold their cups underneath and then, in some sort of freak accident, one of the kids holds his cup just wrong and the spray hits his cup wrong—and the punch shoots right into my shoes."

"Oh, no." Lori couldn't suppress a laugh. "That's awful."

"When Bryce asked me how I was, I said my feet were sticky. So he said I was the most beautiful sticky-footed woman there."

"Ahhh, how sweet."

Marti's voice softened. "Yeah. He is pretty sweet."

"So I guess you didn't make a total mistake marrying him when you were twenty."

"No, I guess not." Her voice lightened. "So how are you?"

"You'll never guess, not in a million years, what I've been doing."

"With you, probably not. So just tell me. I'm much too frazzled tonight to play guessing games."

Lori laughed. "I'm now officially dating the firefighter."

"And . . . ?"

"And what?"

"Come on. I know that tone of voice, Lori Scott. What have you been doing that you're not telling me?"

Lori sighed. "If I tell you, you've got to promise not to say a single word about it. To anyone."

"I promise. Stop driving me crazy, already."

Lori paused, still amazed herself. "I've been reading the Book of Mormon. I'm in Second Nephi."

There was silence for a beat. "You'd make a wonderful Mormon. I've always said you ought to try it sometime. Remember those fun activities we went to? Where John Fullmer had all the girls gaga with crushes?"

"Yeah, him and Byron Kinser." Lori had fun memories of the Young Adult activities she'd attended with Marti, though she'd drawn the line at going to church on Sunday.

They chatted for fifteen more minutes before Marti said, "Duty calls. I've gotta go. Oh, and I've tried calling you several times this afternoon. Is your phone on silent again?"

"Oh, darn. I switched it to silent earlier this morning when I went to the library." Which could explain why she hadn't heard from John today.

"Well, turn it back on. And I'll definitely call you in a few days to check on your very strange behavior. Talk to you soon. Bye."

"Bye, Marti." Lori checked her phone, changing it from silent to soft. There were eight missed calls—three from Marti and *five* from John, scattered throughout the past seven hours. He'd been trying to reach her all day.

Quickly, she pushed reply. The hardest part about his schedule was seeing him for four days straight and then not at all for another two. She missed him, which surprised her.

The call rang through and, after three rings, was answered—but not by John. It was a woman's voice. "Hello?"

"Um, hello." Lori paused, a little disoriented. Wondering if she'd reached a wrong number, she pulled the phone back. The number was correct; it was the one she'd been using for weeks. "May I speak with John Walker?"

"May I tell him who's calling?"

"Lori Scott," she said reluctantly.

"Oh. This is Dawn Lawson. I met you at church."

What is Dawn doing answering John's cell phone?

"Sorry, but John can't come to his phone right now," Dawn said.

What is John doing with Dawn? Lori wondered. *And why is she obviously lying to me?*

Dawn continued. "He's fixing a faucet for me, and then he'll be staying for dinner. I'll tell him you called, though." There was a challenge in those words, and Lori would bet money that any message left would most definitely *not* be passed on to John.

There was silence for a few beats.

Lori could barely think straight. What was she supposed to do now?

Finally, she shook herself. "No, thanks. He's already called five times, so I'm sure he'll call me back later. Or I'll just call him later." Way later. If at all.

"Bye," Dawn said, and Lori could hear the hostility underlying her silky voice.

Lori was feeling some hostility herself at the moment, along with a great deal of flaming jealousy and a lot of confusion.

Hadn't John said he wanted to date Lori exclusively? Was the challenge over for him this easily? She'd said yes, they'd dated for two weeks, and now he'd started dating everyone else again? Without telling her?

Or was it just Dawn he'd started dating again?

She tried to reason herself out of her upset. She'd already known John was dating other women—but not since their exclusive agreement. In fact, that was a good thing, because it proved he wasn't going to get too emotionally involved with her.

If it's such a good thing, then why am I so upset?

She drew in a deep breath and tried to take a step back emotionally. She needed to remember that they were just friends. Even if she really liked him. Even if he'd used the word "exclusive." She'd learned the hard way that words meant nothing to guys.

She decided it was actually a good thing she'd had this reminder to stay emotionally uninvolved, even if she continued to date John non-exclusively. She wasn't about to get hurt again.

And, judging from her strong reaction to his cell phone being answered by an old flame, Lori suspected that, if she let herself get too involved with him, John would have the power to hurt her like no other man before him had done. Except her father, of course.

But maybe she was jumping to conclusions. She needed to see what John said—or didn't say—about being over at Dawn's house.

That's what she'd do. She'd let John take the lead. If he was honest about it, she might continue dating him.

But if he lied, he could forget about seeing her ever again.

With his torso crammed under the kitchen sink and his hands on the wrench, John tightened the pipe. He hadn't been under there long, but long enough to hear his cell phone ring in his jacket pocket in the living room a few minutes before. And then stop ringing.

Probably Lori. And there was no way he would ask Dawn to bring him his phone so he could answer Lori's call with Dawn listening in.

With one last twist, he was done. Standing, he set the wrench on the counter and washed his hands.

Dawn came in, beaming. "You're finished? That was fast."

He nodded. She looked pretty tonight. Too pretty. Her long red hair curled down her back. Her figure was more curvaceous than Lori's, and she looked great in her jeans and USU T-shirt. She'd just graduated in the spring, but had stayed on to teach for a year, probably because she'd been dating John. Her light flowery scent made him very aware of her presence.

"John, you are so handy to have around." She practically purred the words.

Her admiration and smile lit the kitchen. She made him feel good about himself, and that made him very uncomfortable. She obviously didn't feel the least bit of discomfort. But then she hadn't promised to date someone else exclusively.

His mouth was dry. "Where's your aunt?"

"She went visiting teaching tonight." Dawn flipped on the light in the breakfast nook area, revealing a table set for two, complete with candles. A cozy, intimate, romantic dinner for two. "I fixed you a steak. To repay you for your help."

She lit the candles and turned back to him with an inviting smile.

He thought of Lori, waiting for him to pick her up and take her to dinner. He really couldn't stay. He didn't dare. He and Dawn had too much history between them.

The pause lengthened before he finally said, "I really can't tonight, Dawn. But thanks."

She pouted. "You have to go? Now? You just got off shift."

He nodded.

"Please stay, John." And with that, she started to blink and it looked like she might cry.

Oh, no. He hated it when women did that. What was he supposed to do? He felt totally unprepared for dealing with this. "Dawn, I'm sorry."

"I don't understand. Don't you like me anymore?" A couple of tears rolled down her cheeks and she brushed them away.

"Yes, I do," said John. He stopped. She knew he was dating Lori, but she didn't know how much he had come to care for her. Or the promise of exclusivity he'd made. He had to tell her. *Now, you idiot!*

Dawn took a deep breath and smiled, though it looked a little wobbly. "If you have to go, you have to go. We can get together another time. Maybe this weekend. But I have to tell you I'm very disappointed. I spent a lot of time preparing this meal for you. And you never said we weren't dating anymore."

"No, I didn't." Why couldn't he just tell her? He needed to really, truly, once and for all break it off with Dawn. He just didn't know if he could do it. It had been painful enough for them both the last time when he'd only said he wanted to date someone else.

"I would really appreciate it if you stayed for dinner, John."

She looked up into his eyes, and he could see the hurt there, hurt that he'd caused her.

He forced a smile. This was harder than he'd ever imagined. She waited without speaking, and the silence got to him. "I'd love to have dinner with you, Dawn."

She smiled, radiantly happy at his words. "I'm so glad."

So much for telling the truth, for finding Lori and taking her to dinner, for escaping. He'd just have to hope Lori would wait for him. And that she wouldn't ask too many questions when he showed up late, because he wouldn't be able to lie to her.

As Dawn motioned him to a seat and served him a grilled steak, baked potato, and salad, he struggled to come up with the right words to use to break things off. Tonight. Right now.

Finally, halfway through his steak, baked potato, and salad, he couldn't wait any longer. He had to say something. "This is delicious."

That wasn't going to help matters. He paused, hoping for inspiration that didn't arrive. The pause lengthened uncomfortably.

Quietly, she placed her fork on the table and folded her hands in her lap. "But . . . ?"

"I'm very sorry. I'm dating Lori now," he blurted out, glad he'd said the words at last. He let out a long breath. He stood up clumsily, nearly knocking over the chair. He had to get out of here.

"We talked about that last time, and I'm trying to adjust to that reality. You don't have to remind me over and over. It's hard enough to deal with." She stood and touched his sleeve.

Oh, no. He had to say it again, had to use different words, because she hadn't understood. Would this nightmare never end? He stayed standing and took a step away from the table. Away from her. "No. I mean I'm dating her . . . exclusively."

She blinked her eyes and bowed her head.

Oh, please, he thought, *don't let her cry.*

But she didn't cry. Instead, she seemed to pull herself together with great dignity. She walked toward her front door, opened it, and turned back to him.

"Perhaps you'll change your mind after she's returned to New York. When you do, I'll still be here."

He walked toward her, toward the open door, toward escape.

As he stepped within inches of her, Dawn lifted her chin and looked him straight in the eyes. "In the meantime, I'm not going anywhere. I love you, John."

Fifteen minutes later, John stood on Lori's front porch. The El Camino sat in the open, detached garage, so he figured she was home. He was so glad he'd finally told Dawn the truth, even if he hadn't been able to convince her he really meant it. He'd finally had to just say good-bye and leave her in the past.

And now he pushed the bell for what he hoped could be his future. His inability to commit had disappeared about the same moment as he'd met Lori.

Standing on the porch, he appreciated the light breeze. The day had been a scorcher, even for early August, but no more so than his talk with Dawn.

He wouldn't accept any more invitations from Dawn—to help or to do anything else—and Lori didn't need to know about this time, either. Though she might be upset because he was an hour late.

Lori opened the door. With her short blonde hair feathering around her pixie face, she looked gorgeous. She was more slender than Dawn and wore an elegant black outfit with slacks and sandals with high heels.

Relieved to be here with her, without any other entanglements, he grinned, Dawn's face already fading. "Hi, beautiful. Sorry I'm late. Ready for dinner?"

She didn't return his smile, but said, coolly, "I thought you weren't coming tonight."

"My shift ended tonight. I thought I told you."

She didn't open the door for him to step in. "You did."

Okay, so she liked punctuality. He'd have to remember that. "I thought we were going to dinner tonight."

"And I thought we were exclusively dating. And that we had dinner plans tonight."

"We are. We do. I tried to call you. Several times."

"I'm surprised you're up for more food after eating at Dawn Lawson's house."

With a sinking heart, he wondered how she'd found out so quickly. "Did you call my cell earlier?"

"I had a delightful chat with Dawn, who considers you very much her property, you know."

"I can explain. When I first met you, I told Dawn we needed to date other people."

"Ah, so you were a couple then."

"Since you and I started dating officially, I haven't dated Dawn or called her. Tonight I told her about my exclusive arrangement with you."

"On your date with her? Oh, don't worry about it. I won't either, now that I realize how these exclusive things work here in Utah. By the way, do you own a dictionary? You might want to look up the word *exclusive,* which comes after *dating* and before *polygamy.*" She shrugged. "But you don't owe me any kind of explanation. It's not like we're engaged."

He shut his eyes for the briefest moment. In her voice, he could hear the hurt and anger. He needed to help her understand she could trust him. He wasn't like her father. He wouldn't lie to her. "Lori, I do have to explain. I only went over there tonight because Dawn called me and said she needed her faucet fixed. I didn't know she'd planned dinner until after I arrived. And then I didn't know how to get out of it."

"How convenient that you have an excuse." Her words were glacial. No global warming problem in this house.

He was wishing for a few sparks right about now. The woman

he'd broken up with wanted him desperately. And the woman he wanted to date was more distant than ever.

He had to say something that would convince her he was telling the truth or this romance might be over before it had truly begun.

Chapter Sixteen

Hurt and not wanting to show it, Lori said, "I really think it would be best if you leave now."

Instead, he took her hand. His touch jolted her.

"Lori," he said, his voice a low rumble in his chest, "I didn't plan on staying for dinner with her. She asked me to fix her faucet and I didn't know how to get out of it. Then she started to cry, so I ate some of the dinner she'd fixed, but just out of sympathy. And I've told her about us now. She knows I won't be going to her house anymore, not even if she needs something fixed. I made that clear."

She didn't believe him. She wanted to, but she had been hurt too many times before by men lying to her. "It's okay. Really."

"It's not." He pulled her closer to him, and she allowed him to. "I care about you very much. I don't want to date anyone else. I only want to date you."

She must really be acting a fool because she found herself saying, "But how can I trust you?"

Gently, he pushed a lock of hair away from her eyes. "Because I will never lie to you. And only time will prove that to you."

She was silent, her emotions warring within her.

He was quiet, searching her eyes as she weakened.

"And I'm still hungry," he said with a small smile, "so I hope you'll let me take you to dinner."

Now she knew she was really a fool because, after a pause, she smiled up at him and said, "I'll get my purse."

"Hey, let's take your vehicle," he teased.

"The hideous vintage beast? Fuhgetaboutit."

“There is no way we can eat all this.” Amazed, Lori stared at the three gargantuan scoops of ice cream topped with pineapple, strawberry, and chocolate sauce, whipped cream, nuts, and a cherry. “It’s humongous.”

John laughed. “I thought you might be impressed.”

“Impressed? I have friends back home who could feast on this for a month, one bite a night.”

“Then aren’t you glad you’re in Utah, the ice cream capital of the world.” He lifted a spoon and took a bite. “This is great. You really ought to try some before I finish it off.”

“I’ll pay you a hundred bucks if you eat all that.”

His eyes sparkled. “I’ll take that bet.”

She laughed. “On second thought, forget it. I have a brother. He could do it.”

“Whew. For a moment, I thought you were actually going to let me do it.”

“Is everything on the menu this big?”

“I believe this is the largest sundae Peach City Ice Cream serves.”

“First you drive me to Logan to Firehouse Pizza where I proceed to put away far more slices than I ever should have eaten.” The pizza had been better than she’d expected, but she still missed New York’s real pizza. New York’s real subs and bagels, too. “And now, just hours later, you’re feeding me ice cream. Are you trying to fatten me up?”

The jukebox began playing an Elvis tune: “All Shook Up.”

“Well, you are pretty tiny, so you might blow away if there’s a good strong wind.”

She snorted in a most unfeminine manner. “As if.”

“What are you? A size zero?”

“Are you kidding? I’m a four.”

“See, my point exactly.” He took another bite.

With a spoon, she scooped out a bite of vanilla with strawberry sauce. “That *is* good.” She took another spoonful.

“I knew I could get you to eat it.”

She rolled her eyes.

"How's your gardening column going?"

"Let's just say it's a tremendous learning experience."

They ate in silence for a few minutes, until she put down her spoon. "I am totally stuffed. The rest is yours."

"If you insist." He grinned.

"So tell me more about yourself. Have you ever considered moving out of Utah? Is there anything else you'd like to do?"

"I love Utah. I love Brigham City. I love my job."

"Come on. No one is that easy to please."

He shrugged. "I learned a lot of patience on my mission. To be happy with what I had."

"Being around all those naked Swedish women did that?"

"Right." He grinned. "I also learned to avert my eyes quickly. Seriously, my mission shaped me into the man I am today."

"A Peeping Tom?"

"A great guy with fantastic peripheral vision, who is somewhat of an overachiever."

"I was thinking more along the lines of over*eater*," she teased, pointing toward the nearly empty sundae dish.

"I am truly hurt. How could you have missed what an incredibly sensitive and caring person I am?"

She snorted again. "Prove it."

"I will." He smiled, took another bite, and let it melt in his mouth. With a satisfied sigh, he asked, "So, is there something you want to do?"

"Yeah. Watch you finish that sundae and keep it down."

"No, I'm serious. Do you want a family? Do you want to write other types of things? Do you believe in a soul mate?"

"Soul mate?" She paused and chose her words carefully. "Well, I believe there is someone for everyone."

"Me, too." He smiled warmly at her.

She and John had the same desire to create a strong family, but she'd long ago given up that dream. That's why playboy Nicholas had seemed so perfect, because he didn't want children and so wouldn't care that she couldn't provide them.

Time to change the subject. "So you love your job because you're really an overgrown kid who gets to play with matches?"

"Actually, it's the arsonists who play with matches. Firefighters get to play with big red fire trucks."

She laughed. "Then you probably hate arsonists, right?"

"Absolutely."

"I guess now wouldn't be a good time to mention that I happen to be an arsonist."

"Not funny."

"You know, if this were a romance novel, the woman in your life would definitely need to be an arsonist to provide enough inherent conflict."

"And the man in your life would be . . . me."

"For the conflict, right?" She laughed. "You certainly don't have any problems with humility, do you?"

"Forget humble ol' me. Tell me more about your family."

"What's to tell? After the divorce, my mother never remarried. She raised us as a single mom."

"And did a marvelous job, I might add." He leaned forward and touched her necklace. "You always wear this. Why?"

She smiled as she lifted the heart-shaped locket hanging from the dainty gold chain. She opened it to reveal two pictures. "These are my grandparents. Grandpa Scott gave it to me after Grandma died." So far, Grandpa Scott had been the only trustworthy man in her life. If she could only meet a man like him, someone she could trust with her secrets, with knowing she couldn't have children, with knowing she couldn't stand being around her father, with seeing how flawed she was and loving her anyway, then she might consider getting married.

"It must mean a lot to you."

Lori nodded. "Grandma Scott used to tell me the story of how her family moved into Grandpa's town. Everyone warned her about him, how he'd broken half the hearts in town, but she liked him. A lot. And so when he tried to kiss her, she would tell me—with a twinkle in her eye—that, and I quote, 'I was easy kissed.' They were both wonderful people. I miss them."

"Why'd your parents get divorced?"

"Because my father is a pig," she blurted out, and then her eyes widened. She hadn't meant to let that slip.

"Go on," he said calmly. "Tell me about him."

"I'd rather not." She changed the subject, rambling on about her brother, Greg, her degree in literature, her friend Marti.

John smiled at her without saying a word.

She asked, "Why are you so calm all the time? I can't seem to manage it, but you're always mellow."

"Do you want the smart-aleck answer or the truth?"

"The truth."

"Okay, you asked for it. It's because I believe that as long as there is a Savior, there is hope."

Her heart caught on his words, so casually spoken and yet so sincere.

As long as there is a Savior, there is hope.

She so desperately needed hope. Her heart warmed and tears burned her eyelids. She blinked several times, but they spilled over. Great. She hated crying.

She couldn't believe she was reacting this way. Why was she so emotional lately? And why could a few words from John affect her so strongly?

John scooted his chair closer to her and handed her a napkin, waiting while she wiped her eyes, putting his arm around the back of her chair as if to protect her.

After a moment, she said, "Sorry, I don't know what came over me. I never cry."

"The Holy Ghost is telling you that what I just said is true. There is a Savior. And that's why I'm so calm, because nothing that happens in our lives is too much for Him to heal."

She wiped her eyes again and looked over at him.

He smiled gently. "Do you feel more calm now?"

"Yes," she admitted, her voice still a little shaky.

"I get that calm feeling often. When I'm in church, I know I'm worshipping my Savior. When I'm fighting fires, I know I'm serving Him. When I'm here with you, I know I'm spending time in a good, wholesome manner pleasing to Him."

Suddenly she felt drawn toward the Church and what John was getting out of it in his life.

Drawn toward her Savior, who she'd turned from years ago because He hadn't stopped her father from leaving.

Drawn toward the light she'd avoided since she was thirteen years old.

Everything had changed with her father's betrayal.

Now she'd met a man who made her feel peaceful again.

And she feared opening herself up to hope.

John touched her arm again. "Feel better?"

She smiled at him. "Yes."

"Good." He paused, not sure how to say what was in his mind. "I know you were very hurt by what your father did."

She nodded.

"I hope it hasn't turned you away from family and marriage and all the good things in life."

"You have parents who are happy together. We come from very different worlds."

He nodded. "You're right. Watching my parents and my brothers with their families makes me yearn for the same thing."

She didn't answer.

"I'm ready for marriage."

Her eyes widened. "Is this a proposal?"

"No. Just letting you know I'm ready."

"So I'm just one last fling before you settle down?"

"You're not a fling." Just the opposite. He wanted to pull Lori into his arms and not let go.

The strength of the impulse surprised him, but not the strength of his impression that she really, truly was the right one for him.

He didn't have much time left to convince her.

Despite his words, Lori suddenly felt exactly like John's last fling, and a twinge of jealousy hit her. Almost to convince herself, she said, "I don't want to get married."

"I do. I want a family like my brothers have. A wife and children."

"But how can you trust a person that much?"

He shrugged. "I just trust."

"You're open and trust people. I'm closed and mistrust."

"I know, but maybe we can look on those as some of my regrettable bad habits," he teased. "Everyone has some."

He'd finished the sundae, so they got up to leave. He paid the bill and dropped a five-dollar tip on the table.

Waiting at the door for him, she wasn't sure what to do with this new information. He wanted to get married.

She knew he liked her. And she knew that dating led to marriage. Hadn't she actually planned on marriage with Nicholas at one time, fool that she was? Though she realized now that she'd known all along that Nicholas wasn't the marrying kind.

Lori knew John would easily find someone nice after she left town. It would likely be Dawn, who was obviously in love with him. Another twinge of jealousy ate at her.

And Lori would be moving back to New York and putting her life back together, like Humpty Dumpty trying to piece together some sense of healthy relationships and career.

John opened the door for her. After he'd climbed into his seat, he said, "I'll pick you up tomorrow."

She smiled but didn't say anything.

He raised an eyebrow. "Don't you enjoy your time with me?"

"Yes," she admitted. She enjoyed his company very much.

She did enjoy his company, and he had turned out to be a good friend at a crisis point when she had desperately needed a good friend. And she supposed that, as long as he was willing to date on those terms—just while she was here in town—then she was still willing to do so, too.

But perhaps it would be wise to begin spending more time with some female friends, like Serena and Agatha, and to meet more people. That way, she could enjoy the time she had left with John, without having all her emotional eggs in his basket. She couldn't afford to let her heart get involved. And she couldn't afford to lead him on so that his heart got involved, either.

They'd continue to be friends. Good friends. Exclusive good

friends. And then she'd return to New York and to her own life and pick up the pieces somehow.

Maybe being here, with John, would help her understand how a guy ought to treat her, something she'd never realized before. But now she knew she wanted a man who was gallant and kind and gentle and strong, all at the same time. Someone like John.

She'd never have guessed it when she first moved here, but she suspected she was going to miss John and even the slower-paced life here. Maybe even going to church, because she wasn't sure that once she got back to New York, she'd continue. She was afraid maybe she wouldn't.

Still disturbed by her date with John, by the emotions he'd raised in her, Lori punched in Marti's speed dial number as she bounced onto the bed.

"What's up?"

Just the sound of Marti's cheerful voice calmed Lori. She knew she was safe asking her friend anything. Thank goodness. Because she couldn't figure this one out on her own. She sank down onto the pillows. "Listen. I need to ask you something. Something important. And please don't laugh at me."

"I would never laugh at something important."

"Okay. It's about . . . John."

"I'm not surprised. Go on."

Lori sighed. "I feel like John fell for me so quickly that it feels totally impossible. So . . . is quick love possible? Or is it just silly, something that happens only in fairytales and romance novels?"

Marti's voice softened. "My grandfather has often told me the story of when he fell in love with my grandmother in the first grade. The first time he ever saw her, he knew she was going to be his wife. They've been married for more than sixty years. I knew within a month of meeting Bryce, even though we waited nearly a year for the actual wedding." Marti was quiet for a moment. "Are you . . . in love . . . with John?"

"No. I mean, I don't think so. We're just friends. But I really enjoy his company. And I feel peaceful around him. But I'll be leaving

Brigham City and never see him again, so there's really no future for us."

"Just because your parents only knew each other for three months before they got engaged doesn't mean that John will do what your father did. Don't run from love."

Her friend's words stung—probably because they were true. Lori sat up on the edge of the bed. "His attention is flattering, but he'll get over me in no time."

"Take a deep breath. Right now. I mean it."

Lori did as instructed.

"Now take another one."

"Okay."

"Okay. Is John in love with you, Lori?"

"I don't know. Maybe."

"Lori, listen to me. Please give this a chance. If you're there for three months and think there's a future with this guy, stay as long as you need to make sure. A good man is worth it."

Lori shook her head, as if Marti could see the gesture. "I think Dawn's the woman for him. He just hasn't realized it yet."

"Don't talk yourself out of it, okay? Promise me you'll give romance a chance with him. Please, Lori. Don't pull another Nicholas on me."

"Are you kidding? John is nothing like Nicholas."

"Yeah, but there's more than one way to not end up with the right man. One is to date the wrong guy. The other is to date the right guy, but find reasons why it won't work."

"Marti, I'm afraid. He makes me feel things I haven't dared feel for a long time. And I'm not just talking about romance. I'm talking about spiritual things."

Was she kidding herself? Was John in love with her or just intrigued by a challenge? Was Dawn the one for him? Was she pulling a Nicholas again, only a different variation? She was still so confused about everything. And what about the spiritual side of her that John had reawakened? Did she even want to trust God again? Did she dare to trust anyone?

"I think it's great. I already like the guy," said Marti. "So promise me you'll give him a chance."

"I can't make that promise." Because then she'd have to keep it, and she was too afraid of how fast things were moving. She thought it would be wise to spend less time with John. "In the meantime, though, I'm going to spend more time with some other friends."

"That's exciting news," Marti teased. "So you're coming here to visit me?"

Lori laughed. "With other Utah friends, silly."

"Darn it."

"If you want to stay current on your pseudo-swear words, here in Brigham City it's 'flip,' said in two syllables."

"Well, fliiii-iiiip."

"Better. You're nearly ready to come visit me."

"I just might. I'd like to meet John Wayne Walker."

Chapter Seventeen

Lori set down Charles's scriptures and drew in a contented breath. In her time here in Brigham City, especially during the week and a half since speaking with Marti, she'd fallen into a gentle routine.

She supposed she was doing what Marti had suggested long ago—Lori was slowing down. And, surprisingly, she found herself enjoying the relaxed pace.

She was going to bed by ten o'clock, when her New York friends were just hitting the clubs, which she'd never felt comfortable in anyway, and she awoke feeling almost decadently rested around eight. She'd leisurely get up, shower, and eat a good breakfast of granola and fruit. After that, she'd research and work on her column for four hours, fix lunch, and read the Book of Mormon for awhile.

She couldn't explain it, but she found herself calmed by the time spent in that book. She was in Alma now.

Standing and stretching, she wandered outside into the garden. It was peaceful among the plants, too, and she'd never have guessed how much she'd come to enjoy the time spent here. Usually she came out in the cool of the morning or late afternoon, but today it was overcast and cooler than usual, probably only eighty degrees.

As she walked around the garden, plucking out little weeds here and there, she could see that the zucchini was going crazy. There had to be hundreds of them on the spreading vines.

Shaking her head, she raised her arms toward the plants and said, dramatically, "Zucchini, I command you to stop growing!"

Someone chuckled and she spun to her right, feeling foolish. Agatha smiled at her over the dividing fence. "Oh, child, there's nothing on earth a soul can do to stop zucchini from growing. Why don't you just let the garden go? Stop watering and weeding it. Let it wither away."

"I can't, Agatha. I promised Charles I'd take care of it."

"Well, you promised to take care of his cat, too, but Fluffy is over here at my house again." Agatha laughed. "So just let the garden go. It'll give Charlie something to do when he returns."

Worried she'd abused the older woman's generosity, Lori asked, "Do you want me to take the cat?"

"Oh, lands, no. I want you to take it easy on yourself."

"I only wish I knew how."

"Important to learn. Well, gotta run. I've got a genealogy class tonight."

Amused, Lori watched the older woman go inside. As she turned back to the incredibly prolific garden, shaking her head at the harvest awaiting her, her cell phone rang.

It was her mother. "Hey, honey, are you all right?"

"Sure. Why do you ask?"

"Oh, I've just had a feeling to call you for the last day or two, and I've been so busy I haven't gotten around to it. What's going on? Why am I getting this feeling?"

Her Relief Society mother had always been far too intuitive where her children were concerned. So why not tell her mother? "Hey, Mom, would you like a good laugh?"

"Sure."

Leaning over, she plucked off a perfect-looking yellow squash, brushed off the dirt, and set it on the grass. "I've gone to church every Sunday since I got here."

"Which one?" Her mother sounded suspicious.

Lori laughed. "The LDS church, Mom."

"Oh, honey, that's great." Her mother's voice softened. "See, I told you it was fate."

"Thanks for the I-told-you-so." Lori smiled and went a step further. "John's been taking me."

"John?" Her mother's voice perked up another notch.

"He's just a guy I'm dating, but it's no big deal."

"Is he cute?"

Lori thought about his handsome face, broad shoulders and

strong arms, tapered hips and long legs. And his smile. "Oh, yeah, he's definitely cute."

"And . . . he's Mormon?"

Lori rolled her eyes. "Yes, Mom. He's a nice, Mormon guy. Nothing at all like Dad."

Her mother paused. "Speaking of which, your father called me this week and asked for your phone number."

It took only a few seconds for Lori's good mood to dissipate and the conflicted feeling to reenter her heart. She hated her father for that—that he could still ruin her peace of mind and heart with just a mention of him. "I hope you didn't give it to him."

Her mother sounded sad. "I didn't, not without asking you. But Lori, honey, you need to forgive him."

"It's not going to happen, Mom. Ever." Her own words made her heart heavy with bitterness and anger and hurt. "Can we please talk about something else?"

Two days later, seated in the chapel between John and Serena, Lori's mind wandered to the pleasant memory of John kissing her good night after last night's movie.

She could get used to those kisses.

In fact, she hoped she got another one today.

She knew she'd decided to hang out more with other friends, and she had made some plans, but she was enjoying her time with John more and more, even though she knew he was just a holiday romance. But that couldn't keep her from enjoying him while she was here. He was good-looking, nice to kiss, and fun to be with.

She settled back comfortably into her memory, hearing only bits and pieces of the bishop's announcements. Her mind returned to a few days before, when John had brought her a bouquet of roses and daisies just because. She smiled.

" . . . Lori Scott . . ."

What? The sound of her name brought her out of her reverie with a start.

"Sister Scott?" the bishop said from the pulpit. "Would you please stand so everyone can see you?"

Lori repressed a groan and did as instructed.

"Would everyone who can welcome the newest member of our ward please do so by the uplifted hand."

Everyone raised their hand—well, except for Dawn Lawson, who was seated two rows ahead of them. Lori was sorry the pretty redheaded woman so thoroughly disliked her.

Lori sank back down between her friends, thankful to no longer be the focus of the entire ward's attention.

John leaned over and whispered, "Who transferred your records so quickly?"

There was only one person who would have done this. The same person who'd done the same thing no matter where Lori moved, even though she'd sworn never to go back to church. "My incorrigible mother," she whispered back.

John chuckled. "Incorrigible, eh? So you and she have a lot in common, I take it."

She narrowed her eyes, but he continued to chuckle softly. She knew who she thought was incorrigible at the moment.

Unable to lose herself back in memories, Lori sat tensely through the bishop's testimony and through the next thirty minutes of other people bearing their testimonies.

Finally, John reached over, took her hand, and rubbed his thumb across her palm, sending sensations shooting up her arm. Though she was acutely aware of his touch, at the same time she began to relax back into the bench.

Toward the end of the meeting, a little boy skipped to the front, the first child she'd seen today—not surprising in a singles ward. Barely able to see over the pulpit, the boy pulled down the microphone and spoke directly into it. "I love my family. I'm glad we got to come visit Uncle Steve. I love my brothers and sisters. Well, most of 'em. My brother Zach hits my arm too much, but I still love him. I know the Church is true. And I'm sorry my family sometimes uses the naughty four-letter word."

Silence exploded across the chapel as the boy skipped back to his seat, unaware of the silent commotion he'd caused. Everyone turned to see the people the little boy was sitting with. After a long moment, the man sitting next to the little boy stood.

"That must be the little boy's foul-mouthed father," whispered Serena with a giggle.

The relatively young man—probably in his late twenties—worked his way to the podium, his face bright red. He cleared his throat. "Um, before I bear my testimony, I think I'd better clarify something. In our family, the naughty four-letter word stands for . . ." Looking pained, he closed his eyes and spelled out, "F-A-R-T."

A rumble of laughter from the congregation was quickly muffled. After the noise stopped, he proceeded to bear a very nice testimony.

Serena whispered to Lori as they both struggled to stop laughing. "Are we still on for lunch Wednesday?"

Dawn turned to toss a quick glare at Lori, who could feel the other woman's animosity from two rows away. Hoping to soften the situation, Lori smiled at Dawn, but Dawn frowned and turned away.

Lori glanced at John. Leaning forward with his elbows on his knees and his face down, he apparently hadn't noticed the exchange, for which Lori was glad.

Lori touched his hand, and he immediately interlaced his fingers with hers. The warmth and touch reassured her. As long as she stayed close to John, she felt at peace.

Dawn might win John back later, after Lori left town, but for now Lori was thankful she had him.

After church, a man approached Lori. "Sister Scott? I'm Brother Jacobs. The bishop would like to speak to you."

Whatever for? she wondered. Most bishops hadn't called her in. But, she reminded herself, she hadn't gone to church for years so they hadn't had the chance.

She followed Brother Jacobs down the hall, making small talk, and stepped into the office.

The bishop rose, smiled warmly, and put out his hand as Brother Jacobs closed the door, leaving the two of them alone.

Lori shook the bishop's hand—he had a nice, strong

handshake—and sat in the indicated seat next to the desk. He settled himself in his seat, swiveling so he faced Lori.

Only a few inches taller than Lori, Bishop Robertson looked like a Marine sergeant, complete with short gray fuzz on his head, but with a belly that had expanded from a six-pack to a barrel. His smile was warm and friendly, and he reminded her of Greg's likeable and encouraging Scoutmaster back in New York. That resemblance relaxed her somewhat.

"Sister Scott, I want you to know I've enjoyed your articles. You have a great deal of creativity."

"Thank you." She certainly hadn't expected that, and the praise washed over her, bringing a warm feeling. He seemed sincere. "I'm surprised you've read them."

"I'm not the only one. You've certainly enlivened the gardening discussions in my neighborhood." He smiled. "And I'd like to see that happen around here. I want you to share your many talents with the other ladies, so I'm extending a calling to you to serve on our Enrichment committee."

What? "Wait. I can't have a calling. I'm not even active."

He steepled his fingers and smiled. "Yet you come to sacrament meeting every week."

Nervous, she twirled the necklace Grandpa Scott had given her. "I don't know . . ."

"You are an expert on gardening and that's what we want right now. What we need."

She was so *not* an expert on gardening and that made her nervous; she'd doubtless start babbling any time now. She was totally unsuitable for this calling and she needed to help him see that. "I'll be returning home in nine weeks."

"Sister Scott, I still feel impressed that you are the woman for the calling, no matter how long you are available."

Feeling trapped by his calm words, Lori wasn't sure what to do. Normally she would retreat behind her barriers and turn down anything church-related. But, unfortunately, since she'd met John and come to church and felt the Spirit again, her barriers had weakened and she couldn't seem to do that anymore. Thoughts ricocheted throughout her skull.

If the bishop would only speak again, maybe she could find some reason to be offended, to say no, but he just smiled warmly and waited for her response.

With a sigh, she reminded herself that these women probably had some good zucchini recipes. She could even set up a zucchini recipe exchange. Or recipes for other vegetables. How hard could this calling be, anyway? And she'd only have to do it for two months and then she could leave.

That's all the time she had left with John, too. That wasn't much time. She stared at the bishop. Why didn't the word "no" just fall from her mouth? Was it because she could already see the disappointment on John's face when he learned she'd turned down a calling? That shouldn't make any difference, but somehow it did. And she couldn't hide from herself the fact that it was his potential disappointment that caused her to say, "I'll do it. But I can't promise how well."

"You'll do a wonderful job, Sister Scott. I have no doubt."

Lori wasn't nearly so sure as butterflies began fluttering against her insides, tickling and agitating her fears.

"The first big activity is at the end of the month. Sister Serena Martinez is on the committee and can bring you up to speed."

She wondered if Serena had volunteered her.

Bishop Robertson stood and put out his hand again.

Somewhat shell-shocked, Lori stood, shook his hand again, and allowed herself to be ushered out the door.

She, Lori Scott, had a calling in the ward? Where were the lightning strikes? Surely God wouldn't allow her to do this without objecting?

Needing a moment to regain her composure, she slipped into a side coat closet. Though more and more people walked the halls, chattering, the alcove remained empty, quiet, and dark.

And, as if hiding in the shadows contemplating a new intimidating calling wasn't enough of a concern, she glimpsed John walking past—with Dawn holding his arm.

Startled, Lori's first impulse was hurt. But she saw right away that John looked uncomfortable and was trying to pull his arm away without being rude. So this was Dawn's doing; Lori couldn't fault the other woman for following her own heart.

In an effort to reassure herself, Lori reminded herself that Dawn would doubtless have John all to herself soon. But, instead the thought saddened her—and, at the same time, birthed a determination to claim her man for as long as she was still here.

Lori stepped out into the hallway behind them. Neither showed any sign of having seen her.

Just feet away, Lori watched Dawn look up at John. "I need some help. Our shower isn't working, and you were so quick fixing the faucet I thought it might just take you a few minutes—"

John looked even more uncomfortable as he said, softly but firmly, "Dawn, I can't."

Joy sang in Lori's heart. He was being true to her. With a smile and a few quick steps, Lori caught up to the couple and smiled. "Good afternoon, Dawn, John."

Dawn stiffened, her smile cooling. "Good afternoon." She turned to John. "Remember. I'll still be here."

As Dawn walked off, John looked stricken, as if Lori had caught him with his hand in the cookie jar. Again. "Lori, really, this isn't what it looks like."

"Really?" She took the arm Dawn had just abandoned and smiled up at him. "Because it looks to me like you just stayed exclusively mine."

Surprise and immense relief crossed John's face. "Yeah. Well, that's right." He smiled as though very pleased with himself for having passed a test. Which he had, in Lori's opinion.

She might only be here for a short time, but while she was here, she expected him to keep his promise. But she had to admit that she was surprised she trusted him.

Calm and peaceful, Lori walked outside, still holding John's arm. As he opened the truck door for her, he leaned in for a kiss.

And she, like Grandma Scott, was easy kissed.

THE GARDEN GURU

Dear Ms. Scott: I'm tired of cooking the same old thing. Do you have any suggestions for uniquely flavored vegetables? (Rebecca)

Dear Rebecca: Spice up your cooking with jalapeño peppers. Good for chili, salsa, and clearing out your nasal passages. Whether harvesting for immediate use or to freeze for later, be sure to use rubber gloves or clean the hot peppers under running water; this is one vegetable juice that bites back. Jalapeños are hot, but their Scoville units aren't so high that you'll have a serious reaction. You can find a wide range of heat levels, even on the same plant, and more so on different plants—anything from mild to Biker Billy's hot. This plant takes the heat from the sun and transforms it into heat that will salsa dance on your taste buds. Rather than calling 911 if you have a three-alarm fire, skip the water and go straight to the dairy products (milk, ice cream, yogurt) which can break down the capsaicin oils. Enjoy!

Chapter Eighteen

"Now that's more like it," Serena motioned with her fork toward the Hispanic guy who'd just walked into El Parral Mexican Restaurant. "Mmmm. I do love salsa."

Lori chuckled. "He is pretty good-looking."

And he was: maybe five-ten, olive skin, dark eyes and moustache, gorgeous smile. "Want me to invite him over?"

Still staring at the salsa guy, Serena shook her head. "Don't worry, Sister Scott. You leave this guy up to me."

And, just a moment later, when he looked their way, Lori got to watch Serena in action. Serena smiled and lowered her eyelashes. The guy smiled in a way that let Lori know he'd gotten the message—and liked it.

"Wow," Lori said, impressed. "You are good."

At one o'clock, the restaurant was crowded, the air filled with the sounds of cutlery and laughter and the smells of Mexican food at its best.

The hostess seated the guy a few tables away from them. His moving away didn't seem to bother Serena, who laughed. "What can I say? Hispanic guys love demure women. They also love blondes, so if you'd batted your eyelashes, he'd have looked at you, instead."

That brought to mind the image of John's blue eyes looking at her—and she pushed the thought away. She was thinking about him entirely too much lately, and she had to stop doing that or else she'd never be able to say good-bye to him. She refused to cling to him like—well, like Dawn did. And even as she admitted to herself that her feelings and decisions were bouncing all over the place, she said, "I prefer meat and potatoes."

Serena laughed. "Can't get much more meat-and-potatoes than John Wayne Walker. That boy is pure steak."

"That's true." Lori smiled. "So, how was your weekend?"

"It was great. My father drove up and took me to the temple on Saturday."

"So you have a good relationship with him?"

"Oh, sure. He calls me his *niña bonita.*" She shrugged. "What's not to get along?"

Lori smiled. She liked Serena. The first thing she'd asked Serena when they got to the restaurant was if she'd volunteered Lori for the new calling, but she'd said no, that it had been pure inspiration.

Serena lifted her gaze. "So how do you and your father get along?"

"Oh, well, it's not quite as pretty of a picture as you and your father at the temple."

Serena tilted her head. "Want to talk about it?"

"I'm not sure where to start."

"The beginning, of course." Serena smiled gently. "Go on."

"Okay, you asked for it." Lori sighed deeply. "I didn't go to church for a long time before I moved here."

She paused, waiting for some sign of displeasure. Disappointment. Dis-something else negative. But there was nothing but concern in Serena's eyes.

"Okay. And?"

"And there are some things I still don't understand about what happened to my family."

Serena gave Lori her full attention. "Like?"

"Well . . . what if someone does something really horrible?"

"How horrible are we talking?" Serena lowered her voice.

"Oh, say, like having an affair and leaving his wife for another woman."

"Ouch." Serena raised an eyebrow. "That is horrible."

"And what if this person—let's call him Mud—what if Mud left his wife and two kids and married the other woman. What kind of punishment should there be in the Church for that?"

"Well, I'm not sure. I mean, you'd have to talk with the bishop, but I think he'd be disfellowshipped, at least."

"And then what if this same person is later allowed to be sealed to this other woman in the temple?"

Serena pondered the question. "Well, I suppose you can be forgiven for almost anything."

"But isn't that kind of hypocritical? To pretend to honor family and the priesthood when you've done something like that?" Lori couldn't keep the bitterness from her voice. "And what if they have more children, as if the first children don't matter?"

"Oh, I'm so sorry." Gently, she touched Lori's arm.

Lori blinked back tears. She was not going to cry. Not over her father.

"I haven't done anything like you're describing, but before I was converted I lived a more worldly lifestyle. I've done lots of things I'm ashamed of and I'd never want people to know about."

"You?" Lori blurted out. "Really?"

"Of course. We all sin. Some people sin and hurt themselves. Others sin and hurt other people. And"—Serena paused and softened her voice even more before continuing—"and some people sin by letting the hurt caused by others bring them to a place of unforgiveness."

"It's not my fault my father left." Lori's hurt resounded in her voice, a young child stung by rejection, something she always took care to hide, often even from herself.

Serena's voice was gentle. "But perhaps it is your choice that you're still unhappy over it. Christ's Atonement is for everyone. It's to heal us from the sins we commit, and also from the very real hurt other people cause us."

"But how does knowing that in the abstract help me here and now? I believe in Christ and in His Atonement—but how can I make it work in my life? I don't know how." Her voice shook with unexpected emotion. "I need to know how to do that."

Serena took Lori's hand in hers. "All I know is when I repented of my sins and released them to Christ, He took them, and I felt an incredible peace enter my heart and my life. Perhaps if you repent of your unforgiveness and release it, Christ will also send His healing power of love to you."

Lori wanted to believe that, but it seemed far too simple to work.

And she wasn't sure if she was ready for it, anyway. She drew in a deep breath and blew it out slowly. "Thanks."

Serena patted her hand. "I will pray for your healing, that you can release your hurt to Christ."

"Thanks," Lori repeated, genuinely grateful. "And now I suppose we should talk about something else. Anything."

"Perhaps about good men. Salsa men. Meat-and-potatoes men."

Lori lifted her glass of root beer. "To good men." Which, of course, made her think of John again.

"To good men," Serena repeated, clinking her glass with Lori's.

As if on cue, the salsa guy appeared. Smiling at them both, he bowed slightly. He looked straight at Serena of the batting eyelashes. "Do you beautiful *señoritas* mind if I join you?"

Lori was still chuckling about Serena finagling a date with the salsa guy, whom she'd made sure was LDS before he'd finished his burrito. He would be picking her up next weekend for—what else?—salsa dancing.

Sitting in a lawn chair on the patio, the ceiling fan circling lazily above, Lori sipped a glass of lemonade and tried to relax.

A streak of something raced across the back lawn, startling her. It turned out to be Charles's cat racing toward the fence and jumping over it into Agatha's yard.

Charles's cat. Charles's garden. Charles's column.

She couldn't seem to stop worrying about what she'd be writing in the column this next week. She'd spent hours preparing the many recipes she'd gathered, and she was growing weary of zucchini. She hadn't liked it to begin with.

She took another sip of lemonade, relaxing further.

Utah did have its advantages. The air here was warm—the thermometer on the outside wall beside her read ninety-three degrees—but the breeze from the fan kept her comfortable in her black shorts and T-shirt. Without the horrendously high humidity she'd grown up with, the temperature here didn't seem nearly as hot as in New York at the same number.

That old saying was true: It's not the heat, it's the humidity.

She'd like to see some of these Utahans survive a New York summer. Or winter.

"Hey," called out Agatha.

Lori looked over to the adjoining fence. Agatha held Charles's white cat aloft. "Lose something?" she teased.

Lori laughed and pushed out of the chair, crossing to the fence to chat. "No, I think both she and I are happiest when she's with you. Are you sure Charles didn't kidnap her from you?"

"Well, Fluffy is one of the kittens from the last litter my old cat—Sally—had. She started coming over to visit her mother, and never got out of the habit. It drives Charlie absolutely bonkers." Agatha laughed at the thought. She definitely had a mischievous streak in her, which Lori liked.

Agatha set the cat on the ground in her own yard. It sauntered under a tree to lick a front paw.

"I hear you have a new calling in the singles ward," Agatha turned back to her. "How's that going?"

"You heard about that, huh?"

"I passed John Walker in the store and he mentioned it." Agatha patted Lori's hand, which was resting on the top of the fence. "I think you'll do just great."

"Remind me how you know John."

"His parents and I all graduated from high school back in the sixties, way before you were born. I see them once a year at his mother's night-before-Thanksgiving pie party." Agatha waved her hand. "But enough about my old age. Tell me about your calling."

"I have an activity in a couple of weeks and the theme is—of course—zucchini and other vegetables. And I'm really nervous about pulling it off."

"Why, sweetie, don't worry about a thing. You'll be great."

Not convinced, Lori said, "I really need a killer zucchini recipe to fix and serve."

"Is that what you're worried about?" Agatha shrugged. "You've got a great one already."

Lori raised an eyebrow in question. "Remind me where I've hidden it."

"You really are worried, aren't you?" Agatha chuckled. "Charlie has a wonderful recipe for zucchini chicken curry. It's to die for. It's probably on his computer."

"Do you think he'll mind if I use it?"

"Oh, land sakes, no." Agatha waved a gardening glove in dismissal. "He's been promising forever to put that online during zucchini month. He must have forgotten to leave a note for you about it, in the flurry of other notes he left."

Lori laughed. "You know about the notes?"

Agatha laughed warmly. "Sweetie, I've lived next door to the man for decades. I couldn't help but notice the notes, which he leaves for everything. Always has. Once he even left a note on my front door telling me I was over-watering my petunias. He was wrong, of course, but that didn't stop him from leaving the note."

Lori laughed with Agatha. "Are you sure he won't mind?"

"He told me I was free to find that recipe and use it. I just haven't gotten around to it yet. Now, would he have told me that if he didn't want to share it?"

Lori smiled. She really could use a popular recipe. Could it be this simple? Right under her nose the entire time? "Well—"

"Didn't you say he told you to use whatever you found in his files for the column?"

Agatha was right. Charles had told Lori that in one of his notes. "Okay. I'll look for it."

Agatha nodded. "You'll be doing Charlie and me both a favor. In addition to the activity, you could use it in your column."

Lori wasn't aware of how concerned she'd been until the relief filtered in. She *would* use it. She'd help Charles keep his promise—she'd even make sure to mention it in his column. "Thanks for the tip. You've saved me once again."

Agatha waved her glove a second time. "Be sure to bring the printed recipe—and have everyone else bring their recipes, too. Everyone always asks for them, anyway."

"Thanks, Agatha. I'll do that," Lori said, grateful for the older woman's experience in matters of Enrichment Night.

"I'm fixing a nice dinner tonight if you'd like to join me. There will be no zucchini anywhere."

Lori laughed. "Then I'll be there."

Chopping zucchini a couple of days later for another recipe tryout, Lori glanced at the clock. Five after four, Monday afternoon. Only fifteen minutes later than the last time she'd checked. John would be calling around six. She missed him more than she thought was wise when he was on shift.

Oh, who was she kidding? She thought about him more than was wise whether he was on shift or off.

Pulling her attention back to the recipe, she added the other ingredients listed and placed the concoction on the stove. It wasn't Charles's recipe; she hadn't found that yet, either on the computer or in his files.

When Lori's cell phone rang, she wiped her hands on the thick dish towel and answered.

"Hi, Lori. This is Rusty Neal."

Who? Wait, he was her boss. Charles's boss. Heat rose in her face. "Oh. Hi."

"We've received the first wave of responses from readers of Charles's column. They are, to say the least, interesting."

She wasn't sure that was a good thing. She hoped they were interesting in a positive way.

"Your column is certainly unorthodox, different from the way Charles does it."

Uh-oh. Was he going to let her go? If she couldn't do it like Charles, would he find someone else? Had he already found someone else?

It was hard enough having her play shut down after a week; being kicked off this gardening column would be really demoralizing. Like rubbing lemon juice into a raw wound.

Slowly, she said, "I understand if your readers want it done the old way."

Rusty chuckled. "Actually, overall, our readers seem to like your flippant style."

Flippant, huh? Well, that was probably accurate. She still wasn't sure whether to be relieved or not. Where was he headed with this conversation? "How many of the readers liked it?"

"We've gotten a few complaints from some old-timers who want

Charles back, but we've got lots more new people reading and loving it. Whatever you're doing, keep it up."

Pleased and immensely relieved, she smiled for the first time since she'd answered the phone. "I'm glad to hear that."

"I've forwarded some of the e-mails to you so you can read them for yourself." He paused. "Charles will be returning in a couple of months."

"Yes," she said cautiously, wondering where he was headed now. If he was going to can her, she hoped he would just get on with it, because this conversation was beginning to wear on her nerves.

"Would you be interested in writing another column after he returns?"

"I'll be moving back to New York." A twinge of sadness hit her at the thought. She was really going to miss this place. The column. Agatha and her menagerie of cats. Serena. Fry sauce. Thick towels. *John.*

"Oh. Well, would you be interested in starting another column now? The paper really needs someone on the art beat and with your Broadway experience and your witty style, I believe you could write some fantastic reviews on movies and plays."

The idea intrigued her. "Plays *and* movies? Or one or the other?"

"Both until you find your niche and we learn what the readers like. Be sure to save your receipts, and we'll reimburse you for the tickets. Why don't you send me a sample review; if it's what we want, I'll get a contract worked up."

The desire to write that had compelled her since she was a teenager—and that she'd pushed down deep inside after her play flopped—rippled through her. Gently, like a whiff of smoke, it swirled, reawakening her to her old dream. She had to work to keep the sudden emotion from her voice. "All right, I'll do it."

After she hung up, she walked slowly into the bedroom, reached under the bed, and pulled out the screenplay box her mother had packed.

She sat for long minutes just staring, but found she still couldn't bring herself to open it. She was afraid of lifting the lid on that Pandora's box of unpleasant memories. Pushing it back under the bed, she rose, but her agitation continued. Writing used to make her happy. Maybe she'd rediscover that someday, but it wouldn't be today.

Through the bedroom window, she saw it had started to rain. It didn't matter if she chose to water the zucchini or not, because God was handling it. She was glad for the coolness that came with the rain.

With another sigh, she went back outside and watched the rain fall, sitting safe in her favorite chair under the patio cover. The rain made a pleasant sound on the roof.

She was intrigued by Rusty's request. If she did do the reviews, where should she start? What was the name of that theater John had wanted to take her to? Heritage Theater? Yes, she thought that was it.

So when he called at six o'clock on the dot, she was ready. "Yes, I will go with you to the Heritage Theater."

He laughed, and the rich, low rumble pleased her. "Are you always this bossy?"

"Hey, you offered."

"Yup, I most certainly did—quite a while ago." He chuckled again, as if greatly amused. "Friday is the Bees home game against Bear River, but how about this Saturday?"

"Great. It's a deal."

"No," he said, his voice husky. "It's a date."

Chapter Nineteen

Sitting in the crowded, darkened theater with her chair mere inches from John's, Lori was acutely aware of the heat radiating from his very warm body. It was all she could do to resist leaning her head on his shoulder and relaxing into him.

Snap out of it, girl! She had to remember she was just having fun. No more than that. Definitely no cuddling.

While the actors joked onstage and the audience laughed, Lori made brief notes to write her review from later. But she found she had to keep dragging her attention away from the man she wasn't getting involved with, back to the stage, back to the notepad, back to the potential review.

The theater was in a charming, ancient red-brick building that had been added onto over the years. John had managed to get them seats up close to the stage.

The pianist played an unbelievably fast, intricate, jazz-type song while the cast of *Joseph and the Amazing Technicolor Dreamcoat* sang lustily.

"Having fun?" John asked.

She looked into his blue eyes, dark with an emotion she couldn't identify but that took her breath away. She smiled and nodded, afraid her voice would betray too much of her own emotion.

With an answering smile, he took her left hand. "Sorry, I can't wait for you to stop taking notes."

A shiver worked its way up her neck and she relished the contact with him. He began to rub her palm with his thumb.

The audience laughed again, only this time she missed the punch line. Apparently so had John. Neither of them seemed to care, especially not when he began to rub the tops of her fingers with his other hand. How on earth was she supposed to pay attention to the play with this sort of distraction?

She struggled with the answer to that question throughout the rest of the play. All too soon, the curtain closed, and she and John clapped while the curtain reopened and the actors took their final bows. It brought back bittersweet memories for her of her own play's opening night. Except there had been no curtain calls that night.

She stood and turned—and found herself just inches from John. His breath caused her arms to tingle and she raised her face toward his, looking once again into his blue eyes. She found a longing there that echoed her own.

She was in over her head here. She wanted John in her life, but she couldn't have him. All she could do was remind herself—again—that this was only a short-term, holiday romance. Nothing more.

John leaned down and gently kissed her, and she allowed herself to get swept up in the wanting. And she realized that, if she only had a short time left with John, she was going to enjoy every moment of it. Starting with this fantastic kiss. Even if it didn't seem wise. Even if she got involved. Even if she got hurt.

When he finally pulled back, she was breathless.

During the drive to her house, Lori couldn't seem to stop smiling and softly humming a very silly song from the musical. She was still humming it when John walked her to her front door, and later, after he'd kissed her again, leaving her breathless and her legs weak, and later still as she watched him climb back into his pickup.

It took her a long time to unwind. She hugged herself and danced around the kitchen, remembering the kisses. She rubbed lotion onto her thirsty skin and climbed into her red-and-black Betty Boop jammies.

And, finally, she pulled out her laptop and whipped out what she thought was a humorous and flippant enough play review. She'd give it one last read in the morning before e-mailing it to Rusty, but she thought he'd like it.

She'd had a great evening. John's kisses were fantastic. And watching the play and writing the review had gotten her excited about writing again. In fact, an idea had begun to play in her mind, at least a basic situation.

It could be a fish-out-of-water story.

Kind of like her own experience here in Brigham City.

Maybe it could even be a love story.

But, if it were a love story, it would have to end more happily than her own story would. Her heroine would get to stay, because audiences liked happy endings. While she, the author, had to return home, because real people often got unhappy endings.

She was already jealous of her heroine.

"Ugh. This does not look edible, *amiga.*" Serena brushed another coat of dark purple paint onto a large zucchini squash.

"It's edible paint, though. At least that's what the lady said." Suddenly worried she'd made a mistake, Lori asked, "Is this a bad idea? I mean, maybe these women are going to think painted and stuffed squash are stupid."

Serena laughed. "It's a cool idea. I've never seen a purple zucchini before so it looks weird. Weird, but cool."

Agatha brushed a stroke of bright sunshine paint onto a pale spaghetti squash, turning it from pale to brilliant yellow. "What are you going to stuff them with?"

"I'm only baking the zucchinis; the others are just for decoration. I found a recipe online." Lori leaned back in her kitchen chair to inspect the blue polka dots she'd daubed onto the base layer of bright leaf green. "We'll stuff them with hamburger, roasted red peppers, garlic, and some cheese. I tried it the other night and it's really good." She'd mixed it up ahead of time so they just needed to stuff and bake the zucchinis.

"It must be, since you don't even like zucchinis." Serena stretched her arms above her head. "Which reminds me. I'm hungry. Got anything I can eat? Besides zucchini, that is."

Reaching into the fridge, Lori brought out the hoagie sandwiches and broccoli salad she'd fixed earlier. She'd known, since they were starting at eleven, that she'd need to serve lunch. One glance at the newspaper-strewn counters covered with painted vegetables and the table where the three of them were painting and she laughed. "Let's eat on the patio."

As she carried the tray of food and glasses of lemonade outside, Lori drew in a deep breath of air—cool, at eighty-six degrees, for the last Saturday in August. Over the past eight days, she'd enjoyed everything more than usual, almost as though she had been stuck in black and white for years and then suddenly found herself awash in living color.

The air seemed more clear, the sun shone more brightly, food tasted better. Flowers bloomed, birds sang, and even Charles's stupid cat had come up to her yesterday to be petted. Would miracles never cease?

On the patio, the three women chatted through lunch. Afterward they sat back and enjoyed the warmth of the peaceful afternoon and the breeze from the fan overhead.

A bumblebee floated heavily by.

"Look at that," said Agatha. "Good thing they don't know they're not supposed to be able to fly."

One of Agatha's cats jumped the fence and bounded into the older woman's lap. Agatha said, "It looks like your Enrichment activity is going to be a huge success. Wish I could be there."

"Are you kidding?" Lori turned to her. "I'm hoping and praying you'll come for moral support. Please."

"I'm kind of old for a singles activity."

"But you are single. And you're my friend. And I'm practically begging you."

"You are begging, *chica,*" Serena chimed in. "You're only one step above groveling." She stood, stretched, and picked up her glass. "I'm going in for a refill. I'll bring out the pitcher."

Agatha smiled as she stroked her cat's back. "Well, since you're begging and all, I'd love to come."

"Great. All that's left is to print off the recipes people have given us so far."

Agatha pulled a leaf from her cat's fur. "Did you ever find Charlie's recipe?"

Lori shook her head. "I didn't."

The cat jumped down. "Oh, I forgot to tell you. Charlie called me the other night."

"From China? That must have been expensive."

"We only talked for a minute. He just wanted me to make sure you were taking care of his garden and his column right."

Lori froze. She'd been worried about the editor wanting to fire her. What if Charles wanted her gone? And he might, too, if Agatha had told him the truth—that Lori had only the foggiest notion of what she was doing.

"What did you tell him?" Lori asked, her mouth dry.

"Don't look so worried, sweetie." Agatha laughed. "I told him you were doing a great job and he can go back to exploring the world until he gets it out of his system."

Relieved, Lori smiled. "Can he do that in three months?"

Agatha laughed again. "He likes to think he's a great traveler and plans vacations that are too long for him to enjoy. And he has too much pride to admit he's homesick, but he wouldn't have called, otherwise. Silly fool." Her words were spoken with affection, and Lori wondered if Agatha held a torch for her neighbor.

But then Agatha shook her head and said, "No wonder he's never found a woman to put up with the likes of him," and Lori realized she was mistaken. She was imagining romance everywhere these days.

Serena slid the glass door open and poked her head out. "Oh, ladies, I think you ought to see this."

Exchanging curious glances, Lori and Agatha stepped inside.

Smiling broadly, Serena pointed to the corkboard on the kitchen wall, beside the cat with the swinging eyes and tail.

"Serena, sweetie," said Agatha, "that's been there all along."

"Yes, it has," said Serena with a laugh.

Agatha stepped to the board. "Well, I'll be hornswoggled. He wanted it to be easily found." She joined in the laughter.

"What?" Lori stood beside Agatha, who was pointing at . . . "The zucchini chicken curry recipe!"

"He hid it in plain sight, the devil," whispered Agatha.

"Well, you said he intended to put it in the column," said Lori, glad it had been located. "And now we have time to use it for the activity, too."

THE GARDEN GURU

Dear Ms. Scott: How many hours of direct sunlight do my vegetable plants need? (Mary Ann)

Dear Mary Ann: Most vegetables need at least six full hours of direct sun a day in order to produce a good crop. Anyone with eyes can see that plants will bend and grow toward the sunlight. Even more interesting, studies also show they will grow toward speakers playing classical music, as if the music were an audible form of light. It's also been proven that they'll do better if you speak nicely to them. Make sure your vegetable plants have direct sun for a good part of the day, and they will, most definitely and most satisfyingly, grow toward the light . . .

Chapter Twenty

"Everyone seems to be enjoying this," said Serena, carrying another tray of painted squash out to the cultural hall for consumption, passing Lori coming back toward the church kitchen with an empty tray.

Lori nodded, gratified. "It turned out tasty, didn't it?"

"And Charles's zucchini chicken curry is really good. It's nearly gone already."

Serena disappeared into the cultural hall, and Lori entered the kitchen.

Setting her empty tray down to be refilled by two ladies who'd generously offered to help, even though it wasn't even their calling, Lori gathered up another tray holding three brightly colored squash—purple swirls, red-white-and-blue stripes, and orange dots. She made another trip from the kitchen into the cultural hall.

Serena was arranging her load along the several long tables that ran along one wall. The painted squash were interspersed with three different types of salad: green, cabbage with Ramen noodles, and broccoli.

About ten large, round tables had been set up, each of them with a centerpiece of several painted squash. She recognized many of the faces, but few of the names, except for Dawn and the gossiper, Jeanette.

Lori had taught a short lesson on the theme of the evening—"Color Your Life with the Gospel"—and thought she'd done a good job. At least she hadn't made a complete fool of herself, and no one had booed, like they had at her play.

Lori could hardly wait to talk with John when he picked her up, to tell him how well everything had gone. He'd been so sweet earlier, carrying everything inside, wishing her luck, telling her she'd do great. He seemed to have such confidence in her—certainly more than she had in herself.

When Agatha came up to her, Lori set the heavy tray onto the table. "Thanks again for coming, Agatha. It made it easier to have you and Serena here."

She didn't say it, but having Dawn Lawson in the group of thirty or so women had made the evening more difficult for Lori. Dawn, whose hurt and animosity toward Lori showed in her eyes and bristled in the air around her.

Serena joined them and helped Lori arrange the last of the squash. "I love your shoes, *chica.* Did you rob banks in New York or what? I don't know how else you could afford Manolos."

Lori smiled. "I had to practically mortgage my apartment, but I couldn't pass them up."

"Well, if you ever get tired of them, toss them my way. I'd love a chance to walk a mile in *your* shoes."

Agatha motioned toward the tables filled with brightly painted zucchini, spaghetti squash, and crooknecks, and laughed. "Ladies, we did good. Those are some wild zucchinis."

"I like them." Serena touched a small rose-colored zucchini. "They're very colorful. I almost feel like I'm back in Mexico. The women are going to love taking one home."

"I'm just glad zucchini month is over. I can't believe it's almost September," Lori said.

Agatha chuckled. "But you've got lots of new recipes. So it was a success all around."

"Wait. I know. You could write a cookbook." Serena motioned toward the tables like Agatha had done earlier. "You could call it *How to Stuff a Wild Zucchini.*"

"That's a grand idea," said Agatha.

Lori laughed. "Maybe I just will."

"Maybe it could be a book of ideas for Enrichment activities," Agatha suggested. "You'll need pictures."

"I've taken lots already," said Serena, pulling her camera from her purse. "And now I'll get one of you two."

As Lori stood where Serena directed, she saw Dawn talking with two other women and pointing in Lori's direction. The other two women looked at Lori, then quickly away.

It wasn't too hard to guess that whatever Dawn was saying wasn't flattering. This calling would be easier if Dawn weren't around. But then, Lori supposed that Dawn probably thought a romance with John would be easier if Lori weren't around. So Lori would try to understand that the other woman was hurting and probably not handling it as well as she wished, either. She'd continue to try to pretend Dawn didn't despise her.

But then Dawn said, loud enough for Lori to hear—loud enough for most everyone to hear—"Does she think we're all hicks or something?"

The entire group of women turned, wide-eyed and silent, toward Lori, probably wondering if she'd ignore Dawn's words—as most probably wanted—or if she'd respond—as Jeanette, with her eyes bright and her mouth smiling, seemed to look forward to.

Lori wasn't sure what she was going to do, either.

Dawn looked away, and Lori suspected she wished she'd kept quiet.

She wanted to pretend Dawn hadn't spoken, but when the silence stretched out longer and longer, becoming incredibly uncomfortable, and Lori's heart couldn't beat any faster without nearing the bursting point, she figured she'd look the elephant in the living room in the eye, and try to take the sting out of Dawn's words with a smile. She was suddenly glad for the chance to let these women know what she really thought, rather than what Dawn Lawson said she thought.

She forced herself to look at Dawn. "To be totally honest, I might have thought something like that six weeks ago when I first arrived, but I don't anymore. I've learned a lot during my short time here."

She looked away from Dawn and around the room. "Now I believe you're some of the happiest people I've ever known. There is a light in your eyes that makes you"—Lori was surprised at the emotion that swept through her, making her voice tremble—"makes you truly beautiful. And I'm very glad I've come to know you all. So, no, I definitely don't think you ladies are hicks. I just thought you'd enjoy a fun, light-hearted evening, eating and visiting with the other sisters. And I hope we can continue now to do just that."

The color draining from her face, Dawn snatched up her purse and flew from the room. Jeanette followed her. The rest of the ladies began talking again.

Lori's heart still raced, and she took a deep breath to try to slow it.

"Well done," said Agatha. "Excellent speech."

Lori turned to her. "It's true."

And it was. Lori realized she wanted that same light to shine from her own eyes. She recognized it now—it was the same light her mother had, the light that helped her let go of any bitterness toward her ex-husband, Lori's father.

It had to do with the light. The light of the Gospel. The light of Christ. The light that brought peace.

Lori was tired of the negative emotions of hurt and anger and jealousy that so often coiled and writhed painfully in her chest, coloring everything a dark shade. She wanted to move into the light.

She loved the peaceful way she felt around these people.

Around John.

She wanted peace in her life and light in her eyes.

Chapter Twenty-One

John opened the truck door as Lori came out of the building, all smiles. He grinned in return. She waved to him and crossed the parking lot, leaning up for a quick kiss.

He enjoyed the feel of her close to him. When she pulled back, he said, "Need I ask how it went?"

"It was so great. All the women—well, almost all—told me how much they absolutely loved the activity. Several of them said they'd had more fun than they have for a long time."

"Didn't I tell you you'd be great?"

She smiled at him and his pulse quickened. "You did. Thanks for being so supportive."

A warm feeling filled him at her words.

They went inside and he carried out a box filled with the leftover painted vegetables, far fewer than he'd helped her carry in. After they climbed into the truck, some women motioned to Lori and she climbed back out to chat with them for a moment.

While he waited, John turned up the volume on the truck's scanner so he could listen to the emergency dispatcher. Even though he was off duty, he liked to know what was going on, though he didn't plan on responding to anything tonight. No, tonight he wanted to spend time with his girl.

When she climbed back in, he spun the knob, turning the volume down so he could barely hear it.

"Do you want to go straight home? Or would you rather go for a drive?"

"I'm still buzzing from the activity. Let's ride."

"Your wish is my command," he teased, and pointed the truck

toward the canyon. It was still somewhat light at not-quite-nine o'clock because of the bright moon.

They talked as he drove the twenty minutes to the lookout point. He'd never been able to speak this freely and easily to any woman, ever. Even Dawn had done most of the talking and he'd just stayed quiet. But he found himself confiding things to Lori, exchanging thoughts, becoming closer than he'd ever been to anyone.

As he made the final turn into the pullout and parked at the edge, where the vista of the valley below was revealed in the moonlight, Lori's reaction was everything he'd hoped for.

"It's beautiful," she whispered, turning toward him, her eyes bright. "The trees are spectacular."

The mountainside was covered with trees already turning vivid shades of orange and red and yellow. It was a sight he loved every autumn. "I'll have to bring you back to see a sunset from here."

He held out his arm and she smiled, scooting close to him and leaning back against his chest. "I'd rather see the sunset from *here.*"

His pulse quickened again, both at her words and her nearness. He tightened his arm around her and she snuggled back in until they seemed to be parts of a puzzle, not complete without the other.

She made a satisfied sound, and his pulse jumped again.

"Like it?" he asked, wanting to please her.

"Very much. It's the perfect end to a perfect day."

John never wanted this moment to end. He wanted to keep her here. He didn't want her to leave. He hadn't planned to say the words, but, as Lori sighed, he realized he wanted time to pursue Lori. He didn't dare use the word *marriage* with her, though it was what he was beginning to want, but he'd like to court her.

Even though she still professed that she wasn't active in the Church, a calm feeling settled on him, as though that would come. "Lori?"

She traced a fingertip down his arm and intertwined her fingers with his. "Uh-huh."

"I'd like to call your father and ask for his permission to court you."

Immediately he knew he'd made a huge mistake; she stiffened and pulled away, turning toward him with wide eyes. "What?"

She sounded upset. Really upset. Monumentally upset.

He'd apparently misread all the signs and was moving much too fast for her, but he'd already said the words and couldn't take them back. More quietly, he repeated, "I want to court you."

"Not that part. The other," she said with a frown on her face and a harsh tone in her voice that he'd never heard before.

Confused, he said, "So you're okay with me courting you?"

"I'm not sure about that, but I am definitely not okay with you ever calling my father and asking him anything about me. He has nothing to do with my life."

The evening that had begun so beautifully had just taken a nosedive.

Shocked, Lori could only stare at him.

Finally, he spoke, sounding contrite and confused. "I'm sorry, Lori. I didn't mean to upset you."

She drew in a deep breath and closed her eyes. "I haven't told you about my father, have I?"

"Not really." His fingers touched her hand tentatively.

She opened her eyes and took his hand. "I don't talk about him much. Not at all, actually. But I guess it's time I told you what happened."

He squeezed her hand; she squeezed back. "When I was thirteen years old, my mom and dad were having a few marital problems. My mom said it was nothing that couldn't have been fixed with some counseling, which she tried to get him to go to. I think him getting over his selfishness would have helped, too."

She shook her head as if to shake off the memories, but they stayed, flooding her. She clutched his hand for support.

"Go on," he said, gently, and took her hand in both of his, pulling her against him again.

As she leaned into him, he wrapped his arms around her waist and shoulders, enfolding her in caring and support. She suspected it would be easier to talk about her father if she wasn't looking in John's eyes.

"He had an affair with a neighbor. Sister Fiona Bennett."

"I'm so sorry," he murmured into her hair, his breath warm on her ear. "That must have been really tough for you and your mother and brother."

She shivered. "A year after the divorce was final, he married Fiona in a quiet civil ceremony. He didn't invite me, either. I wouldn't have gone, but it would have been nice to know I was included or that he cared about me at all."

She was grateful he didn't rush in, like so many people did, to reassure her that her father must still love her. She wished she could believe he loved her, but he'd proved he didn't want her around. "He lives thirty miles away from my mother's house. And I haven't talked to him since he left. Thirteen years ago."

"It must feel very unfair to you."

"It does." She thought about it for a minute. "I feel sad. And I'm still angry at him for deserting me."

He squeezed her hand.

"I guess I'm afraid to call him because he might prove once again that he doesn't care."

"Sometimes it's best to face your fears head on."

"If you really believe that, then why don't you ride the white roller coaster at Lagoon?"

"Ouch," he said with a rueful chuckle. "I guess I deserved that."

"Yes, you did."

"So if I ride the white roller coaster, will you consider calling your father?"

"I don't think so. But thanks for caring."

Even now, when she should be upset still, he could calm her.

They sat quietly again for a minute, and he asked, "Are they still married?"

She sighed deeply and he tightened his embrace again, holding her securely as she faced these painful memories. "A couple of years ago they were sealed in the temple and now he's living like a righteous person, but I know he's this big hypocrite. Him and his whole family of Hideous H's."

When he spoke, he sounded tentative—and surprised. "Hideous . . . H's?"

"Yeah. Hillary, Hailey, and Hannah—his replacement family. He doesn't need me or my brother anymore. And I don't need him, either. That's why I don't want you to call him. Because he didn't care enough to stay. He has no say in my life now."

A few minutes later, as the moon hid behind a cloud and the sky darkened around them, she said, "It's not a big deal. We were better off without him."

When he finally did speak, he said, "If I had a beautiful little girl like you, I could never leave."

At his words, a lump grew in her throat. Emotions she'd thought long dead and buried worked their way through her heart. The hurt she'd felt as a child when her father had left overwhelmed her. But John's words echoed through her body, clear as a bell's ring, and brought a measure of healing to that same small child still inside.

She blinked back hot tears, and he handed her a napkin with the Wendy's logo printed on it. The silliness of it made her smile. But yet there was a rightness to it, as the hurt belonged to the child she used to be.

Staying secure in his arms, she wiped her eyes, then tilted her face up to his, just inches away. "Thank you for listening without telling me I should get over it. I hate when people do that."

John smiled gently.

His sweet words had touched her so deeply she could feel her barriers melting. She could see the feelings he had for her in his eyes. He cared for her. And, when he kissed her, she realized the truth about her own feelings.

She was in love with John Wayne Walker!

Chapter Twenty-Two

Before she could process her feelings, John turned to her with the most serious look she'd ever seen on his face. "Lori, I want to have a little girl who looks just like you."

Overwhelmed at his words, by her emotions, she froze. Even her heart seemed to stop in that instant when she saw everything so clearly, as if in a blinding white light.

How had she forgotten that the reason she couldn't ever be a couple with John wasn't because she couldn't fall in love with him, but because he wanted children so much and she couldn't give him any? How had she forgotten that horrible reality?

He smiled at her and shook his head. "It's so amazing that I found you."

Speechless, she struggled for air.

"Stations Three and Four." The voice seemed to come from nowhere, making Lori jump in John's arms. It was his firefighter's radio, barely audible. "Brush fire on the old highway. Repeat—three-alarm fire on the old highway threatening the new development."

John groaned. "Not now." He hugged her close to him, then loosened his grip.

"You're off duty, aren't you?" she asked, as they sat forward on his truck seat.

"This is a bad one. They'll need me." He looked over at her, and his eyes smoldered, causing chills to race up her spine and neck. "I don't want to leave you." His voice was husky with emotion that seemed to match her own.

She leaned over and gave him a kiss, which turned into a very long kiss.

With another groan, he fastened his seat belt, waited for her to fasten hers, started his truck, and pulled back onto the highway, his headlights piercing the dark night ahead of them.

I am in love with John Wayne Walker!

That thought had raced round and round her brain—and her heart—since John had dropped her off at home four hours ago before heading off to battle a fire.

As she climbed out of bed, unable to sleep for the past two hours, her mind turned to other, more fearful thoughts.

Was John safe? He must still be fighting the fire, because he'd promised he'd call when he got home, and he hadn't called yet. Were all the firefighters safe? And how had she ever let this happen? How could she have been so blind to her own feelings?

She paced into the kitchen, pulling open the fridge door. Nothing looked good. And she really had no appetite, she just wanted to distract herself. She ran her fingers through her messy hair.

What had happened? This was supposed to be a holiday romance, not something serious. She and John were supposed to date until she left, and then she would go back to New York, leaving him behind to pick up where he left off with the voluptuous woman with the glowing red hair—the undoubtedly über-fertile Dawn Lawson. Win-win-win situation for all three of them. Nobody was supposed to get involved. Nobody was supposed to get hurt. Nobody was supposed to fall in love.

But she had.

I am in love with John Wayne Walker!

When she thought of him fighting the fire at that very moment, her heart pounded with fear for him. Her heart swelled with the depth of her emotion.

For the first time, she knew she was getting a taste of what wives of firefighters—and cops and every other guy who put himself in danger to keep others safe—must go through every day. She kept worrying if he were safe, if the fire was under control, if he'd come back unscathed.

It was far too late to get out of this relationship before anyone got hurt. Her heart was going to be broken more than Nicholas had ever had the power to do.

Not only that, she knew John's heart was involved, too. She'd seen it in his eyes tonight, when he'd said he wanted to court her, to have a child who looked like her. And, to be honest, she'd known he cared for her for a long time, though she'd tried to convince herself otherwise.

Now Lori was in love with John, and she was pretty sure he was in love with her, too.

She hadn't thought her infertility would be an issue, but John wanted kids who looked just like her—and she couldn't give him any.

The irony and tragedy of the situation struck her head-on: she'd finally met a trustworthy man—and she couldn't have him.

Her heart ached and she wrapped her arms around herself, sinking onto the couch in pain.

The last thing she wanted was to let John go, but it wasn't fair to lead him on, to get involved with a man who wanted kids so badly. As much as it would hurt both of them, she had to break things off with John.

It wasn't just the children she'd never give birth to. She realized she trusted John like she had her Grandpa Scott—but she wasn't sure she trusted John to stick around forever. Not when he found out the truth about her.

The tears began to flow—and continued forever.

She sat on the couch like a zombie, praying, "Please help me, Father," over and over.

When the phone finally rang at three in the morning, she was still awake. "Hello."

"Sorry to wake you, babe. I'm home safely and calling as I promised." John's voice was soft, caressing.

"I'm glad." Her voice caught. The relief she felt made her eyes burn again. She blinked hard.

"I won't keep you up," he said. "See you tomorrow night."

"Okay," she whispered.

"Sweet dreams, beautiful."

As she folded up her phone, she knew she had less than twenty-four hours to figure out how to break up with the man she loved.

Chapter Twenty-Three

Happy, John stood on the porch and rang the bell. Stuffing his hands in his pockets, he hummed the silly song they'd heard at the Heritage Theater the other night.

When the door opened and he caught sight of Lori's puffy eyes, he stopped humming, concerned. "Are you all right?"

"I was up most of the night."

"I woke you when I called. I'm sorry."

"No, I was still up. I was just thinking through a lot of things."

He wondered if she'd been thinking about her father, after finally talking about him. "Can I come in?"

"Oh. Yes. Please."

He stepped in and leaned over to kiss her. Was it his imagination or did she pull away somewhat? Her lips were warm, but the kiss ended quickly, and not because of him.

"The Peach Days festival starts in ninety minutes, if you still want to go."

She sighed and shook her head.

"So what did you do all night instead of sleeping?"

"I worried if you were safe or not."

That pleased him. "What else?"

"I cried."

"About what?"

She didn't answer the question, but motioned him toward a chair. She sat on the other chair. Not together with him on the couch.

"I read a few chapters of—" She stopped, looking at him as if she'd said something wrong.

"Of what?" He smiled. "Some naughty novel?"

She smiled back, but it was a faint imitation of her usual bright smile. “You might not believe it, but I started reading the Book of Mormon after you challenged me that day when we were weeding.”

“Did you find any comfort there?”

“Some,” she admitted.

He kept himself from grinning. This was really great. “What else did you do?”

She looked down at her hands. “I did a lot of thinking.”

“About?”

When Lori looked up, he saw such sadness in her eyes that he reached out between the two chairs and brushed hair off her cheek, the touch scorching him.

Lori looked away. “John, this isn’t going to work.”

“What do you mean?” Wary, he felt adrenaline pump through every cell as though he were facing a fire. A big one.

When she blinked her eyes closed, John wondered if she was fighting back tears. More worried than ever, he asked, “Lori, please tell me what’s wrong.”

Finally, she opened her eyes, but she still wouldn’t look at him. “We need to break it off. Our relationship, I mean.”

Her words hit him like a blast from a fire hose. Carefully, quietly, hurting, he asked, “Why?”

She lifted her gaze toward the window. “I just think we’re getting . . . too involved. And, with me going back to New York soon, I just thought . . .”

Her voice faded away, as did his hopes—but then they rose again. Did she feel *she* was getting too involved? That must mean she cared for him. He definitely wasn’t ready to have her leave his life. He’d do whatever it took to win her, even if that meant backing off in the short-term, with the long-term goal of staying close by.

He reached out again and gently turned her chin until she looked into his eyes. “I’d still like to see you.”

She bit her lip, then said, “I just don’t want either of us to get hurt.”

Afraid if he didn’t backpedal a little he might lose her altogether, for the first time since he’d told his mother he hadn’t taken that pack of gum from 7-11 when he was five, he lied. "You know, I did some thinking last night, too. This has all moved rather quickly. You're probably right—being just friends might be wiser for us."

"I don't know if I can still see you." She stood and he stood, too. "I think it would be best if we broke it off totally."

He stepped in front of her, close, but not too close. "Lori, have I done anything wrong?"

She shook her head. "Not at all."

Not wanting to leave without having a foot back in the door, he hid his pain and asked, "Then can I still stop by and see you now and then?"

She paused. Debated. Finally nodded.

John raised an eyebrow. "Dinner tonight?"

She shook her head. "I didn't get much sleep last night. I'm going to turn in early."

"Okay. Get some sleep." He forced a grin. "See you around, friend."

She smiled faintly and nodded. "See you around."

She closed the door behind him, and he walked to his truck, his muscles tight.

He had some questions to ask his bishop.

A scowling boy, probably twelve or thirteen, answered the door and peered up at John through long, ragged, black bangs. "Yeah?"

"I need to speak with Bishop Robertson, please."

"Doesn't everyone?" The kid rolled his eyes. "Don't you know what day this is?"

Punk. "Sure I do. It's Wednesday."

"Yeah, Wednesday. The first day of Peach Days, and my sister is in the Junior Peach Queen Pageant at the middle school." The boy called back over his shoulder, "Dad. Someone else to see you." Under his breath, he muttered, "Again."

"Sorry." The kid was resentful, but John could understand his frustration; after all, his own father had been a bishop at one time. His questions could certainly wait another day. In fact, he could talk with his own dad later tonight or tomorrow. "Hey, look. Don't worry about it. I'll come back another time."

But then the bishop was at the door. "John. Hi."

"Hi, Bishop. I'm sorry. I didn't realize I was interrupting a family event. I'll come back later."

The bishop motioned him in. "I have some time."

"Are you sure? I really don't want to interrupt."

"I'm sure I can give you thirty minutes, anyway." He pulled the door open wide, and glanced back at his son with a smile. "Then we'll leave and we'll still be thirty minutes early for the pageant, just like we planned, okay?"

The boy stared through his bangs; he seemed to accept what his father was telling him because he shrugged and said "Okay" before disappearing into the living room.

The bishop led the way down the hall and through the first doorway. The room must have originally been a medium-sized bedroom, but it now housed a desk and computer and a couple of chairs.

John had known Bishop Robertson for more than five years, but had only met his family on a few occasions, usually at holiday time.

The bishop might look a little out of shape, but John and the rest of the single guys had learned from experience that looks could be deceiving—the bishop was rock hard muscle with a belly. He wasn't someone you wanted to have block you in a game of football or on the basketball court, either. Now John realized what a sacrifice those games must have been for the bishop's family.

Bishop Robertson motioned John to sit and did the same, settling back comfortably into the easy chair. "So, what can I do for you?"

John hesitated. "I'm not sure exactly what I'm asking, but I need help figuring out some things." He started slowly, but soon was pouring out his story. Meeting Lori and being smitten by her. His talk with Dawn. Dating Lori. Being dumped by Lori. And how he very much still wanted to date her.

When the words quit spewing from his mouth, John sat back in his chair, relieved.

"Whew. That's quite a tale. But how exactly can I help you?"

"I have a lot of questions. But mainly I just need some perspective on how to proceed." John told the bishop about Lori's father's betrayal and her subsequent mistrust of men. "I really care about her, Bishop. How can I get her to trust me? What do I do next?"

Bishop Robertson steepled his fingers and said, softly, "Pursue her gently. Don't put pressure on her. At the same time, prepare yourself to accept whatever she decides."

Disappointed, John said, "Then I might lose her."

"Yes." The bishop paused, as if considering his words. "Sometimes that happens."

"But—"

The bishop held up his hand and John quieted.

"John, I think it's fairly obvious to everyone in the ward that Dawn Lawson cares for you deeply."

"Dawn?"

"The point I'm trying to make is that you can't force people to do what you want them to. You can't change things with Lori if she doesn't want to go there, no matter how much you wish you could. Just as Dawn can't change things with you, no matter how much she wishes she could and no matter what she does." The bishop looked John straight in the eye. "I just want you to remember that you can't dictate how a person responds to you, even if you want it with all your heart."

Guilt speared John. He knew he'd hurt Dawn. "That hardly seems fair."

"It's not. But it is real life. It has to do with that darned agency we fought so hard for in the pre-mortal life."

"So you're suggesting I pursue Lori. But if she doesn't want to be pursued, step away and let her go."

The bishop nodded. "I wish I could help you more. I can't make this decision for you, John. And you can't make it for Lori."

THE GARDEN GURU

Dear Ms. Scott: We want to start a community garden in our subdivision. We already have a small plot donated. What is the best way to set this up to avoid problems down the road? I want to participate, but I also want to be in control of what I plant. (Phil)

Dear Phil: Give each individual or family their own plot of land in the community garden, as a small well-tended plot will produce more than a larger, neglected one. Have a kickoff date when someone (a local farmer, perhaps?) will till the plot and when everyone starts planting at the same time. This will get some excitement going. A community garden is a great opportunity to work together as a team, but it does require some give-and-take. And the harvest will be well worth it. Since the harvest is over for this year, let me tell you the best time to plant in the spring . . .

Chapter Twenty-Four

As Lori looked at the zucchini she'd harvested and tossed into two big boxes, she was amazed at the never-ending supply of both zucchinis and thoughts of John. It had been two days since she'd told him she couldn't see him anymore, and he'd apparently believed her and returned to the playing field.

Though it had to be this way, she was melancholy. When she'd caught Nicholas with another woman, she'd thought her heart was broken. Now that she'd stopped seeing John, she knew better. Now she knew what a broken heart really felt like.

Harvesting zucchini as the sun edged toward the horizon was supposed to be therapeutic, but it just gave her more time to think. And the thoughts all centered on John. Holding her hand. Kissing her. Cradling her safely in his arms. Making her laugh. Listening to her when she needed to talk.

She'd done the right thing, hadn't she? Yes. Of course she had. He needed a woman who could give him children. She'd known that from the beginning. So why did she feel so bad?

She bent over to pluck more of the long green veggies that she'd grown to despise for the very fertility she couldn't achieve herself. Even a vegetable could reproduce—but not Lori.

"Hey, beautiful."

At the sound, Lori twirled.

John was opening her back gate. Coming into the yard. Latching the gate behind him. "I thought you might need some help with your garden."

Though her heart filled with joy at the sight of him, the sound of a few words from his lips, his mere presence, Lori had to be strong.

Didn't she? "John, I was serious the other day. I think it would be best if we don't see each other again."

"We're friends, remember?" He carried a bulging grocery-sized plastic bag. "It looks like you could use a friend to help you get rid of all this zucchini. Don't even try to deny it."

She looked at the two full boxes—and the vines still producing like crazy. Overwhelmed, she nodded. "If they sent zucchini plants to starving Third World countries, the world's food shortage could be totally averted in one growing season."

"I can see it now. Zucchini-rice cakes in Asia. Zucchini tacos in South America. Zucchini-grub-casserole in Africa." He laughed. "I'm offering to help. As your friend." He raised an eyebrow. "We did agree it's okay to remain friends, right?"

She couldn't help but smile, thankful he'd found a way around her weak defenses. She was so glad to see him. So thankful he still wanted to see her. "Yes."

Turning, he planted his fists on his hips, the filled plastic bag hanging from his wrist, and surveyed the garden. He shook his head and pursed his lips. Using his John Wayne imitation, he said, "You need some major help here, little lady. So here's what we're gonna do. We'll just take these plants and do some doorbell ditching."

"Doorbell ditching?"

"You bet. A time-honored Western tradition. So grab a box. We're going to get the job done."

For a second, all she could remember was that the last time he'd spoken in his fake John Wayne voice, she'd gotten a kiss. She jerked her thoughts away and looked at the box, heavy with bounty. "I don't think I can carry one."

He opened the plastic bag to reveal more bags inside, and smiled slowly. "I thought these might come in handy."

They spent the next fifteen minutes bagging the zucchini and dropping the filled bags—eighteen of them—back into the boxes. John dragged the boxes, one at a time, and hefted them into the back of his pickup.

As they drove, he said, "Usually it's wise to wait until nightfall, but it's dusk now. Close enough."

"Where are we going?"

"To my parents' ward. I know some people who can use free vegetables. And this is an excellent time to do it, because a lot of folks are down on Main Street for the Junior Parade."

"Junior Parade?"

"Part of Peach Days. Softball tournament. Teen Dance. Small town fun and games. The custom car show is in the morning—you could bring Ben and show him off."

"I think I'll skip that golden opportunity. I already drive him once a week after dark so no one can see him."

When he pulled up to the curb in his parents' neighborhood, it wasn't quite dark. "Okay, grab a bag."

They climbed down and she pulled out a bag of zucchini.

He made a great deal of noise while shushing her, and walked stealthily toward the edge of a fence on the corner. Not like Tom Cruise in *Mission: Impossible;* more like Kronk in *The Emperor's New Groove,* only without the theme music. Obvious. Exaggerated. Fun. "Give me the bag and I'll show you how it's done. You wait here."

He Kronked his way across the street and up to the front porch of a home a few houses away. A large van was parked in front, the tops of several car seats visible. Apparently the family had lots of kids. John placed the bag on the porch, rang the bell, and hightailed it back to the corner with Lori.

As he raced past, he grabbed her hand and pulled her behind the cover of the fence. They were both laughing.

"Okay," he said. "Let's see if they answer."

He stood right beside her as they peered around the edge of the fence. Sure enough, the door opened and a woman looked out and saw the bag. Before she could look up and catch them, John pulled Lori back and they ran to his truck, climbed in, and drove down the street.

"What happens if they catch us?" asked Lori, laughing.

"They make you take your zucchini back home," he answered with a chuckle. "And make you take some of theirs, too."

They took turns leaving the bags of zucchini and running away. Lori hadn't had this much fun in, well, in days, since she'd last been around John.

They worked their way up the road until, finally, with just one bag left, John drove into a fancier neighborhood, and pointed to a house down the street. "Okay. You get the honors on the last onc."

She did her own Kronk imitation onto the porch, hearing John's laughter behind her. She set down the bag and reached for the bell—when the door opened!

She was caught!

"Ah-haaaaa!" A tall man with a dark goatee scowled at her and called over his shoulder. "Honey, call the cops. We've got us a zucchini doorbell ditcher."

Shocked, heart hammering, Lori stammered, "I'm sorry, I—"

But the man started chuckling and opened the door. "Come on in, Lori. John called and said you'd be along for some pie."

Once she was over her shock, she recognized John's friend, Quinn Jackson. His short, dark-haired wife, Tricia, came to stand beside him, shaking her head. "Men and their silly games. Come in and we'll discuss how you can get back at John. Maybe I'll put a raw egg on top of his pie."

"I heard that," said John, coming up behind Lori. "And you would never do that, Tricia."

"Oh, I wouldn't, eh?" Tricia allowed herself to be swept into a bear hug with John.

As he pulled back, he said, "Nah. You're much too nice."

At the end of the evening, after playing card games with John and Quinn and Tricia, eating delicious homemade peach pie with ice cream (and no eggs on top), watching the couple hold their two children and lavish attention on them, and after the much shorter drive home, Lori sat quietly and companionably in the pickup as John pulled over to the curb.

"This has been fun." He climbed down and helped her out the passenger side. After the initial touch of his hand to help her down, he stuffed his hands in his pockets.

She had to give him points for trying to keep it *just friends.* But could he keep from trying to kiss her at the door? If he did try, she wasn't sure she had enough strength to turn him away.

At the door, he leaned in. He *was* going to kiss her. What did she do now? Her heart hammered in her chest harder than it had when Quinn had caught her doorbell ditching.

"I'm trying to remember how friends say good night." He reached out and shook her hand. "See you later."

As he walked to his truck, she realized he'd kept his word.

She felt downright cheated!

She wanted that kiss!

Oh, she was in so much trouble. If she had any sense, she'd leave Brigham City tomorrow. But she was, apparently, a fool because she was going to stay put, drawn to John like a moth to a flame.

The next morning, John and his father and brothers had helped out at the Peach Days Fire Department Breakfast from six until after ten. After washing up, he'd taken in the parade on Main Street.

Afterward, he climbed into his truck and pulled out his cell phone. He called his father, who'd ridden home with Roy. "I'm coming over. I need some advice."

"About what, son?"

"About Lori," John admitted.

"Great. See you soon."

When John pulled up to the curb at his parents' house, though, he saw three extra trucks. His brothers were here. No way was he going to talk romance with his brothers around. He began to pull away when he caught sight of his father in the doorway, waving him in.

Why did he have such a bad feeling about this?

His parents' living room was large and roomy with two long curved couches, two easy chairs, and a baby grand piano on which his mother had given lessons to all her children and grandchildren.

At the moment, his three brothers and their wives were seated on the couches. His mother sat in one of the chairs. Other than his father's La-Z-Boy recliner, the only seating space left was the piano bench.

He could hear the sound of kids playing downstairs.

His worst nightmare faced him—but he wasn't going to stay here and let it happen. He turned toward the door, but his three brothers moved between him and the door. John didn't like the smug smiles on their faces.

"Uh, Dad, can we go in your den?" John asked quietly. "This is kinda private."

"Nonsense, son," his father boomed out, motioning toward the entire huge family, sitting around like predators waiting for any sign of weakness from John. "Everybody wants to help you. We've been giving this a great deal of thought."

John groaned. "You told them?"

"He sure did, little bro," said Clint. "Come in, sit down, and learn how to become a great lover."

Feeling his face flush hot, John pulled out the piano bench and sat. He was sure he was going to regret this.

Roy tapped John's shoulder. "Give her ice cream. It works every time with Becky."

"That's because she's pregnant, moron," Kirk said. "You need to be romantic. Like this." He got down on one knee. "And take her flowers. Roses. Lots and lots of roses."

"He's not in the doghouse, fool." Clint shook his head. "Out of my way, amateurs. What you need to do, John, is buy the lady some tickets to an expensive concert. *Les Mis* works wonders."

Becky struggled to her swollen feet and waddled over to John, one hand on her back and the other out, as if for balance. She needed a Wide Load sign, her belly had gotten so big. "Come with me, and let the *women* give you advice on winning a woman's heart."

She took his hand. Trapped, he let himself be led to the curved part of the couch, surrounded by the women in his family: Opal and Julie on his left, Becky and his mother on his right.

"Okay," Opal said. "What's the problem? I thought everything was going great."

John stared at them. They really expected him to talk?

The men laughed. Clint said, "Talk to them, John. Resistance is futile. You will be assimilated."

John glared at his brothers.

"So," Becky said, putting a finger under his chin and turning his face back in her direction. "Wasn't everything going well?"

"I thought so," admitted John, trying to speak softly so his brothers couldn't hear.

It didn't work. Clint laughed. "That's how much you know, fool."

"Shush," Julie told her husband. Amazingly, that worked. She patted John's hand. "Go on."

"I thought everything was great. And then she said we're getting too involved."

"Ooohhhh," said all four women in unison. John thought it sounded pretty ominous.

But then Becky said, "That's wonderful news!"

"It is?" John didn't understand any of this woman stuff.

"Sure," said Julie. "It means she likes you more than she feels comfortable with."

"So," said Opal, "you've just got to be her friend for awhile until she feels comfortable again. Sometimes a woman just needs to get used to the view."

"And what a view," sighed Becky.

"How would you know?" Clint teased. "You got ugly Roy."

"Shut up." Roy punched Clint's shoulder.

Becky stood again, all five-foot-four of her, her waist-length wavy brown hair pulled back in its usual ponytail, big brown doe eyes blazing, and put her hands on her hips. She actually looked ticked off, a most un-Becky-ish thing. "All of you men need to leave. Now."

They laughed until their mother shooed them out. "Get out of here, boys. You, too, Bill."

As he left the room, John's father called out, "I like Lori. She's a keeper."

The noise moved down the hall and the women settled in. "Now maybe we can get something planned," said his mother.

"Planned?" asked John, concerned. "It's not an invasion."

"Of course it is," said Julie. "You don't think we'd leave all of this important stuff up to you, do you? You'd just screw it up."

"Obviously," muttered Opal.

John's nervousness grew the longer he listened to the women. Finally, he said, "Can't I just go over and be nice to her?"

"Does she want you going over?" asked Becky.

"Well, no. But when I do, she lets me stay and help her harvest zucchini."

"Harvest time will be over soon, son," his mother pointed out. "Then what?"

"Then she'll be going back to New York," said Opal. "We can't wait that long."

"Yes. We have to do something now." John's mother lifted her finger to her mouth. The others were quiet and watched her. John felt very much like a little boy at the moment, and he didn't like it. Finally, she smiled and looked at John. "Do you happen to know Lori's mother's name? Or have her phone number?"

"Her name is Evelyn Scott, but I don't know her number."

Julie patted his hand again. "Where does she live?"

"Schenectady. New York."

His mother smiled. "That's it, then."

John began to grow light-headed. He feared he was beginning to hyperventilate. "What's it? What are you going to do?"

"Call information, get her number, and call. That's all."

"That's all?" John groaned. "Never mind. I can do this on my own. Forget I came over."

"Too late." Becky pulled out her cell phone and handed it to John. "Here, punch in Lori's number."

"What am I going to say to her?"

"You're not going to say a thing. I am."

He balked until Becky pushed his shoulder. "Do it."

He punched in the numbers and handed the phone back to Becky, trying to take several deep breaths so the light-headedness would fade. It helped a little, and gave him something to focus on while he listened to Becky cheerfully chat with Lori and invite her to the Peach Days Community Symphony performance at two that afternoon.

His head still spinning, he wondered why on earth he had ever turned to his family for help.

Look at the havoc they'd wrought in less than an hour.

John was completely out of the loop.

His mother was going to befriend Lori's mother.

And his pregnant sister-in-law had a date with his girlfriend.

Chapter Twenty-Five

"Thanks. I had a great time," said Lori as they left the courthouse. "The music did me good."

Becky smiled at her. "I'm so glad you came."

"Thanks for inviting me."

Becky had given her a ride over. And she had just as much trouble getting behind the wheel with her huge belly this time as before.

"How can you even drive?"

"Because I'm too stubborn not to." She started the car and turned toward Lori's neighborhood. "Plus my feet are too swollen to walk."

They drove in silence for a moment. Becky shot her a glance. Then another.

"What?" asked Lori.

"I'm just wondering . . . how are things going with John?"

Lori looked at Becky, huge as a blimp. "When are you due again?"

Becky groaned. "I still have a little over three weeks—and don't you dare change the subject on a grouchy pregnant woman."

"Did he ask you to do this?"

"Are you kidding? Of course not! It freaked him out that I called you. But I had to know how you feel about him."

Lori sighed. "I'll be leaving soon. I need to keep my distance and not get any more involved with John right now."

"So you admit you are involved, then."

Lori sighed again. "I like John very much."

"Do you love him?"

Words caught in her throat. Hurt rose within her. She couldn't go there. How could she tell Becky she loved John, but still had to leave him? "I don't want to talk about it."

"If you love him, why don't you allow yourself to be with him?"

"That's not what I said."

"Oh, Lori, I can see it in your eyes. Every time you look at him, I can see it. And every time he looks at you, he glows."

The hurt threatened to overwhelm her. She didn't know how to make Becky understand without telling her the truth—and she could never reveal her secret. "Becky, please. I can't talk about it. It's not an easy decision, but one I feel is my only option."

"Okay." It was Becky's turn to sigh. "But if you need someone to talk to, I'm a good listener."

"*Now* what are you doing?" asked John, feeling totally out of control. What had he started when he'd called his father earlier? The Walker family troops had been mobilized. Everyone had gone home with their assignments.

And his mother had just picked up the telephone again. Luckily there'd been no answer at Lori's mom's house earlier, and he was hoping his own mother had given up her silly quest.

Not that he didn't trust her. But he didn't trust her.

"I'm just calling a friend," his mother reassured him, motioning for him to sit at the kitchen table.

When he did, she set a piece of his favorite homemade pie—peach—in front of him.

He looked up at her and frowned. "Mom, I'm not six years old. You can't bribe me with pie anymore."

"Shhh." She placed her finger to her lips. "It's ringing."

If his mother was calling her best friend, Diane, then he was going to have to listen to her recite his own love-life fiasco. Diane already knew every intimate detail of the Walker family life, he was sure.

Frowning, John wondered if the symphony was over yet. What had Becky said to Lori? What had Lori said to Becky? And had Becky taken Lori home yet?

Waiting was driving him nuts. Being out of control was driving him even more nuts. His family drove him the most nuts of all.

He lifted the fork and took a bite of pie. It was pretty good, so he took another. He might as well enjoy something tonight.

"Hi," his mother said. "My name is Irene Walker."

John looked her way. She wouldn't need to introduce herself to Diane. So who was she calling? Which friend would need an introduction?

"May I please speak with Evelyn Scott?"

She was calling Lori's mother! John dropped his fork. *"Mom!"*

His mother ignored him. "Oh, I'm so glad I reached you. I'm John Walker's mother. He's been dating your daughter, Lori. . . . Yes, we're thrilled about it, too. Lori is a delightful girl. We all adore her."

He sat there in disbelief, listening to snippets of conversation from his mother's end and guessing at Lori's mother's reactions. He realized he truly was caught in a nightmare and there seemed to be no way out.

"Oh, yes, he always got very good grades. . . . You should have seen how cute he was! . . . He went on a mission to Sweden. . . . He's an Eagle Scout."

He groaned. "Mother! Stick to the subject!"

Calmly, without even glancing in his direction, his mother said, "I am sticking to the subject, dear."

Unable to listen to any more, he left the room and drifted into the family room, dropping his body into the couch next to his father. He tried to focus on the game on TV.

"Hi, son. What's your mother doing?"

"I don't want to talk about it."

His father raised an eyebrow.

"She's talking to Lori's mother."

His father laughed. "Women are very good at this romance thing. Just leave it all up to the mothers and sisters-in-law and Lori will be yours in no time."

"Do you really believe that, Dad?"

"Not really. But it's a fact of life that once you fall in love with a woman, you have to pretend to believe it or you'll never have any peace."

"Great, Dad. You're making it sound more appealing all the time."

A few minutes later, his mother came in, smiling. "It's all arranged. Lori's mother is in."

"What did she say?" John practically growled.

"Don't worry, dear. It's all taken care of."

"That's it? You're not going to tell me anything?"

"No, I'm not. Now run along home. I'll need to talk to Becky when she gets back and I don't want you around."

With another growl, another eye roll, and a shake of his head, he got up. "I can't take any more of this dating by proxy. I'm outta here."

That night, as Lori snuggled into her bed under just a sheet—it was still too warm for blankets—she couldn't get her conversation with Becky out of her mind. John liked her, wanted to be with her, still loved her.

She'd done everything she could to distract herself. She'd played Solitaire—with real cards, even—on the kitchen table. She'd watched an old favorite, *Casablanca,* on television, but this time the ending was too sad, too similar to the plane she'd be boarding soon, not with a husband, but with her tattered dreams of a happy life.

Now she was trying to lose herself in a good novel. Only she couldn't get past the first five pages, though she'd been reading for nearly an hour.

When her phone rang and she saw it was her mother, she was glad for the distraction. "Hi, Mom. How are things in New York?"

Lori relaxed as her mother brought her up-to-date on her latest escapades as Relief Society president, the ward gossip, and Greg's dating life.

"Lori, honey." Her mother paused. "It's time for you to get on with your own future."

"That certainly came out of the blue. What are you talking about, Mom?"

"About you and your young man there in Utah."

"John? What about him?"

"I want to know how you feel about John Wayne Walker."

"I'm—" Lori stopped, not sure how much to share.

"Tell me the truth, Lori Elaine Scott. Are you in love with him?"

Lori hesitated for a second, but the need to have her mother soothe her pain overcame her need to keep silent. "Yes."

"Why, that's wonderful."

"It would be, except he wants children." Lori sighed. "Six of them."

"Oh, dear." Lori could hear the excitement fade from her mother's voice. "That does present a problem."

"Exactly."

"But nothing that can't be worked out." It had apparently only been a momentary lull in optimism. "People who can't have children get married all the time, Lori. Just tell him the truth. He'll understand. Maybe you could adopt."

"He wants his own children, not someone else's." She wished she was numb to the sensation of her heart being shredded.

"Have you asked him?"

"Of course I haven't. I don't need to."

"Honey, you need to give him the chance to make his own choice. You can't give up on love based on an assumption. What if you're wrong? What if he's an even better man than you think?"

"I can't tell him, Mom. And I can't adopt."

"Why not? Adoption is a perfectly viable option."

But adoption wouldn't give John a daughter who looked just like her. "He's made it crystal clear what he wants."

"Listen, honey. There's more to a marriage than the children you bring into it. And there's more to your cold feet than just your infertility. I think you're too scared to trust a man because of your father."

"Oh, please, not Dad again." Why did everyone keep bringing him up? She just wanted to forget him. But even as she had the thought, she wondered if there was some truth to her mother's words. Was she still—like Agatha's Spade and Hope Garden Club friend—stuck in the first phase of grieving? Did she have cold feet because of the hurt caused by her father?

"Please forgive him so you can get on with your own life, your own happiness. Your father has repented and paid the price. It was hard for him; he was out of the Church for several years."

"He replaced me with three other kids."

"Oh, honey. He never replaced you. He loves you with all his heart. He calls me all the time asking how he can reconnect."

"Sure he does. To soothe his guilty conscience."

"Give him a break, Lori. He may have made the first mistake and started this rift, but you've made it bigger over the years. Not all men can be trusted, but there are trustworthy men out there who can be. Your father let us down, but your Grandpa Scott never did. Not ever. Not even once."

"No, he didn't," Lori admitted, tears stinging her eyes as she fingered the necklace he'd given her so many years before.

"Your father made your teenage years hard, but now you're choosing to let him make the rest of your life hard. You're a smart girl, Lori. Make a smart choice."

"What about the Hideous H's?"

Her mother chuckled. "You mean like . . . healing? Happiness? Heaven on earth? Hardly hideous."

It was no use arguing with her mother. Still fingering the necklace, remembering the calm feeling Grandpa Scott had always carried with him, her heart softened. "How did you keep from getting bitter, Mom?"

"Are you kidding? He left me for another woman. Of course I was bitter. And angry. But I finally had to look at some hard truths and learn some tough lessons. I had to see that I was part of the problem we were having. And I realized I had to get on with my life, and the only way I could do that was to forgive your father. And Fiona Bennett. I had to repent for harboring bitterness and hatred against both of them." Her voice grew husky with emotion. "And I had to repent for helping plant that same bitterness in my daughter's heart, something I've regretted for a long, long time."

"If you're over it, if you've forgiven Dad, why haven't you ever remarried?"

Her mother laughed. “Because I’ve never met the right man. If I ever do, I won’t hesitate at the chance to love again. I advise you not to lose any opportunities, either.”

“You come home straight after work. How are you supposed to meet a new guy?”

“Greg told me he can place an ad for me on eHarmony. I may just take him up on his offer.”

Lori laughed and wiped away a tear. “Be sure to mention that they’ll never win an argument with you. Ever.”

“I don’t plan on arguing with the next guy. One of the things I learned.”

“That ought to do it,” said Serena, hands on her hips and a smile on her face.

Lori surveyed the stand they’d crudely constructed out of pieces of lumber given to them by Serena’s father. It was little more than a square table with a place for a sign on the front and a place for a large box of zucchini on top. They pulled several full boxes onto the grass next to the stand. “It won’t win any awards.”

“But it’s good enough. And now—for the sign.” Serena pulled out five permanent markers and wrote the word “FREE,” in elegant calligraphy on a large poster board which she nailed to the front. She added a sketch of a zucchini.

“Hey, you’re a good artist.”

“I like to draw.” Serena shrugged. “And I’m majoring in art at the university.”

“I can’t even draw a straight line.”

Serena laughed. “Do you see any straight lines on this thing? That skill is not a prerequisite for an art degree.”

“Now for the zucchini.” Lori kicked the edge of one of the full boxes. “Okay, here’s the moment of truth. Will this thing hold?”

“If not, we’ll have created a big mess.”

Laughing, they hefted the heavy box onto the top of the stand—and waited. The stand wobbled, but held.

“All right. Looks like you’re in business.” Serena tossed the markers into her large “I’m a Purple Person” bag.

"I forgot to ask—how's it going with the salsa guy?"

Serena smiled and batted her eyelashes. "He is totally within my power."

"I have no doubt of that. I just hope you're using your power for good, and not for evil," Lori teased.

"We're going out Friday. You and John want to join us?"

Lori hadn't told Serena about the new developments in her relationship, but it was time. "Actually, John and I aren't seeing much of each other anymore. We're back to just being friends."

"Ha. I'd like to see anyone go from romance back to just friends. I don't think it can be done."

"Well, we're doing it."

"Sure you are. And I'm a Chihuahua." She gave Lori a hug. "I've got to leave to get ready for my cousin's *quinceañera.*"

"Quin-see-*what?*"

"*Quinceañera.* It's a Mexican thing. We have a fancy, dress-up party when girls turn fifteen. There'll be lots of food and dancing." Her eyes sparkled with mischief. "Both with salsa, of course."

"Of course." Lori smiled. "Have fun."

As Serena climbed into her car, Lori opened an umbrella and stuck it into the box of zucchini to keep the vegetables from wilting. The mid-September sun was still hot in the afternoon, though the evenings were beginning to cool.

The vegetables would probably do okay, but she was getting more sunburnt here than she'd ever gotten in New York. There was something about the sun here in Utah that seemed hotter.

Lori carried her hammer into the house. In the kitchen, she poured herself a cold glass of water and pressed it against her warm forehead. Out on the patio, she turned on the fan and sat under the breeze.

Ah. That felt better already.

Charles's yard was very relaxing. The garden was still in its last bloom, and she was enjoying being a part of the harvest, though she would never have suspected it when she first moved here.

Nearly every last bit of harvested zucchini was now in the front yard. If Serena was right, it would be gone soon. There were more on the vines, but she'd given up keeping pace with them.

Picking up the romance novel Serena had lent her, she read until the breeze from the ceiling fan cooled too much for comfort—about a hundred pages. Standing and stretching, she turned off the fan and went back inside.

Feeling good about having dealt with the zucchini problem, she looked out the living room window to check the stand.

The stand was gone.

Someone had taken it! Stolen it! Swiped it!

She yanked open the front door just in time to see two other disturbing things.

John Wayne Walker's truck was pulling into her driveway.

And there were two more boxes of zucchini on her lawn than what she'd started with. Someone had stolen her stand—and left their zucchini for her!

Chapter Twenty-Six

John turned off his truck and climbed out.

Lori was walking across her front lawn—which was littered with boxes of zucchini—a distressed look on her face.

Concerned, he crossed to her. "Lori, what's wrong?"

Apparently speechless, she motioned to four boxes of zucchini on her lawn.

"What happened?"

"Serena and I built a stand—and someone stole it!" she wailed. "And then they left me their zucchini."

He couldn't help it; he laughed.

"It's not funny."

He pulled her into his arms and she clung to him. "It took us two hours to build that stand. Serena even painted the word 'free' on the front of it."

"So someone took the *free* stand and left their zucchini for you?" He couldn't help but laugh again. "That's hilarious."

She pulled loose from his embrace, apparently offended, but he still couldn't stop laughing.

"This is zucchini season, honey. It's a war zone. There is no Geneva convention for gardeners."

She started to smile. "I suppose, given enough time, even I may laugh at this."

"I hope so. Otherwise, you may have to go to garden therapy or something."

She snorted. "You're not as funny as you think you are."

He grinned and touched her chin. "But you're smiling."

She nodded. "So maybe you're funnier than I think you are."

"Okay," he said. "Let's get rid of this stuff."

"How? You almost got me arrested doorbell ditching."

"Let's drive it to the shelter. They can feed homeless people some of those zucchini tacos."

It took them thirty minutes to drop off the boxes. As he drove toward her house, Lori touched his arm. "Would you drive back up in the canyon so I can see the leaves again? Please?"

Hiding his delight, he nodded and turned toward the canyon. It was too early for sunset, but he was heartened by the fact that she wanted to go back where they'd had such an intimate conversation before.

When he parked, she stayed on her side of the truck. He didn't reach for her hand. Not yet. He'd let her make the moves tonight so he didn't spook her back into "just friends" mode.

"I love the vivid colors up here."

"I have to ask you. Are the leaves on the trees in New York black or something?"

She shot him a look that clearly asked, "Are you crazy?"

"I mean, that's all I see you wear, so I was just wondering," he teased. "Maybe New York is a black-and-white state, all one-dimensional."

She snorted. He loved her little snort. It was a delicate thing, more like a little sneeze. She used it when she was trying to indicate her disdain or disgust, but he thought it was cute. In fact, he liked to see if he could provoke a snort.

"New York has lots of beautifully colored trees," she said defensively. "And I wear lots of other colors."

He chuckled and motioned toward her outfit. "Prove it."

She looked down at her T-shirt, shorts, and sandals—all black—and pulled a face at him. "I have other colors at home."

"Prove it," he repeated.

"Back in New York, I have a closet full of colorful clothes."

He laughed at the indignant look on her face. "Whatever."

"Are you prejudiced against the color black?"

"Not at all. It looks ravishingly gorgeous on you."

She snorted again. "You are so full of it."

He smiled. He'd succeeded in getting another cute little snort. "You're probably right."

She turned back to the leaves, gazing out the windshield, and they sat in silence again. Finally, she said, "Do you ever wonder how God invented colors?"

"I've wondered if we helped."

"If we did, then I helped invent the color—"

"Black?" he teased.

"Nope. I helped invent red. It's my favorite."

"Shush your pretty mouth before someone hears you! Don't ever say that around these parts."

"Why?"

"Up here, it's got to be USU blue, not U of U red. You could get seriously hurt talking like that. Think of your safety, girl."

"Girl, huh?" She snorted again. "I remember when I turned twelve, my father bought me a dozen red balloons." She paused and shook her head. "I haven't thought about that forever. He tied my present to the balloons."

He was glad her voice didn't hold any bitterness at the moment. "What was the present?"

"Another locket to hang on the necklace from Grandpa Scott."

"Do you still have it?" he asked.

"It had pictures of him and my mom in it. After he left, I put it in my mother's jewelry box."

She didn't say more, and he didn't push.

After long moments, she turned to him. "John, do you think it's possible for people to change? Really change?"

At the wistful sound in her voice, he started to reach for her hand, then stopped himself. "Yes. I do. Very much so."

She sighed. "Can we get out of the truck for awhile?"

Feeling very tender toward her, he said, "Sure."

She opened the door. He joined her in front of the truck.

"I feel like I could stay here forever, looking at this scene. It's so beautiful and peaceful. Just like I feel peaceful around you, and when I'm in church."

Just like he felt warm and happy when he was around her.

That emotion began to swell within his heart. An emotion he'd never felt before—never recognized as being possible—spread through him, filling him, body and soul, with warmth and light and . . . love.

Finally, he knew without a doubt.

He was in love with Lori. A soul mate, love-nearly-at-first-sight, eternal kind of love.

Is it time? he prayed silently. *Right now?*

Yes. The answer whispered through his soul.

He was confused. *She hasn't regained her testimony.* The impression of peace came again, stronger, as if the testimony would come.

What if I scare her off again?

The whispering voice brought peace to his heart. *It is time.*

He'd learned on his mission that if the Spirit said the time was right to say something, it meant the other person was ready to hear it. He prayed that was the case with Lori.

Turning to her, he dropped to one knee and took her hand.

"Lori, I love you with all my heart." His voice shook with the emotion flooding his senses. "Will you marry me?"

Stunned, Lori said, "I thought we were just friends."

"You know we've both felt more for each other than that from the beginning," John said, still on one knee, both his hands warm around hers.

Her heart ached. She wanted to marry John with all her heart, but she couldn't. Not when he wanted children so much and she couldn't give them to him.

He stood, still holding her hands in his. "Lori, you are one of the most beautiful people I've ever known. When I'm around you, I'm a complete person. When I'm around you, I want to be my best. I don't want you to leave. I don't know if I can survive without you. You have become as necessary to me as the very air I breathe. I need you. I love you."

Her love for John swelled until it burned against her eyes. As the tears spilled onto her cheeks—tears of love, of joy, of pain—the truth of her feelings escaped in a whisper. "I love you, too."

"Then marry me. We'll be good together."

"I . . . can't." She could hear the anguish in her voice.

He pulled her into his arms and she fit perfectly, as if she'd always been meant to nestle there, sheltered and loved.

"You are the woman of my dreams. You are everything I've been searching for . . . forever."

He wiped a tear away from her cheek, gently.

"I can't be who you want, John."

"You don't understand, Lori. You are already exactly who I want, just the way you are."

She had never wanted anything more in her life.

I can have him if I say yes.

The thought exploded within her.

She could have him.

In that moment, she wanted more than anything to be with John. She wanted to marry him. To spend her life with him.

She couldn't walk away from him. Not from everything she'd always wanted.

Her mother had said Lori needed to tell him about her infertility, but as she looked into his beautiful blue eyes and saw the love there, she realized she could never say the words. If she did, she might see that love fade. He might leave her. And she couldn't deal with that.

She could say yes . . . and pretend she'd never known about her infertility.

Gentle as love, John raised her face toward him. "Please marry me, Lori."

"Yes," she said, joy filling her as she made her decision. "Yes, I will."

He picked her up and swung her around, hugging her tightly, laughing happily. Then he set her down and kissed her, gently at first, and then more hungrily.

She wrapped her arms around him and kissed him back.

She'd waited for so long for someone to truly love. For someone to truly love her.

Perhaps someday God would forgive her for not telling John something that would bring him so much pain down the road.

Perhaps someday she'd forgive herself.

Chapter Twenty-Seven

Once again, John waited in dread on Dawn's porch with hurtful news.

When Dawn opened the door and saw him, her face lit up. "Come in, John. It's so good to see you."

She opened her door wide and he went in, dreading this talk more than any of the others he'd had with her. She took his arm and, smiling, walked with him to the kitchen. "I made a peach pie. Your favorite. I was planning on bringing it over to your place, but this is even better."

"Thanks, Dawn, but I can't stay for pie." He stopped and looked down at her. This time he was just going to spit out the words, because they would never get easier to say, or to hear, and he didn't want to prolong the hurt.

"Oh." Her smile faded and she pulled back her arm from his and stood there, looking vulnerable. "Is anything wrong?"

"Dawn, I care too much about you to let you learn about this from anyone else." He took a deep breath. "I'm going to marry Lori."

Her eyes widened, and she blinked. Hard. As if trying not to cry. She turned to the window for a moment, then straightened her shoulders and turned back. "Thank you for telling me in person, John. When is the wedding?"

"We haven't chosen a date yet."

She fingered the material on her sleeve. "I have something to tell you, too. I'm moving back home for awhile. My dad's leukemia is back and my mom needs help nursing him."

"Oh, Dawn, I'm so sorry to hear that." If guilt could multiply, his just had.

"Thanks. Me, too."

"And you just started teaching. What will you do about your students?"

"Another teacher's already been hired."

In this moment when she was so valiantly trying to be both brave and gracious, though he knew her heart was breaking from both his news and her father's condition, John admired her more than ever. She was a good woman, but not the woman for him. "Good luck with your father. I'll pray for him."

She nodded. "And good luck in your marriage. I hope you're happy."

The conversation was just plain surreal. "Thanks."

She smiled, though it was forced. "Now, I really need to get back to my class work. I've got a lot to do before I meet with the new teacher tomorrow."

"Oh, sure. I didn't mean to disturb you."

He found himself on the porch, feeling sad for what might have been, even while he rejoiced in what he had with Lori.

He hoped Dawn found someone who could love her the way he loved Lori. She deserved a happy ending, too.

"Two calls in one week," Lori's mother teased her. "I feel honored."

Lori smiled. She was looking forward to her mother's excitement at her engagement news—but dreading the inevitable discussion about whether she'd told John about her infertility. And, even worse, if her mother didn't bring up the subject, Lori would have to. She couldn't leave an end like that dangling loose. "I have some good news for you, Mom."

"I know and I'm so excited. I can hardly wait for you to move back in with me. Three weeks, right?"

"Well, that's not the news. Not exactly."

"What is not exactly? You can't move back into your Manhattan apartment because you sublet it, so where else would you stay? Of course you'll stay with me."

"It's not about where I'll be staying." Lori laughed. "Well, actually, I guess it is, but—"

"When is that gardening column guy getting back? Has he decided to party a little longer on the Great Wall of China?" Her mother sounded suspicious, like Charles had some sort of evil plan to stay away just so she couldn't see her daughter.

Lori chuckled. "Charles will get back the second week in October, as planned, but I'm not leaving Utah then."

"Why not? Have you gotten another job?" Her mother gasped and her voice lowered. "You're staying because of the fireman, aren't you?"

"He asked me to marry him. And I said yes."

Her mother actually squealed with happiness. "Oh, that's absolutely marvelous. I knew he'd understand when you told him. He must be a really great guy. I love him already."

"He is a really great guy." Here it was—the part of the discussion Lori had been dreading. "But I didn't tell him."

"You didn't tell him? Lori, what are you going to do when he finds out? Don't you think he'll be upset?"

"We'll find out together. And I'll be as surprised and as disappointed as he is. We'll deal with it later. Together."

"Oh, Lori, honey, you're just asking for trouble. Things like this have a way of getting out at the worst possible time and biting you right in the fanny."

"Mom, I'm asking you, please, not to tell John that you or I already knew about my infertility. Please."

Her mother's voice was disapproving. "You want me to lie?"

"No. Just don't volunteer the information."

"What if he asks me straight out?"

"Please, Mom? I'm begging you."

"You need to tell him, Lori. You don't want to start your relationship with a lie. That's not a good foundation for a marriage."

"I don't want to lose him."

Her mother sighed. "I won't tell him, Lori. That's your job. But I think you're making a big mistake."

"Thanks, Mom. I really appreciate it. Now are you going to be happy for me or not? I'm getting married, after all."

"I am very happy." Her mother must have accepted what Lori had asked because she sounded excited again. "When's the wedding? And where?"

"We haven't decided yet on the when, but the where is probably here in Brigham City."

"Let me know the instant you decide so Greg and I can get airline tickets. And I'll want to throw you a reception here in Schenectady, too, of course."

Lori smiled. "Of course."

"When do I get to meet the groom?"

"I'll ask him tomorrow night. He's taking me to buy a ring."

"Oh, honey, that's so exciting. Be sure to e-mail me a picture of it. And of him. And of you two together. And of you wearing the ring."

Lori smiled, happier than she'd been in ages, but still with a nagging doubt in the back of her mind. She couldn't tell John now. Of course she couldn't. She'd already been over that. She didn't feel good about it, but this was how it needed to be.

For everyone's sake.

Her mother said, hesitantly. "Lori, you need to invite your father, too."

Her father was the last person she wanted there—him, Fiona, and the Hideous H's. "How sweet. We could sit around and talk about old times. I could tell the sisters how their mom and dad met."

"It's not those girls' fault. Let it go. It's time."

"Just like that?"

"Yes."

"Without him even ever saying he's sorry?"

"Yes."

Tears burned her eyes. "I can't do that."

Her mother's sigh slapped her in the face.

John held the door of the jewelry store open for Lori. She smiled up at him as she walked in. His sister-in-law Julie had told him to make sure to ask for a certain saleslady who was only in on Friday afternoons, but he'd be darned if he could remember her name.

Lori stopped at two octagonal cases. He recognized the Hummel and Lladró figurines inside, but only because his mother had collected them for years. Lori traced her finger lightly along the glass. Perhaps she'd want to collect them, too. The thought made him smile. Until he saw the price tag on one. "Holy smokes. I had no idea these were so expensive," he said.

"That's nothing. There's the really expensive stuff," Lori said, pointing to a U-shaped case. The right side held Rolexes and Omegas.

Glass display cases filled with more Hummel and Lladró figures and sterling silver necklaces outlined the perimeter of the store, while additional cases were arranged throughout the center of the store, creating a maze of sorts.

A salesman came up and smiled. "My name is Bruce. Is there anything I can help you with?"

Probably in his twenties, the guy was the same height as John, but looked like he spent all his off-hours at the gym.

"We'd like to buy a ring." John squeezed Lori's hand. More specifically, a very large, incredibly impressive, more-than-ten-cows ring to top anything his brothers had given any of their wives.

"How exciting." Bruce smiled warmly. "Have you set the date?"

"Not yet," said Lori.

"But soon," said John, not wanting to put it off.

When Lori smiled up at him, joy filled him. He was still amazed that this beautiful woman wanted him in her life as much as he wanted her in his.

"Would you like a matching set? Or would you prefer to choose your engagement ring and customize your wedding band?"

"Customize," said John, quickly.

Lori laughed. "Whatever the man says."

Bruce stepped behind one of the long cases. "Which cut do you prefer?"

And that began an endless round of questions and answers. Bruce brought them rings that fit what Lori and John wanted. Trays of rings were brought out and set on top of the cases. Lori and John studied each one, and she tried on quite a few, but so far nothing had brought the kind of reaction he was hoping for.

And then she gasped.

The salesman smiled, his hand hovering. "This one?"

She nodded and whispered, "I love it."

The ring was pretty, but the diamond was pathetically small compared to what John had in mind. "Are you sure you wouldn't prefer a diamond that's a little . . . larger?"

"Now that's something I don't hear often," said the salesman as he handed the ring to John. "Go ahead. Put it on your lovely bride and see how it looks on her finger."

John took Lori's hand and realized his own was trembling slightly. He slipped the ring on her ring finger.

Lori held up her hand. "It's beautiful, John. I love it."

"It would be more beautiful with a bigger stone."

She laughed. "I'm okay with this one, but if you want a bigger stone, who am I to complain?" She turned back to Bruce with a smile. "Give the man a larger stone."

"How large of a stone would you like?"

"At least one carat in an excellent quality diamond." That ought to do it. He didn't pay much attention to engagement talk, but he had picked up on the fact that the largest diamond any of his sisters-in-law had was three-quarters of a carat.

The salesman's eyes lit up. "Our jeweler is on the premises today. There's usually a wait of two to three days, but I like your style. I'll see if he can reset it right now, if you'd like."

John smiled. "Yes. Thanks."

As the salesman disappeared into the back of the store, Lori turned to John and touched his lips with her finger. "You are so funny."

"Hey, I have to live with my brothers for a long time. And when they're all telling eight-cow stories, I want my wife to have a ten-cow ring on her finger."

"Ah, I understand. You want me to have the best cow story at your family dinner table." She laughed, then kissed him. "I do love you, you know."

"I know," he said, a little breathless as he pulled her close. "And I love you, too. Very much."

As they waited for the ring to be reset, they chose a wedding band for John, then wandered the store, admiring the expensive pieces of jewelry. They'd nearly made it around the perimeter when the door opened behind them and a familiar voice said, "There they are."

"That sounds suspiciously like Clint." John frowned and turned to discover not just Clint, but all three of his brothers, their wives, and his parents.

Clint grinned as he punched John on the shoulder. Hard. "Julie just happened to mention that you two were buying your rings today, so we decided to share this special moment with you."

Lori was much more gracious than John felt. With a warm smile, she said, "I'm so glad you came. We just chose an engagement ring."

As if on cue, the salesman returned, handed the now very large, incredibly impressive ring to John, who smiled and slipped it on Lori's finger.

The ring exceeded all John's expectations. This wasn't a ten-cow ring—there were at least twelve cows grazing there.

The wives oohed and aahed as Lori held out her hand to show it off, and he heard a chorus of "It's beautiful!" "It's so big!" "Wow! I love it!"

Lori's smile was beautiful to behold.

John turned to his brothers and grinned. "I win."

Lori had done something she never had before, something she'd never thought she would: she'd read the entire Book of Mormon.

Though she'd finished it an hour ago, she couldn't stop rereading the verses in Moroni. Chapter ten. Verses four and five.

Afraid to ask, afraid not to, she bought herself more time by reading the words yet again.

And when ye shall receive these things, I would exhort you that ye would ask God, the Eternal Father, in the name of Christ, if these things are not true; and if ye shall ask with a sincere heart, with real intent, having faith in Christ, he will manifest the truth of it unto you, by the power of the Holy Ghost. And by the power of the Holy Ghost ye may know the truth of all things.

Carefully, Lori closed Charles's Book of Mormon and placed it gently on the edge of the bed beside her. The worn brown leather looked right at home on Charles's old-fashioned, faded, flowered bedspread.

As a child, she had walked those many steps to the front of the chapel and borne her testimony—just like so many other little kids on fast and testimony Sunday. Back then, she knew the Church was true, knew the Book of Mormon was true, knew her family would last forever.

But in truth, she'd come to realize that she'd known nothing that seemed to matter after her father left. When he'd walked out the door and turned his back on their family, she'd lost everything important to her, especially her hope and faith. Her father had taken many things from her, but she could see now, with a stab of remorse, that she had robbed herself of many more things because of her anger. She'd done what it said in the old saying: She'd cut off her nose to spite her face.

Now she wasn't sure which would be worse, if the Book of Mormon was true . . . or if it wasn't.

Finally, she could put off the prayer no longer. With her heart pounding, her hands cold, her fears swirling through her, Lori slid off the bed. Kneeling, she opened the Book of Mormon to Moroni's challenge and read it one last time. She took a deep breath, and, holding the book in her hands, closed her eyes. She poured out her heart to the Father she'd turned her back on just like her earthly father had turned his back on her, the Father who had always been there for her.

Heavenly Father, I really want to know if this book is true. I have read the entire thing, with a sincere desire to know if it is true. I have felt the Spirit as I've read—Thy spirit of peace and comfort. Please, Father, if this book is true, let me know beyond any doubt, for I have so many doubts.

As she continued to pray, a peaceful warmth settled in her chest, filling her very breath with confirmation. The Spirit was so strong it couldn't be contained in her body and flowed in tears down her cheeks. Warmth and love touched every cell in her body, filled every part of her aching soul, dispelled every doubt.

She prayed her thanks while the peaceful feeling calmed the very tears it had brought. It was the same calm, peaceful feeling she remembered from her childhood. The same calm, peaceful feeling she'd recognized and cherished when she'd been with John at church. The same calm, peaceful feeling she'd come to desire with all her heart.

She was in the light once again and never wanted to leave it.

Once again, Lori *knew* the truth.

THE GARDEN GURU

Dear Ms. Scott: I have a gardening dilemma. Actually, a life dilemma. Last year, I don't know why (yes, I do—to impress her), I told my mother-in-law I grew some tomatoes, when I really bought them at a farmer's market. Now she wants to know where I bought my plants, and I don't know what to tell her. Help! (Name Withheld on Request)

Dear Name Withheld: I hate these kinds of dilemmas. It's always so much easier to see the solution for someone else's life than your own, isn't it? You could tell her the truth and face her disappointment. Or you could say you've decided gardening was too much work and so this year you're just going to buy your tomatoes at the farmer's market. Open your phone book and find the name of a nursery to give her. If you live around Perry, I'd recommend Alpine Nursery. In the meantime, which farmer's market do you shop at? I can always use some good tomatoes . . .

Chapter Twenty-Eight

A week later, Lori waited for John just inside the Old Grist Mill sandwich shop, watching through the glass doors. Clouds had gathered overhead and a brisk breeze had sprung up. Luckily she'd brought a light jacket, but John had still insisted on going for the truck so she wouldn't get chilled.

She loved being pampered and cherished.

As John's truck approached, she smiled. Just the sight of his truck was enough to brighten her day. In the two weeks since he'd proposed, they'd been together every day he'd been off shift, and she still couldn't get enough of him. She didn't know if she ever would.

When he parked in front, she climbed in and quickly shut the door. "Whew. Does the weather always change this fast?"

"There's a saying in Utah that if you don't like the weather, just wait twenty minutes."

"That sounds about right." She scooted over to the middle seat. "So . . . where to now?"

"And ruin the surprise? No way." He grinned.

"I know where you live. I still have zucchini on the vine. I will bring you boxes of zucchini and doorbell ditch them if you don't tell me."

"Okay, okay. Don't do that! I'll tell." He laughed. "Quinn and Tricia invited us over for more pie and cards."

"Sounds fun." She snuggled closer to him and pulled her seat belt tight. She lifted her hand to admire the gorgeous ring on her finger again.

"Like it?" he asked, his voice soft.

"Very much." She looked over at him and smiled. "I like you very much, too."

"The feeling is definitely mutual." As he turned the wheel and pulled out onto Main Street, his cell phone played. "Forget that," he said. "I don't want to be disturbed tonight."

"Sounds good to me."

He slipped his arm around her shoulders. "So did you think about January eleventh as a possible date?"

That was his parents' anniversary, and he had thought it would be sweet if he and Lori got married that day, too. She liked that tender, romantic streak in him.

His phone rang again. "Persistent, aren't they?"

"Maybe it's important."

He handed her his phone. "Who is it?"

"It's Roy." She handed it back.

He pulled up to a red light and flipped his phone open. "What's up, Roy? . . . Are you kidding? Isn't this, like, a month early? . . . Just a week? Really? . . . You're a father? Poor defenseless little girl," he teased, but his voice softened. "How are they? . . . Okay? Good."

Becky had given birth. Lori had mixed feelings. She was glad for Becky, who had become a dear friend already, but she had to beat back the familiar sadness of knowing she would never—not ever—experience the joy Becky had.

"Congratulations, bro! We'll be right over." With a grin, he replaced his phone. "They want us to come see the baby."

When the red light changed, the truck shot forward.

The drive to the Brigham City Community Hospital took ten minutes, with another ten to park and find the maternity floor. As he drove, Lori called Quinn and Tricia's number to cancel their plans.

When they passed the nursery, John grabbed Lori's hand. "Let's see if she's in here."

He was filled with excitement, an elation he hadn't expected, perhaps because he was with Lori now, and it wouldn't be more than a year or two before they had their own child.

He scanned the bassinets for names. Boy Stoddard. Boy Simpson.

Boy Hullinger. No new Walker babies or even girl babies in the nursery today.

"Hey, John. Lori. Over here."

John looked up. Roy was heading toward them, a huge smile on his face. "The baby's in the room with Becky. Come on."

John shook his head. "We don't want to intrude."

"Are you kidding? Becky wants to show her off. Her family was here earlier and have headed down to the cafeteria. The rest of the Walker clan is on their way. You guys got here just in time to have Becky and the baby all to yourselves."

"We didn't bring our gift," said Lori. "We wanted to get here as fast as we could."

"Don't worry about that. Just come see her." He led the way.

Surprised, John whispered, "We have a gift?"

As she followed Roy, she smiled mischievously. "I bought a gift. And since *we* are now officially a couple, that means *we* have a gift."

"Great." He grinned. "So . . . what did we get her?"

"Some very expensive crib sheets and bumper pads in the pattern Becky said she wanted, but hadn't gotten yet."

"Cool." Not so much the gift she'd gotten for Becky's baby, though that was cool, too, he had no doubt, but the ramifications of what she'd just said. "So does this mean you'll keep track of everyone's birthdays and anniversaries? If so, this couple thing has some unexpected benefits."

She punched him playfully and teased, "On second thought, buy your own gift."

Halfway down the hospital corridor, Roy opened a door.

As John stepped inside the room, he saw Becky lying in the bed, holding her baby in her arms, like some modern-day Madonna. She looked more tired than he'd ever seen her, but also more beautiful. Her long brown hair was pulled back into a simple ponytail and she wasn't wearing any makeup, but she glowed with happiness as she pulled her adoring gaze from the baby in her arms to her visitors.

John leaned over and kissed her cheek. "Congratulations, momma. You look fabulous."

"Yeah, right, sure I do." She nodded. "But nice of you to lie for my benefit."

"Oh, she's beautiful," cooed Lori as she leaned in for a better look. "What are you going to name her?"

"Holli," said Becky, gazing back down at her new baby with such obvious love in her eyes that John choked up.

Roy said, "She was seven pounds, six ounces, and twenty inches long."

John almost laughed at his brother, but there was something reverent about the moment that kept him from doing it.

After a long moment, Becky looked back up at them. "Would you like to hold her?"

When he glanced over at her, Lori smiled. "You first, Uncle John."

Carefully, worried he'd drop her, he lifted the tiny bundle from Becky's arms. He stood and gazed down into her wrinkled, red, beautiful little face. "Look, her eyes are open," he whispered. "She's looking at me."

"All the nurses have commented on how alert she is," Roy said proudly.

Touched by the baby's gaze that seemed to be focused on his face so intently, John whispered, "Hey, little Holli, do you remember me from before?"

She reached up a tiny hand and touched her palm to his cheek, not at all like a spastic newborn baby, and he was overcome with the feeling that, yes, she did know him from before.

Overwhelmed by the sensation, he sank down into the armchair and just looked at her. She pulled her hand back and he wrapped the little blanket around it until she was cocooned again, her dark blue eyes peering at him curiously.

Lori slipped up behind him and put her hands on his shoulders, leaning over to look at the baby, too.

John wasn't sure when the tears started—at some point after Holli had touched his face—but he was rocked to his very core by this tiny new life that hadn't been here before today, that hadn't existed before Roy and Becky had found each other and created a family.

Finally, he turned to look into Lori's eyes, just inches from his, his heart overflowing with love, and whispered, his voice choked with emotion, "I can hardly wait until I hold our baby like this."

Her eyes widened and she squeezed his shoulder as he looked back down at Holli.

This was what life was all about.

Having someone special to love.

And creating a family with that special someone.

Stricken, Lori watched John hold his new niece, and knew again his deep desire for children of his own. The all-too-familiar ache made her tremble. Her body had betrayed her long ago; she would never have a joyous moment after birth. The appendix that had ruptured when she was fourteen had developed into a raging infection, which in turn had damaged her fallopian tubes beyond repair.

The ache didn't dissipate as she took a turn holding Holli, as she and John chatted with Roy and Becky, as John drove her home and held her close, as he told her he loved her and tenderly kissed her good night.

It didn't diminish when she paced the floor, or when she sat for hours on her bed.

Instead, the ache grew stronger, pulling at her insides until she thought she would die. The look on John's face as he'd held little Holli was burned into her mind, haunting her.

Why, God? Why can't I have children? Why would you lead me to a wonderful man who wants them so much when I can't have them?

There were no answers and her tears turned into great heaving sobs of anguish.

Finally, when she could stand the pain no more, she knelt by the bed. In between her sobs, she began to pray.

Father, please help me understand. Help me trust Thee. I am so confused. Please let me know if I am still supposed to marry John.

She waited, still crying, though the tears had stopped shaking her body and simply flowed. There was no answer other than more confusion.

She prayed for an hour, asking variations of the same question, but there was still no answer. Finally, she quit crying. Totally drained and exhausted, still on her knees, Lori began a different prayer.

Father in Heaven . . . Ever since my father left, I have held myself back from trusting Thee. He never came back, even though I prayed for that every night. Now I ask for help in trusting Thee again. Help Thou mine unbelief.

A wisp of peace brushed against her deep despair. It was time, after all these years, to totally trust her Father in Heaven again.

I will do whatever I feel guided to do. She had an impression and one more tear worked its way down her cheek. Feeling drained, she prayed, *Do I need to tell John about my infertility before I marry him?*

Immediately, a great warmth filled her heart, pushing aside the ache, and planting in its place the beautiful peace she loved so much.

Even if John leaves me when he finds out the truth?

The warmth spread from her heart to every cell in her body. She had never known such peace, even as before she had never known such despair.

I thank Thee, Father. Please give me the courage to tell him the truth. And please, please, please soften his heart so he will still love me afterward.

She hoped that her mother was right. Maybe she and John could adopt. Maybe God would bring a child into their lives in some other way. She hoped that was true. Maybe John would even come to forgive her for not telling him the truth in the beginning.

She ended her prayer, knowing without a doubt that she had to tell John the truth. She couldn't marry him unless she did. But if she did tell him, she might not get the chance to marry him.

No matter his response, she owed him the truth.

Even if it cost her everything.

Lori peeked out through the blinds again. John's truck still wasn't there. She'd called him an hour ago and asked him to come over and the minutes in between had stretched out interminably.

This was torture, waiting to tell the man she loved something that might drive him away forever. Why wasn't he here?

She forced herself to take a deep breath. She'd already prayed three times since she called him and she hoped the peaceful feeling she had would last while she spoke the words to John that were going to cause him such great pain.

She heard an engine outside, close, and then it stopped. She peeked out again. John was climbing out of the truck. Now she wished he'd taken more time. She wasn't ready for this.

As her heart fluttered, pumping adrenaline throughout her body, Lori drew in another deep breath. In this moment before she possibly ruined everything between them, she needed to savor the love John still felt for her right now—and the love she felt for this handsome, thoughtful, gentle firefighter.

She'd finally found a true hero—and now she might be driving him away.

He rang the bell, and she sucked in a ragged breath. Nothing could calm her heart now. Not until she'd said the words. This was it.

She opened the door.

"Hi, beautiful." With a smile, he leaned over and kissed her. Gently. That was nearly her undoing. She blinked back tears as he pulled away.

Please, Father, help me not cry.

"I couldn't wait to see you again."

Please help me accept Thy will. "I need to talk to you."

He raised an eyebrow. "Is everything okay?"

Please help him understand. "I need to tell you something."

She took another breath to try to calm herself.

He tilted his head. "You aren't breaking up with me again, are you?"

"Oh, no. Nothing like that." More like he would be breaking up with her.

"Good. I can handle anything else."

Please, Father, help him handle what I feel impressed to tell him.

She took his hand, savoring the feel of his fingers intertwined with hers, creating a memory of his touch.

She led him to Charles's old-fashioned couch where they sat, side by side.

He was beginning to look concerned. "Honey, what is it?"

She looked into his eyes. "John, I love you."

He squeezed her hand. "I love you, too, Lori."

"I have to tell you something before we get married." *Something that may change everything.*

She pulled her gaze away.

"Just say it. You can tell me anything." But already he was sounding unsure.

"I know how much you want children."

"Very much."

She forced herself to look into his eyes again. "I. Can't. Have. Children."

Confusion filled his eyes. "What do you mean?"

"There's a problem with my fallopian tubes, from an infection after my appendix ruptured, and I can't . . ." *Please, Father, help me.* "I will never be able to have children. I am so sorry. I want them as much as you do."

Apparently shell-shocked, John spoke slowly, repeating her words. "You can't ever have children?"

She could see the hurt in his eyes, the disappointment, perhaps even betrayal.

"John, I never meant to hurt anyone, especially not you. I was just too afraid to tell you because I thought you . . . might not . . . want me after I told you."

"I don't know what to say."

His hand loosened slightly, and she instinctively pulled hers away. Gazing at the wall, he was silent for so long that she began to tremble. His emotional distance scared her.

Please, Father, help me. Help us.

"Will I see you again?"

"Of course you will. This doesn't change my feelings for you. I'm just . . . stunned by the news. But we can get through this. Together." He looked at her, his eyes filled with pain, and he took her hand again. "But it's going to take some time for me to think this one through. I'll be honest—it's a shock. I may need a few days to get used to the idea. Is that okay?"

She nodded, wanting to keep repeating her apologies—*I'm so sorry. I never meant to hurt you*—but found she couldn't say anything.

They sat in silence for a long time.

Finally, he squeezed her hand, put an arm around her shoulder, and looked into her eyes. "We'll deal with this. I love you, Lori. I always will."

When she started to cry, he held her and comforted her.

He was doing and saying all the right things, but he couldn't hide the hurt and betrayal in his eyes. When he'd had a chance to think things over, she feared he would realize just how much he wanted children. And then Lori was afraid her worst fears could come true.

She'd lose John's love and respect.

She'd lose his large, loving family.

She'd lose *everything.*

Chapter Twenty-Nine

John didn't know how long he'd driven the mountain roads, but glancing at the clock, he was surprised to see it was nearly nine.

He'd driven, tormented, for three hours.

John was certainly aware eternity was forever and, in the eternal scheme of things, he'd have plenty of time for posterity with Lori. But the thought of having no children here and now ripped his heart in two. And the thought of not having Lori in his life hurt even worse.

He had to talk to someone.

His father.

He turned toward the house that had been home for him for nearly two decades. The home that was so often filled with children and grandchildren. The ache grew as he drove.

When he finally pulled into his parents' driveway, he used his cell phone to call inside.

His father answered. "Why are you parked in the driveway?"

"Dad, I need to talk. No brothers, no wives, no other family. Just you. Will you come out, please?"

Without another word, his father came out and there, in the cab of his truck, John repeated the words Lori had used to blow him away like a fire hose blasting everything in its path.

His father sighed and leaned his head back against the headrest. After a moment, he asked, "Do you love Lori?"

"More than anything."

"Did you pray about marrying her? I know you did."

"Of course. But I want children, Dad. This is a hard concept for me to swallow—a whole lifetime of no children."

"That is a tough one."

"Plus part of me feels like Lori lied by not telling me before, even though I can understand why she wouldn't."

His father put a big hand on John's shoulder. "Marriage is all about learning. In fact, I've heard it said your spouse is your greatest opportunity for spiritual growth. They do things that drive you to your knees. Even your saintly mother has done things that I've thought I might not be able to get over. You've just gotten one of those moments before the wedding ceremony, that's all. You'll have a head start on your marriage when it takes place."

John sighed. "I know I'll marry Lori. Of course I will. I just need some time to get used to this new view."

His father nodded. "Lori's a good woman who's also hurting. The fact that she can't have children must be very hurtful to her, especially when you want them so much. And you always have, from the time you were a little boy. I remember at your kindergarten graduation when all the kids went up to the microphone and said what they wanted to be when they grew up and you walked up and said you wanted to be a dad."

John closed his eyes. Why did this have to be so hard?

His father said, "There's always adoption."

"I know."

"If you adopt, they'll become the children of your heart. You've already seen how that can happen." His father sighed. "Look, son, it's okay to be upset. It's okay to take time to make the right decision. It's even okay if you don't feel you can adopt."

"I just need time to get used to the idea, that's all."

They sat in silence for a moment.

Finally, John said, "This is the hardest disappointment I've ever had to deal with."

"I know. I'm sorry. I wish I could do more to help you." His father squeezed his shoulder. "But I have faith in you. You're a good man, John, and I know you'll do the right thing."

His father climbed out of the truck and walked back toward his house.

John sat there, aching. He still needed to talk with someone. Someone who could provide comfort for his broken heart.

His Father.

But before he could close his eyes to pray, the radio crackled into life.

Lori picked up her phone on the second ring.

"Lori, it's me. John."

She blinked back tears. It had only been a few hours since she'd told him the truth, but she'd gone through torture waiting for the call. "Hi."

Her voice came out barely above a whisper. She didn't know if he was calling to tell her he wanted to break things off or to tell her everything would be all right.

She could barely hear him, there was so much noise on his end of the line.

"I wanted you to know that our department has been called to the Uintah Mountains to help fight a huge brush fire. I don't know how long I'll be gone, but I'll call you when I get back."

"Oh. Okay."

He wasn't giving her the clues she needed as to how he felt.

"It might be a couple of days before I can call again, but I will as soon as I get back. Don't give up on me, okay?"

"I won't," she said, wishing she could trust him to come back, to forgive her.

"Lori, I love you."

"I love you, too, John."

"Gotta go, they've got the plane ready to fly over."

She hung up the phone, disturbed. She knew he loved her. But did he love her enough to pursue a future with no children? Until she knew the answer to that question, she couldn't relax.

She suspected the next few days would be torture while she waited for her man to come home, for him to decide if he really wanted her.

Out in the garden, Lori pulled what surely must be the last weed in the entire yard and wondered when she'd started using gardening to relax.

It had been three days since John had called, and she had cleaned everything inside and weeded everything outside trying to calm her nerves.

When she heard a vehicle that sounded like it had pulled into the driveway and then shut off, her heart pounded.

John! He'd come back!

She peeled off her gardening gloves and dropped them as she raced for the gate. Moving around the house quickly, it took a moment for reality to strike: the vehicle wasn't John's truck and the visitor wasn't John.

A taxi sat in the driveway and the driver, a man about Lori's age, was opening the trunk. The passenger stood by the side of the car. He was an older man—in his sixties, she'd guess—and not much taller than Lori. His unruly gray hair reminded her a little of Doc Brown's in *Back to the Future,* though not quite as wild.

As Lori walked across the lawn, the older man looked at her, smiled, and extended his hand. "You must be Lori Scott."

"I am," she said as she shook his hand. But who was he?

"Charles Dobson."

"Oh. *Oh.* I didn't expect you yet." He looked different from his grainy picture in the newspaper.

"Yes, well, I've returned from my trip a wee bit early."

A wee bit, eh? Over two weeks early, but who was counting?

He picked up two bags and walked to the front door. Lori and the driver followed him with more luggage. Charles definitely did not travel light. There were more bags still on the grass.

After all the bags had been deposited in the living room and the taxi driver paid and gone, Charles said, "I believe the job description was for three months. I certainly don't want my unexpected return to interfere with our agreement. I'm happy to go to a hotel—or pay for a hotel room for you, if you would prefer."

"Oh, no. Really. That won't be necessary."

"I am so very glad to be home. China is an absorbing country, but truly, there is no place like home."

Lori looked around his living room again, the old-fashioned room that had seemed so foreign and hopelessly outdated when she arrived. Now it seemed cozy. It felt like home. "I can see why you wanted to come back."

"Yes. To my home and my girl, Fluffy."

He'd come home for his cat? The one that wouldn't leave Agatha's yard? Boy, was he going to be disappointed.

"And Ben. How is he?"

"He still runs great." And after dark, when people couldn't see him.

"I would like to see what you've done with my column while I've been gone." He started down the hall, only to stop. "Oh, my, you probably want to finish out the rest of your columns, don't you?"

"The columns? Well, no, I guess not—not with you back." The last thing she needed was a professional gardener looking over her shoulder and seeing the convoluted way she faked her work.

He smiled. "Thank you, my dear. I do feel ready to resume writing to my many fans. I've missed them."

She pulled out the folder containing the clippings of her articles.

He settled on the den sofa. As he read, his eyebrows raised and he uttered an occasional "Oh, my!"

"Do you like what I've done?" she asked, surprisingly worried he wouldn't.

"You have a very interesting style, my dear. But, yes. I like it. I suspect my hard-core fans were a bit shaken, but no doubt others have enjoyed it immensely."

"You're very aware of your fans. That's exactly what Mr. Neal said happened."

He pulled out the last few clippings and read on.

Freezing in place, he raised his eyebrows. "I notice my zucchini chicken curry recipe made it into print."

"Agatha said you'd been promising to put the recipe into your column and that you'd just forgotten. She said you'd be glad I put it in."

"Oh, she did, did she?" He turned to Lori, but she couldn't read his expression. Was he upset? Amused? Worried? "Agatha has been trying to obtain this recipe from me for years—as well as my cat. Well, we'll see about that."

Lori pressed both palms to her face. She'd screwed up big-time. "Charles, I'm so sorry."

"Oh, don't worry, dear. You're not to blame. But now, if you'll excuse me, I have something to settle."

Through the window, she watched him do a funny little jumping walk over to Agatha's door. She really should call and warn the older woman, but there wasn't time now.

Suddenly feeling empty, Lori sighed. Charles was surely disappointed in her. Soon Agatha would be upset with her, too. And it had been three days since John had looked at her with such hurt in his eyes and then disappeared.

She knew from everything he'd said and everything she'd observed that he did not want an infertile woman, but he was too nice of a guy to know how to break it off with her.

Her heart wrenched. She needed to do the right thing. For his sake. He deserved to have children.

With Charles back, she was free to leave. And if she left now, gave John back his ring, freed him from the promise he'd made before he knew the truth, he could marry Dawn and have the children he wanted so much.

It was the unselfish thing for her to do. She couldn't give him children of her own. But she could give him back the opportunity to have them with someone else.

Though her heart wrenched again, Lori knew she was doing the right thing. It was time to go home. Back to her mother's home in Schenectady.

Back to a world without John.

Chapter Thirty

Two hours later, Charles had not returned and Lori had done everything she needed to before leaving: stacked her packed suitcases and large black duffle bag along the living room wall, put new sheets on Charles's bed and washed, dried, and folded the others.

As she wiped off the kitchen table and counters one last time, Lori called Serena to tell her good-bye. After expressing her sympathetic disappointment, Serena offered to drive her to the Salt Lake airport.

"Thanks. I'll have to call to see when the earliest flight is . . . and I'd like to stop at John's house first."

"I'll drive you wherever and whenever you need to go, *amiga.* You call and let me know what time you want to leave, and I'll be there."

"Don't you have classes?"

"Don't worry about my classes and my schedule. I want to be there for you, so I will be there."

"Salsa girl to the rescue, huh?"

"You'd better believe it, *chica de calabacín.* That's 'zucchini chick,' in case you don't know."

Thankful for her new friend's support, Lori called the airport and made a reservation for the five o'clock flight. That gave her a couple of hours before she'd need to leave for the airport. She called Serena back with the info.

Hanging up the phone, she went into the living room to wait for Serena to arrive. Her belongings filled the two suitcases, the duffle bag, and four big boxes stacked and ready to pack in Serena's car.

Looking out the window, she saw Charles walking slowly back from Agatha's house. It had begun to drizzle.

Surprised, she saw he carried Fluffy in his arms. And she wondered what on earth Agatha had said to him—or he to her—to put such a smug smile on his face.

"Land sakes, girl. Come in out of the rain."

Lori stepped into Agatha's living room, her clothes barely damp. The details of the room stood out as vividly as they had the first time she'd been here—the wicker love seat and chairs, the soft flowered cushions, the knickknacks—but for a totally different reason. Today, she was nostalgic, and she still had the good-bye ahead.

"Would you like some lemonade, sweetie? You look a little peaked."

Lori smiled. "That's what you asked me the day I arrived."

"Well, I do like a good glass of hand-squeezed lemonade."

"So do I. Thanks, I'd love one."

Agatha bustled from the room, and soon was back with two glasses. Lori took one and sipped. "Fabulous."

Lori no longer believed her first impression of Agatha as everyone's grandma. No, Agatha was a savvy woman who kept herself spry and active, both physically and mentally.

As Agatha settled herself on the love seat, setting two coasters down on the glass-topped, wicker-based table, Lori tried not to think about Dawn, the beautiful, redheaded fertility goddess waiting in the wings to marry John and give him a passel of kids with red hair instead of blonde.

Lori forced a smile. "I came over to tell you good-bye. With Charles back, there's no reason for me to stay. I'm going home."

"My dear, what about John? He seems like a pretty good reason to me."

Lori didn't want to go there, not even with Agatha. "I'm curious—what did you say to Charles? He chatted with me and was super nice—but he didn't seem overly happy when he left my place . . . his place. But when he returned, he was smiling."

Agatha's smile was luminous. "I don't suppose I ever brought up the subject of Charlie with you, did I?"

"His recipe. His silliness in going to China. Things like that."

"Ah, but there's a story behind all of that."

Lori chuckled and tilted her head. "I would love to hear this story."

"Charlie came over here today to keep his part of a bargain we made two years ago."

"Why do I think this isn't going to be any normal kind of bargain?"

Agatha laughed. "Because you are incredibly perceptive, my dear. No, this is definitely not the normal kind of bargain because ours has not been the normal sort of courtship."

Lori raised an eyebrow. "Courtship?"

"He came over today to ask for my hand in marriage. And I accepted." Agatha sighed deeply, putting her hand to her heart melodramatically. The older woman was obviously enjoying every moment of the story. "Romantic, isn't it?"

Surprised, Lori said, "Charles proposed?"

"It was about time. We've known each other all our lives. Went to school together. And we started dating three years ago. "

"Really."

Agatha just smiled.

"He seemed upset when he left my house."

"He was pretending to be a tad angry when he reached my door, too." Agatha smiled. "But as you can tell, it all worked out for the best."

"I am so happy for you. I guess that trip to China made him realize what was really important to him."

Agatha shot her an amused look. "Actually, we're back to the bargain now."

"Ah, the not-so-normal bargain. I can hardly wait to hear the details."

Agatha took another slow sip. "Well, after the man had courted me for a year, and had not had the decency of offering a proposal, I told him it was high time he got around to it. In return, he got a trifle snippy and told me that he would not be pushed." Agatha motioned to Lori. "You might want to put down your cup, dear."

Not sure why, Lori did as Agatha suggested.

Agatha continued. "Charlie told me he loves a resourceful

woman, and so—here comes the bargain—if I could get my hands on a certain zucchini chicken curry recipe of his, then he would propose. I was too proud to go looking for it until you came. But it seems he'd hidden it in plain sight, hoping I'd find it, or that someone would. And, two years later, you came along to help us."

Glad now that she'd put down the cup so she didn't spill the lemonade as she started to laugh, Lori said, "You are so very sneaky, Agatha McCrea. You *used* me to get that recipe. You played me like a Stradivarius. And so did Charles. I love it."

"You merely helped me keep my side of the bargain." Agatha settled back into the cushions with a satisfied smile. "And so Charlie, being a man of honor, if not of great speed, came over this day to keep his."

Lori couldn't stop laughing, and Agatha joined her with a few chuckles of her own.

Finally, Lori wiped her eyes. "Oh, thank you. I needed that today. At least one of us is going to end up with a happily ever after."

"You'll have yours, too, my dear. And you and John are young enough to have it all. You'll get married, have a family, enjoy many years together. All Charlie and I will have is our cats. Well, and our passion for gardens. And our romance novels."

"I'm giving John back his ring."

Agatha gasped. "Young lady, tell me what is wrong between you and your young man. You changed the subject before, and I expect you not to do so again."

The laughter seemed to have opened any barriers between the two women, not that there were many left, and Lori was relieved to share her burden.

"I didn't tell John the truth about me. I didn't tell anyone. But after seeing John holding his brother's baby, well, I told John what I should have told him when he proposed." Lori's voice trembled. "I can't have children. Not ever."

"Oh, I am sorry, Lori. I didn't know or I would never have said anything about a family." Agatha frowned. "What did he say?"

"He said we'd get through this together, but he needed time to think things through. He called to tell me he was going to the Uintah Mountains to fight a fire." Lori shook her head. "But I saw the look on his face when I told him the truth. He's going to want his ring back. He won't get over this."

"Oh, land sakes, no, sweetie. He's a good man. Give him a few days to work things through in his man's mind and he'll be back with flowers in his hand."

"I wish that were the case." But it had been three days already. Surely he could call from the mountains, if he really wanted to. Lori had no hope left. She shrugged. "I couldn't wait two years, anyway."

With a sad smile, Agatha said, "If the man is the right man for you, you'd be surprised how long you can wait. But it won't take John two years. He's obviously crazy about you. He'll work his way through this. Trust him. Give him a little time."

But Lori didn't see how he could ever forgive her. She'd seen the hurt, betrayed look in his eyes when he'd left.

She suspected it was similar to the hurt, betrayed look she'd given her father, and she'd never been able to forgive him.

She was going to free John from his obligation to her. It was the only gift she had left to give him.

An hour later, Lori's heart pounded as she stood before John's door.

A note seemed so impersonal, so she tried his cell phone number one more time. When she reached his voicemail again and heard his warm, deep voice, she fought back tears. This time, she left a message: "John, this is Lori. Charles came back early and I'm flying home today. I . . . I think it will be best for both of us to get on with our separate lives. I wish you happiness, John."

Only after she hung up did she whisper, "I love you."

Pain like barbed wire coiled within her, pricking her heart each time she moved. She pulled out the envelope she'd brought with her, the note she'd hoped she wouldn't have to leave, the note that said pretty much what her voicemail had said.

Looking down, the sun glinted off the large diamond John had insisted be set into her engagement ring. With a sigh, she pulled the note out and added one more line: *P.S. I'm giving you back the ring. It's beautiful, but you gave it to the wrong woman.*

Pausing, she looked at the ring—her last real link to John, to her hopes about their marriage, to her chance at true happiness. With a painful sigh, she slipped it from her finger, placed it in the envelope, licked and sealed it, and taped it to the inside of his screen door, down at the bottom so other people couldn't see it.

"Good-bye, John Wayne Walker," she whispered. "It was great while it lasted."

Then she made the long walk back to the car and let Serena drive her to the Salt Lake airport.

Chapter Thirty-One

Lori was back to square one.

She was sitting alone in her bedroom at her mother's house in Schenectady. She still didn't have a play on Broadway. Her heart was broken more than ever before. And she was hosting another pity party. No, actually, it wasn't so much a pity party as a time to catch her heartbroken breath before going on.

She wished John had loved her enough to forgive her, to follow her here, and to want her even though her body was defective in the reproductive department. But she knew that was just a dream. It truly had been a holiday romance, but one that had ripped her heart asunder and changed her forever. She'd always cherish the fact that he'd brought her back to the light of the Gospel and back to her Savior.

She was trying to read, but hadn't gotten far when she heard a man's deep voice coming from downstairs.

John! He'd followed her here!

She opened her bedroom door and darted to the top of the stairs.

Greg stood at the bottom. "Hi, sis."

Her heart seemed to roll down each of the steps before her. She was such a fool. Of course John hadn't come. She knew he wouldn't. She didn't really expect him to. But, like Dawn, her heart hadn't gotten the message yet.

"Hi, Greg," she said as she followed her heart down the stairs.

"My relationship isn't going so hot, either. I figured we could have a pity party together."

Despite her pain, Lori chuckled. "That sounds so very unattractive, doesn't it?"

"Okay, so I came to cheer you up instead. I brought your favorite ice cream."

In the family room, the television set was on. Her mother must have been watching it before she left for the store. Lori's heart was breaking, but apparently life still went on: a huge forest fire in Utah, a whale rescued in Maine, a Hollywood actress filing for divorce and already matched up with a new man.

Just like John was probably already matched up with Dawn.

"For what my opinion counts, I think John will come for you. If he's any kind of man, that is." He looked at her. "Mom said you weren't going to tell him. What made you change your mind?"

"I prayed about it. Now don't faint. I prayed after Dad left, too."

He put his hand to his heart, in a gesture that reminded her of Agatha last week. "You mentioned both Dad and prayer in the same sentence. It boggles the mind."

"Oh, shut up, you big goon, and just listen."

"Yes, ma'am."

She found the remote and clicked off the television set, then sank onto the couch. Greg sat next to her, propping his long legs on the table. He looked at her, one eyebrow still raised.

"When Dad left, I prayed that God would make Mom and Dad get back together. So when Dad married Fiona, I stopped praying. But then, in Utah, I started again. And I felt impressed to tell John the truth. So now I'm trying my best to believe that God has my best interests at heart and that He's not just ignoring my pleas again."

For once, Greg stayed silent and just listened.

"And when I pray now, I feel peaceful. I guess it's God's way of telling me everything will be okay, even without John. But I keep wondering if I did the right thing, or if I just made another huge mistake."

"I can't answer that for you." Greg took her hand—now it was her turn to be shocked—and said, "Sometimes people just make mistakes, even you, even fathers, even men you fall in love with. Even brothers, if you can believe that."

She smiled at him and he smiled back. With a sigh, she said, "I keep thinking about Dad. I don't want to, but I do."

"Maybe you're ready to call him now."

"I don't think so."

"Lori, just do it. Put aside your hurt and your pride—"

"Pride?"

"Yeah, pride. Stubborn, obstinate, monumental pride. Call him."

"I don't know if I can."

Greg grinned and let go of her hand. "I'm pulling out the darts. If you lose, you have to call Dad. If you win, you don't have to call him ever."

"I always win, you know that."

"Yeah, you're probably right. Stupid darts, anyway. I mean, look what happened last time you played darts—you had a grand adventure and fell in love."

"And I am now alone in my mother's house talking to my dweeby brother."

"Good point. No darts. How about a soda?"

She smiled. "Now that I'm not in Brigham City anymore, I'd like to have something caffeinated."

"Fuhgetaboutit," he said. "The prophet said we don't drink them. I gave them up, too, in honor of your adventure."

"Oh, well, I kind of got hooked on root beer while I was in Utah."

"Then let's go get one."

"Greg?"

"Yeah?"

"Thanks for trying to cheer me up."

He pulled a face. "Big baby."

"Freakishly tall dweeb."

Some things never changed. She and her brother loved each other and tormented each other. And for that, at least, she was thankful.

The next evening after church, Lori sat on her bed, having changed out of her dress and into casual clothes. She'd been pondering what she was going to do with her life.

In fast and testimony meeting, she'd felt impressed to bear her testimony, while her mother had sat crying on the bench—along with a lot of other women who'd known Lori her entire life. She knew how much her coming back to church, to the Gospel, meant to her mother.

At home, her mother had served a delicious roast beef dinner with creamy mashed potatoes and slightly lumpy gravy, and a big tossed green salad.

Sitting there for the last few hours, she'd felt the ache of losing John for good. Instead of a forever family, she had only bittersweet memories.

But she couldn't allow herself to dwell in that sad place or she'd have to give up right now. And she wasn't going to give up. She was going to get on with her life. And to do that, there were two things she needed to do: call her father and tackle her screenplay.

Ever since Lori had talked with Greg yesterday, she hadn't been able to get her father out of her mind. Surprisingly enough, for the first time, she thought it would be less painful to call and talk with him than it would be not to call.

She had finally admitted to herself that her mother—and Greg and Marti and Serena and John—had all been right. She had to reconnect with her father, forgive him, and heal from the hurt. She had to grow up; she wasn't thirteen anymore and she couldn't live her life as though she were.

She'd already asked her mother for the phone number. To her mother's credit, she hadn't made a big deal about it. She'd just written the number down and handed the paper to Lori, hugged her, and said, "I love you, Lori."

As she sat there, phone in hand, she went over the memories of her father's betrayal and her pain. From the time he'd left, she'd refused to go visit him, and he hadn't asked. And then, two years ago, she'd learned he'd taken his three new daughters for the camping trip at Yellowstone he'd promised her so many years ago. Instead of Lori, he'd taken Fiona and the H's. And, despite the fact that she'd refused to do anything with him for years, despite the fact that she'd have refused to go even if he had invited her, the fact that he *hadn't* asked had ripped her heart out.

Help me, Father, to make this call. And help me know that no matter how my father reacts today, You love me.

Taking a deep breath, she punched in the numbers and listened to the phone ring.

A girl answered. One of the H's, but whether it was Hillary or Hailey or Hannah, Lori couldn't tell. "Is your dad there?"

"Just a minute, please," the girl said, not hideously at all but quite politely. And then she called out, "Dad. Telephone."

After a moment, her father answered.

As soon as Lori heard his deep voice, she had to blink back tears. "Hi, Dad. It's me."

"Lori?" He sounded surprised, hesitant but also hopeful. "Is this really you?"

It was hard to get the words out. "I just . . . wanted to say hi."

"I am so glad you called. I've been thinking about you so much lately. Is everything all right?"

He sounded genuinely concerned, almost as if he really cared. But she wasn't ready to trust him enough to confide in him. Not yet. "Everything's good, Dad."

"We'd love to have you come over and visit us."

"Maybe soon."

He paused for a second. "Okay. Whatever you want."

He sounded like a little boy who wanted a puppy and was trying to pretend very hard that he didn't really want it *that* much. Did he really want to see her that much? Was it *her* love that he needed? When she visualized him like that, her anger melted and tears began to flow. "Dad, I've missed you."

"I've missed you, too." She could hear him crying, too.

"Just a minute," she said while she found a tissue to blow her nose. When she got back on, she said, "Dad? Are you there?"

"I'm sorry, Lori. I know I wasn't there for you when I should have been. And I will always regret that." His voice was shaky with emotion. "But I will always be here for you from now on, if you'll let me. Always. I promise."

She wiped her eyes and whispered, "Thanks."

"I'd really like to see you. Can I come get you and bring you over here to visit?"

"I'm not ready to be around the others, Dad. Not yet."

Her feelings were still too raw.

"Oh. Sure. That's okay."

Then she confided more than she ever thought she would. "It's hard to be around the family you replaced me with."

"Oh, Lori, baby," he said, and she could hear the pain and regret in his voice. "I've made some huge mistakes. I never meant to replace you. You are my baby girl. The first little girl I ever had. I was so excited to hold you for the first time. That's why I've stayed here in town, even though I've had several job offers out of state. I wanted to stay close to you and Greg, to try to make up for not being there in other ways."

A longing to see him built inside her. "Maybe I could see just you to begin with. Maybe that would be okay."

"That would be great. I could come over tomorrow evening and take you for a drive. Maybe we could share an extra-thick chocolate malt."

Her favorite. He'd remembered. "I'd like that, Dad."

"Maybe we can work up to including Fiona and the girls, too. But only if you want."

"Maybe." She wasn't ready to be around Fiona yet. Or the H's, even if they were hospitable instead of hideous. She'd go for ice cream with her dad and see where things went from there.

After they hung up, she cried for a long time, only these tears were thick and heavy, washing away the old hurt from long ago. Cleansing tears that left her exhausted, but feeling lighter at the same time.

After awhile, she wiped her tears.

If she was going to truly get on with her life without the man she'd grown to love, she might as well go all the way.

She pulled out the box with her screenplay, lifted the lid, and reached for the pages.

Chapter Thirty-Two

Hopeful. Hopeless.

Lori alternated between the two extremes.

Her father had taken her for a malt on Monday evening, the day after their talk, and they'd had a very nice visit. They were still tentative and feeling their way around each other. He was very careful and tender with her. She was hopeful that they might repair their relationship and she could have a father again, even though he hadn't been there for her before.

They even had plans for the weekend. He was going to pick up both her and Greg tomorrow and they were going to spend a nice Saturday morning at the art museum. Maybe the next time, she'd be ready to include his other daughters. But not just yet.

On the other end of the spectrum, it had been twelve days since John had last called—nearly two weeks—and he hadn't written or e-mailed or called again. She had finally accepted that he really wasn't going to be part of her future. He wanted his own children and he probably couldn't forgive her for keeping the truth from him. And how could she blame him?

Lori had put off job hunting since she'd arrived home, but after the weekend, she would start looking. She needed cash while she finished her screenplay.

A knock was followed by Lori's mother peeking around the bedroom door. "Hey, hon, want to go out to a movie?"

"I don't think so, Mom. Maybe next weekend."

Her mother stepped into the room. "You're too young to be wasting away at home."

Lori smiled. "And I'm too old to be guilt-tripped into going out."

"I guess you are, at that. Okay, another exciting Friday night watching a DVD and munching popcorn?"

"You choose the movie."

"Return to Me."

Lori sighed. "Mom, he's not coming for me. It's over. I've accepted it."

"Never stop dreaming, Lori. Don't give up on love."

Lori smiled. "What time is Greg coming over?"

His brother had called earlier to announce he wanted to show them the new suit he'd bought for a date with a woman he'd met.

Her mother glanced at her watch. "Any time now."

"Anybody home?" a woman called from downstairs.

"Up here, Marti," Lori shouted back as she stood and joined her mother. "We'll be right down."

"Come on." Mom wrapped an arm around Lori's waist. "Let's party."

Lori laughed. "Let's do."

As they walked down the stairs, Marti looked up at them, her hands on her hips. "I hear there's a wild movie night here every Friday. When does it start?"

"As soon as you rowdy yourself up a little."

Marti did a few dance moves from their high school era, and both Lori and her mother laughed.

"All right," Lori said. "Let the wild party begin."

Someone knocked on the door. "Oh, for Pete's sake, Greg," called out her mother. "You don't have to knock."

Another knock.

Lori rolled her eyes. "I'll get it and smack him around a little while I'm at it."

As she swung open the door, she said, "Come in, already, you freakishly tall—"

She stopped, frozen in place.

It wasn't Greg.

John Wayne Walker stood on her porch.

Shocked into silence, she stood still for the longest moment.

Dressed in slacks and a white button-down shirt, he'd obviously dressed up for the occasion.

She still couldn't move. "What are you doing here?"

He looked nervous. "I'm sorry I haven't called."

She whispered, "It's been nearly two weeks."

"I know. We were out of contact with everyone during the worst of the blaze. Then, after I got home and found your note and your ring, I decided I had to come talk to you in person. It would be too easy for you to tell me to get lost over the phone."

"Oh."

"Oh," her mother repeated as she stepped up beside Lori. She smiled widely. "You must be John Walker."

He smiled and put out his hand. "Yes, ma'am, I am."

"I'm Irene Scott." Her mother beamed as she shook his hand. "Please do come in."

"Thank you," he said as he turned back to lock gazes with Lori, "but I need to speak with your daughter first."

Marti came up. "Hi, I'm Marti Owens—Lori's best friend."

"Glad to meet you."

Marti studied him. "I told you he'd be back," she muttered to Lori.

"Shh," Lori said. "He's not back for me."

John tilted his head. "I'm not?"

Lori turned to the other two women. "Could we please have a moment of privacy here?"

"Hey, Lori," called out Greg as he pulled up in his new suit and Jeep. "He looks freakishly tall."

John raised an eyebrow. "And you said my family was weird."

"I never said that." She looked into his blue eyes and said, "Come inside."

She led him to the breakfast nook where they could be alone. She stood, nervous, not sure what to say.

Finally, the words spewed out of Lori. "I'm sorry I didn't tell you sooner that I couldn't have children. At first I thought it didn't matter because I didn't plan on getting involved. I was just going to come home without falling in love. But then I fell in love, and then I didn't want to lose you by telling you, and then I didn't even know how to tell you."

He put his finger up gently to her lips. "Shh. I've forgiven you for that."

"Are you dating Dawn now?"

He looked surprised. "Why would I be doing that?"

"Because . . . I thought . . ."

"No. I am not dating anyone else."

"Oh," said Lori, a flicker of hope lighting her heart.

"Lori, I'm sorry it took me so long to work through things. And to come to you. And now I need to know if you can forgive me for being so upset." His blue eyes radiated love for her—the same love she could feel within herself. "Can you forgive me?"

"Of course." She smiled just a tiny bit.

"It doesn't matter to me that you can't have children."

"John, we can't survive a marriage built on guilt."

"Guilt?"

"I will feel guilty forever."

John shook his head. "Our marriage will be built on love. And I want to have children with you. We can adopt." He looked at her, his hands clenched as if he was nervous. "If you want, that is."

"I'm just afraid it won't be the same for you as having your own children. I know you'll be the kind of parent Quinn and Tricia are. They adore their kids. And I want that for you. You deserve that."

He started laughing. "You want the same thing for me that Quinn and Tricia have?"

She didn't see what was so funny. "Yes."

"Oh, Lori." He reached for her, pulling her into his arms. "I have missed you so much."

She went to him easily and clung to him, not wanting to ever let him go. "I've missed you, too."

With a low rumble in his chest, almost a chuckle, he said, "Quinn and Tricia *adopted* Evan and Emma."

Surprised, she pulled back just enough to look up at him. "What?"

"They adopted. And I could adore our adopted children just as much as Quinn and Tricia adore theirs."

Joy filled her heart. "So that's how Tricia got her figure back so quickly."

He laughed again, and this time she joined in.

But then she grew serious. “But you said you wanted girls who looked just like me.”

“I want *you,* Lori. I have spent practically every waking moment since I first met you thinking about you. My world finally came alive when you entered it. Suddenly, there were sparks.”

“And I know how you like sparks,” she teased.

“And it’s been horrible for me these past two weeks thinking I might have lost you.” He hugged her again and then held her out from him, his hands on her arms. “Heavenly Father will send us children, one way or another. The children who are meant to be ours.”

He leaned over and kissed her.

“Ah, how sweet,” said Greg.

Lori ignored her brother and wrapped her arms around John’s neck. After a long moment, they pulled back.

Lori turned to see the three of them—her mother, brother, and best friend—clapping loudly.

“I’m sorry about my family,” she said to John.

“Don’t be. I like ’em.” He relaxed his hold on her and took her hand. “Oh, wait, I have something to show you.”

He reached in his shirt pocket and pulled out a print.

It was a picture of people on a roller coaster. Lagoon’s white wooden roller coaster. And she could pick out John’s terror-stricken face as he rode the first big drop down.

She looked up at him, questioningly.

He said, “You suggested a bargain.”

“You’re too late.” She laughed. “I already called my father. I even went for a malt with him and I’m seeing him tomorrow, too.”

“Are you kidding?” He pulled the picture back. “You mean I rode that beast for nothing?”

“Not for nothing.” She hugged him again. “I admire you greatly.”

“Then it was worth it.” He reached in his pocket and pulled out her ring. “You left something of yours at my place, and I need to return it.” He took her hand and slipped the ring back on her finger.

“It was fate, after all,” whispered her mother.

John grinned and looked into Lori's eyes. "It sure was. It took some darts, a fire, and some wild zucchinis to bring us together."

Lori looked at the others. "Scram."

"First show us your ring." Marti picked up her friend's hand. "It's beautiful. Look how big it is."

Her mother said, "It's gorgeous."

"*Now* will you please leave us alone?" begged Lori. *"Please?"*

Laughing, the three of them disappeared into the living room.

With a sigh, Lori slipped into John's embrace again. "I just have one question."

"Anything."

"It may seem kind of silly, but can we honeymoon in Yellowstone? I've never been."

He laughed in surprise. "Only if we can go to Hawaii afterward."

"You've got a deal."

"No," he said with a tender smile. "I've got a date with eternity."

THE GARDEN GURU

Dear Dr. Dobson: Is there such a thing as a happy ending? I know you are a gardening expert, not a life coach, but I have always loved to garden and I don't know who else to turn to. Since my husband died last spring, I haven't been able to get myself back on my feet and into the garden. Can you help me? (Victoria)

Dear Victoria: Oh, yes, indeed, there is such a thing as a happy ending, even for such a sad story as yours. I, myself, am proof of that. After several years of waiting, I have married my sweetheart, Miss Agatha McCrea. I've finally found my true love; you've lost yours—yet these are but two sides of the same love story. Please don't give up hope, dear lady. Start small, with one plant. Soon you'll realize that life is still all around you. Watching the new spring growth of plants will remind you of the oft-quoted circle of life, and you will begin to find your new place in that circle. I beg of you, go back out into the garden today. And be sure to visit my wife's new Web site; she counsels people on how to enhance their lives with simple changes. She has certainly enhanced mine. Good luck, dear lady. Write again . . .

Epilogue

Lori raised a tissue to wipe her tears. They were definitely tears of happiness.

John sat next to her and looked down at the bundle in Lori's arms. He'd be blessing their newly adopted baby girl in just minutes and he seemed a little nervous.

She leaned into him. "Has it really only been two years since we met? It seems like a lifetime ago."

He whispered back, "What if I mess up?"

"You won't. You've done it before for other people."

"I know, but not for my own daughter."

"Just don't you dare call her Zucchini." He'd teased that he was going to often enough.

That made him smile. "But I am. It's zucchini that brought her mother and father together."

"Your mother said I was to smack you upside the head if you did."

He pulled her close and put out his finger for the baby to grab. She had blonde hair, like Lori's, but with the faintest hint of red in the sun, like John's. Almost as if God had known what He was doing.

Secure in his arms, seeing him adoring their new little daughter, Lori was happy.

She looked down the row. Between her family and John's, they filled three complete rows in their Brigham City ward. She and John sat on the end of the second row, so John could get in and out easily.

In front of her sat her mother and Greg. Next to Greg sat their father, along with Fiona, and Lori's three younger sisters. She knew the difference between them now, even over the phone. She'd even been to their home several times with John.

John's family filled out the second row: Wild Bill and Irene, Clint and Julie, Kirk and Opal, Roy and Becky, and their many children.

On the row behind them sat Quinn and Tricia with their kids, as well as some of the other firefighters from John's stationhouse.

Serena was there with the salsa guy she'd met in El Parral Mexican Restaurant. Roberto had proposed last week; Serena had accepted.

Charles and Agatha sat in the row across from them. They had just celebrated their first anniversary. Charles had indeed kept his side of the bargain. Next to Agatha sat her Spade and Hope buddies: Victoria, Lisa Anne, and Norma. Victoria was still dealing with her grief—but she was also smiling again.

Lori had finished her screenplay and it was currently being produced for the Sundance Film Festival. Her new cookbook, appropriately titled *How to Stuff a Wild Zucchini,* was selling briskly. And she had several ideas sketched out for more stories and plays.

Though her writing success was wonderful, it could never, ever, compare to the joy she felt sitting among family and friends, to being loved by John Wayne Walker, and to being the mother of a beautiful baby girl.

The bishop stood and announced it was time for the blessing.

John handed her a folded scrap of paper. "Don't open this until you hear me say her name."

"It'd better not be Zucchini," warned Lori again.

John smiled as he gently picked up their beautiful child and carried her to the front of the chapel. They were joined by his father and brothers, her father and brother, Quinn, a couple of firefighters, Charles, and Roberto.

They closed together in a circle of priesthood, which Lori found as comforting as her circle of family and friends. She was so glad she'd found her way back to the safety and joy of Christ and His Gospel.

John's voice spoke the blessing and Lori listened for the name. After Isabella, what would he say?

"And the name by which she shall be known . . . is Isabella Z Walker."

Lori opened the paper he'd given her and peeked at it.

He'd written, *It's spelled Zee.*

Lori smiled. He'd come as close to zucchini as he dared. Well, she supposed she could live with Zee.

Isabella Zee Walker.

After the blessing, John carried Bella back down the aisle, his face radiating joy and love. As he slipped in beside her and gently placed Bella in her arms, Lori rejoiced.

"Is her name all right?" he whispered.

"It's perfect. It really did start with some wild zucchinis, didn't it?"

He smiled and leaned close to whisper, "And a whole lot of sparks."

Charles Dobson's Secret-but-Not-Well-Hidden Zucchini Chicken Curry Recipe

12 cups water
1 teaspoon salt
2 to 3 pounds chicken breasts
2 celery stalks, sliced
1 medium onion, diced
2 medium Gala apples (or any tart apple), peeled and diced
2 medium zucchini, peeled and diced
1 tablespoon curry powder (add more only after tasting)
4 tablespoons butter, divided
$\frac{1}{3}$ cup raisins (may be golden or regular)
$1\frac{1}{2}$ cups chicken broth (or 1 bouillon cube plus $1\frac{1}{2}$ cups water)
$\frac{1}{2}$ cup Barq's or A&W root beer or caffeine-free Coca-Cola (no diet soda)
3 tablespoons flour
1 cup evaporated milk, undiluted (or coconut milk)
1 teaspoon salt
$\frac{1}{8}$ teaspoon white pepper or regular black pepper
Rice, cooked
Condiments: Spicy Mango Fruit Chutney, raisins, grated coconut, lime wedges

In a large pot, add water and salt and bring to a boil. Add chicken and sliced celery. (If chicken is frozen, boil for 20 minutes before adding celery.) Reduce heat, cover, and simmer until the chicken is tender, about 20 minutes. Cut up the cooked chicken and set aside. Reserve $1\frac{1}{2}$ cups of the chicken broth; set aside.

In a large skillet, melt 1 tablespoon butter; sauté diced onions for 2 to 3 minutes. Move to a separate bowl. Dice apples and zucchini and add to onions. Add curry powder. In the skillet, melt the remaining 3 tablespoons butter and add the apples/zucchini/onion mixture. Saute for 5 minutes, stirring often.

In a bowl, combine the raisins, reserved chicken broth, and soda of your choice. Add to the skillet and cook for 2 minutes.

Mix the flour into the evaporated milk, whisking to remove any lumps. Add the salt and pepper. When smooth, add to the skillet and stir. Cook over low heat until mixture is creamy and thick. Season to taste. Add the cooked chicken and celery.

Serve over rice with any of the condiments desired.

Serves 4 to 6.

Spicy Mango Fruit Chutney

1 mango
1 plum
1 Gala apple
1 nectarine
1 peach
1 teaspoon olive oil
½ jalapeño pepper, seeded and minced
1 clove garlic, minced
⅛ teaspoon ginger (ground or crystallized)
½ teaspoon salt
¼ teaspoon white pepper or regular black pepper
½ teaspoon cider vinegar

Peel all fruit and cut into medium-sized chunks. Mix together in a bowl and set aside. In a medium saucepan, warm the olive oil over medium heat. Sauté jalapeño pepper, garlic, and ginger for 2 minutes. Add the fruit to the pan, reduce heat to low, and simmer until the fruit starts to break down, about 15 to 30 minutes. Add salt and pepper to taste. Remove chutney from heat. Stir in the vinegar. Serve with Zucchini Chicken Curry.

Makes about 1½ cups.

Author's Note

Although Brigham City is a real town, and a charming one, with tree-lined streets and old-time buildings, I have made a few changes to fit the needs of my story: I hired full-time firefighters and added a daily newspaper (though the *Box Elder News Journal* is a good one already). There is a real Spade and Hope Garden Club, but all of my club members are fictional. Peach City Ice Cream does have a large sundae, which is deliciously not fictional.

I hope you enjoyed spending time in my version of Brigham City as much as I enjoyed my visits in the actual town.

Acknowledgments

I owe thanks to the ladies who helped me plot this book: Diane Chase Stoddard (a captivating author of medieval time-travel romances) and Kristin Holt (a fabulous writer and life-change coach). Thanks to the talented people who read my manuscript and helped me make it better in so many ways: Diane Stoddard (a fabulous friend who has helped me stay motivated through all the tough times), Bruce Simpson (a talented fantasy author), and my awesome sister-in-law Marie Barnhurst (who read the entire book and spotted flaws that others had missed).

A special thanks to Kathleen Wright, my incredibly generous author-friend, for sharing her Bear Lake cabin for the week during which I had my "Bear Lake epiphany" and finished this book and who, along with her husband, Fred, gave me and my husband a fabulous celebration dinner when this book sold.

I am very thankful for the help, information, and personalized tour that Deputy Chief Tom Coleman of the Provo Fire Department provided me and for the firefighters of Station Four for letting me ask questions, take pictures, and even climb aboard their engine. It was great to ride along and watch you in action. (And I liked your jokes.)

I'm grateful to Jana Erickson, to my editor, Lisa Mangum, and to the entire Deseret Book team who offered their insights and excellent advice (and who liked my books!). Heather G. Ward designed a great cover for me. I look forward to working with all of you on many future projects.

And thanks to my cousin-by-marriage, Jennifer Benson, for taking time to meet me in the Brigham City area, answer questions while we ate a great Maddox lunch, and accompany me on a tour of the area.

I'm thankful to Phyllis Nielsen of the Spade and Hope Garden Club for answering my questions and saying it was okay for me to use the name of their club in my book. And to Kevin Packer, a real estate agent who sends out one awesome welcome packet.

This book wouldn't be complete without Charles Dobson's Zucchini Chicken Curry recipe and I want to thank those friends who shared their recipes until I finally came up with a mixture of this and that and found what Charles had been hiding.

I really must thank Chevrolet, somewhat tongue-in-cheek, for designing the uniquely indecisive '65 El Camino so Lori could be so pleasantly mortified while driving around town.

Thanks to those in my family who are especially good about saying exactly the right thing to brighten my day. And, last and always first, my heartfelt thanks to my husband Mark, who has brought immeasurable joy into my life.

About the Author

Raised by her shop-'til-you-drop mother and pay-for-the-purchases oilman father, Heather Horrocks lived overseas for her first seventeen years, attending schools in Colombia, Venezuela, London, Kuwait, and Iran.

She's been a church pianist since her childhood Kuwait branch days, with turns teaching in Sunday School, Relief Society, and Primary.

Through the years, she's spent her days as a secretary, video store owner, and medical transcriptionist (though not all at the same time), and she's now delighted to turn her attention fully to her writing craft.

How to Stuff a Wild Zucchini is her first of many romantic comedies; she is also the author of two inspirational books, *Women Who Knew the Mortal Messiah* and *Men Who Knew the Mortal Messiah,* and is working on a baptism book, *You Just Turned 8.*

She loves anyone who can make her laugh, which explains why she adores her witty husband, Mark, Anne George mysteries, Bill Cosby, and her friend Diane. She loves movies (especially romantic comedies), music, books, sharing what she's learned about life and writing, and cooking for friends and family, especially for her nine children/stepchildren and their families. She resides in Utah with her husband, two youngest sons, a sister, and two dogs. You can reach her online at www.heatherhorrocks.com.